Plague of Flies: Revolt of the Spirits, 1846

Laurel Anne Hill

Plague of Flies: Revolt of the Spirits, 1846

Laurel Anne Hill

Copyright 2021 Laurel Anne Hill
Published by Sand Hill Review Press
www.sandhillreviewpress.com
1 Baldwin Ave, #304, San Mateo, CA 94401

ISBN: 978-1-949534-20-7 Paperback
ISBN: 978-1-949534-21-4 ebook

Library of Congress Control Number: 2021911387

Cover by Julie Dillon
Interior by Backspace Ink

Names: Hill, Laurel Anne, author.
Title: Plague of flies : revolt of the spirits , 1846 / Laurel Anne
Hill.
Description: San Mateo, CA: Sand Hill Review Press, 2021.
Identifiers: LCCN: 2021911387 | ISBN: 978-1-949534-20-7
(paperback) | 978-1-949534-21-4 (ebook)
Subjects: LCSH Bear Flag Revolt, 1846--Fiction. | Mexican
War, 1846-1848--California--Fiction. | California--History--
1846-1850--Fiction. | Hispanic American women--Fiction. |
Bildungsroman. | Historical fiction. | Fantasy fiction. | BISAC
FICTION / Fantasy / Historical | FICTION / Magical Realism
| FICTION / Hispanic & Latino | FICTION / Coming of Age |
FICTION / Alternative History
Classification: LCC PS3608.I4347 P53 2021 | DDC 813.6--
dc23

SHRP
Sand Hill Review Press
1 BALDWIN AVE, #304, SAN MATEO, CA 94401

Dedicated to my beloved husband, David (now a spirit),
and to the spirits of my Mexican great-grandparents
Emigdio Medina and Hipólita Orendain de Medina.

I would like to thank all of the following for their love, support and/or belief in my work:

- Tory Hartmann, Editor of Sand Hill Review Press

- Julie Dillon, internationally acclaimed science fiction/ fantasy artist

- Rosario Melina Rodríguez, M.A., Ph.D., Editor, Stylos Editing LLC

- Kanyon CoyoteWoman Sayers-Roods, from Kanyon Konsulting LLC

- Desireé Duffy, *Black Château Enterprises*

- John Palisano, President of Horror Writers Association

- Christine Knight, editor of my preliminary manuscript

- Robert Yehling, editor of my preliminary manuscript

- Charlotte Cook and her writing group

- All of my family and friends who encouraged me to write this novel

I. First Days of the Bears, June 1846

1. Spirits, Worries and Swarms

ALL THESE FLIES. *Las moscas* swarm in circles around me at the corral's gate. I flinch. Where did they come from so fast? A low, shadowy figure—like a wolf or coyote—slinks along the edge of my eyesight, then flickers and disappears. A spirit in animal form, perhaps. A shiver travels down my spine. Flies close in and dot my hands. Fat, ugly insects. Maybe a spirit wants to measure the steadiness of my nerves.

I let go of the splintery gatepost. Shake my wrists over and over. Swat at the buzzing battalion. The new rope latch I need to install on the wooden gate to the adobe corral falls to the ground near my feet. *Madre de Dios*. The flies are as swift as those foreign warmongers who attacked my people fifteen days ago. Those horrid Yankees invaded the rancho of General Mariano Vallejo—a dear friend of my family—then claimed Alta California no longer is Mexican land.

"Leave me alone." I wave my arms this way and that. If some spirit tests me for squeamishness, I think I've just failed.

Inside the corral, one of Mamá's mares snorts. I turn. Blood trickles down Fandango's flank. The work of a single fly. For some reason, *las moscas* never bite me. But then, they're too busy threatening to bite me—showing me how easily they could. Do they ever swarm around anyone else? No, only Catalina Delgado. Me.

"Go and be useful for a change." I point in the direction of General Vallejo's rancho, a two-day journey north of here by horse and rowboat. "Go attack the wretched men of the Bear Flag."

Bear Flaggers invaded General Vallejo's home fifteen days ago and arrested him. They took over his entire rancho. Many of those Yankees remain there to terrorize his family. *México*—my beloved country—faces war with Los Estados Unidos as a result. My face warms, skin tingling. México won its freedom from Spain in 1821, nine years before my birth. We deserve to manage our own destiny. Here comes another round of buzzing. I swat at the flies again. The least these stupid insects could do is be patriotic.

"And when you're done with the Bear Flaggers," I tell them, "go bite their *presidente:* Polk." Too bad horseflies are neither useful nor loyal.

The flies head over to the nearby olive grove or to some other place. Time to finish my chore. I pick up the rope latch, balance on my bare toes, then try to stretch a loop of braided rawhide over the gatepost. Stubborn thing.

Bleached longhorn skulls—one hundred set in mortar and layered like bricks—stare at me harder than usual from the corral's far wall. Spirit people spy on me through those skeletal eye sockets. That's what *Papi's* old *vaquero* claimed the day before he died. I cross myself. Ghosts of people and animals... May the vaquero's prophecy about one particular spirit man remain unfulfilled.

"Catalina!"

Past the corral, Mamá stands close to the spreading oak, the tree I used to climb as a child. Her long black hair, coiled on top of her head like reeds woven into a basket, shines in the sunlight. Tortoiseshell combs fasten her tresses in place. How beautiful she is.

"War or no war," Mamá says, "the chamber pots need cleaning."

"*Sí*, Mamá." An orderly home is her answer to all adversity.

"And have you finally finished putting on that new latch?" Mamá rests her hands on her broad hips, her waist thicker than a month ago.

"*En un momento.*"

The horseflies are gone. If I use them as an excuse Mamá won't believe me. They never bother me when others are around. It isn't fair. I force the rawhide loop into final position and a splinter from the fence post jabs my finger. The tip protrudes from my skin.

"All done." I pick at the sliver. The thing wants to stay where it is.

"*Bien.* When you marry a wealthy *ranchero's* son, maybe you'll have time to waste on daydreams." She walks up the path toward the work rooms, her long blue broadcloth skirt swaying with each step.

"Sí, Mamá." Worrying about war and a spirit man is not the same as daydreaming.

Marriage. A wealthy ranchero's son. I let out a heavy sigh. Months have passed since I turned sixteen, but Papi has not yet arranged my marriage to Ángelo Ortega. The dying vaquero's prophesy about a spirit man riding off with me casts shadows on my reputation as a chaste young woman. Does Papi anticipate a rebuke from Ángelo's father?

I manage to remove the splinter from my finger. If only my worries would go away as well. Wind flutters the faded crimson sash around my waist. The tufted ends of my ebony braids hang past the front of my shoulders. I can almost feel the place where my beloved Ángelo once touched my hair. May Santa Catalina de Siena intercede on her humble namesake's behalf and facilitate my marriage.

Mamá often says faith must go hand-in-hand with deeds. The heat of summer already browns the distant green hillsides. I must enlist Mamá's help in prodding Papi toward action before the year ends. This week might be too soon, though. He works our southern pastures with my brothers and our hired vaqueros, rounding up our stray cattle so Bear Flaggers won't steal them.

Some horseflies return and buzz around me louder than ever. A dozen more circle the pair of docile mares Mamá always uses to pull her *carreta* now that she grows heavier with child. This morning the horses stand neck-to-flank, swishing their charcoal tails with a lazy rhythm, brushing the pests away from each other's dark eyes. Cooperation brings benefits.

Mamá might agree to help me if I cooperate and clean the chamber pots right away. Foxtails cling to the lower half of my skirt. Just my old green one. She doesn't like burrs of any sort in the house. I walk the dirt path toward the main house, pulling the prickly grasses out of my garment. It is hardest to reach the ones in the back at ankle length.

"Come see!" The high-pitched voice behind me belongs to my friend Josefa. "Someone travels this way."

Visitors? I turn around to face the cook's unmarried daughter. She runs toward me, flailing her dark-skinned arms. Her black braids, thick as bell ropes, bounce as she scurries. Alarm crosses the girl's round broad-nosed face. Dearest Josefa rarely displays fear, even that time Papi flogged her for disobedience.

In the distance, a cloud of yellow-brown dust billows along the ground. I squint into the mid-morning sun. Riders, or maybe a wagon, approach from the northeast. They're too far away to identify. Over a league. They could arrive in an hour. Or much less.

At breakfast, Mamá mentioned nothing about having visitors today. Who are these people? Do they bring bad news, the way my godfather did about General Vallejo's arrest? Bad news or good, I'd rather face messengers than unfriendly *Indios* or disgruntled Yankees. And far better to face almost anyone than a spirit man with the power to ride by day.

"We must tell Don Ygnacio." Josefa pants. She tugs my arm. "Now."

I nod. My dear *abuelito*, even though he walks with a cane and tends to forget things, is still the family head and needs to know. But wait: what if this is my godfather again? If so, Ángelo might be with him. As a dutiful grandnephew, he often is. Grandpa will send me into the kitchen to prepare beef and chili pepper stew for *la comida*, our mid-afternoon meal. I'll barely get a chance to see Ángelo at all.

"Wait a few more minutes," I say.

"But—" Josefa juts her head forward, eyes round as full moons.

"I said wait."

I spoke with too harsh a tone. May God forgive me. Josefa is a household servant, a descendant of coastal Indio peoples, but also my dear friend. Such laughter we always share while working together in the kitchen. We share secrets too.

"You're right to worry." I rest my hand upon Josefa's sloped shoulder. "But this way we'll have more information for Abuelito Ygnacio. For everyone."

Billowing dust cloaks shapes in the distance. I squint. Horsemen, not a wagon, advance across the valley floor. I'm sure. The azure sky and rounded hills frame four horses and three riders. Do they wear the short silver-trimmed jackets or woven serapes of civilized *Californios*, my people? Or the fringed buckskins, dark work shirts or mismatched rags of Bear Flaggers?

"Too many for messengers," I say.

"Not enough for tribal warriors planning a raid." Josefa's hands tent her forehead.

Whoever these riders are, their mounts now move with more haste. The old vaquero foretold the spirit man would ride a black Andalusian stallion carried by the wind. No telling yet if one of the approaching horses has the magnificent mane and tail of the Andalusian breed. Regardless, a bitter taste I don't recognize fills my mouth. Trouble comes my way.

"Warn the other women," I say to Josefa, and bolt toward the main adobe house.

My fingers grip the green calico of my skirt and raise my flouncing ruffled hem to knee level. Mamá often chastises me for showing my bare legs or pantalettes, even for revealing more than the lower edge of my petticoat at Misión de San José. But this is no time to trip and fall.

A rasping voice whispers unintelligible words into my ear, as if spirits watching from the skulls of the longhorns pursue me and speak. Where does the sound come from? Then the voice melts away, like hail landing upon heated stones.

A horsefly buzzes at my face. I bat the insect aside without slowing my pace, my heart pounding to the rhythm of unseen hooves. Who are those riders? Will I need to load Abuelito's musket? I clasp my crucifix. Worries are the horseflies of my mind.

2. Warning Abuelito

I BREATHE HARD from running and open the front door of my adobe home. The iron hinges squeak. I don't have permission to enter the house before noon and disturb Abuelito during his private time. But those riders will reach corrals and *casa* soon.

Are they Bear Flaggers? Will they take my grandfather prisoner and force me and Mamá? Even if the visitors are just harmless travelers, their rapid approach may mean someone pursues them. I step over the threshold, walk past my shoes and riding leggings, and into the cool semi-darkness of the entryway.

"Abuelito," I call. No one answers. Did he fall asleep while reading?

Ahead, sunlight streams through open window shutters and bathes the part of the main room I can see. Wrought iron bars in recessed windowsills cast parallel shadow-stripes on the tiled floor. I hurry beyond the entryway and turn left. Abuelito Ygnacio is sitting on his high-backed pine-and-cowhide chair at the far end of the main room. His shoulders hunch forward and his elbows rest on the sunlit dining table. He lifts his head as I approach. The skin around his stern eyes is more wrinkled than his yellowed shirt. His lips part, half-hidden by his lush white mustache and beard. Gnarled, large-boned fingers close the leather-bound book from General Vallejo, the only one of his three books he never lets me read.

"Pardon, please." Words rush from my mouth, like a flash flood speeding through an arroyo. "Strangers ride this way. Three, I think."

How strange to speak before I'm told to do so. I glance down, fingering the folds of my skirt.

"Do they ride Spanish Barbs?" Abuelito wraps a piece of sackcloth around his book. "Or are their horses Andalusians?"

I shrug. So, he worries about spirit men too. They might be less dangerous, though, than *hombres* made of flesh and blood.

"I'll get the musket," I say. "And the powder horn."

I step around the sooty iron brazier and metal stand in the middle of the room. Flecks of yesterday's ashes on the floor still await the straws of my broom. At the wall, I reach out toward a jagged crack in the plaster and grasp the barrel and sun-bleached stock of the family flintlock, mounted below a pair of crossed sabers.

"No," Abuelito says, his voice firm.

I turn. My grandfather stands clear of the table. The bottoms of his white linen drawers protrude through lateral slits in his knee-length breeches, like two flags hanging out of adjacent windows.

"If we need a musket," he says, "we will have already needed several."

"But—" Warmth flushes my face.

"Greeting visitors at gunpoint is ungracious. Have you learned nothing from me?"

Abuelito walks over to his open storage trunk, then trades his book for his quilted leather jacket and a flintlock pistol. He wedges the weapon into an inner pocket, nearly the length of the bulky garment from his military days. He never stores his pistols loaded. Did he forget to add powder and shot?

"Do you need some—"

"Go make sure all the women stay inside the work rooms." Abuelito straightens himself, but he still seems as bent as an old pine hammered by the wind.

"I've already sent Josefa." Why did he not let me finish my question?

"Go."

I must stay. Dare I say something more assertive to him? My stomach muscles tighten.

"I'm staying with you."

"Insolent child." Abuelito's palsied right hand trembles as he puts on his jacket. The garment's hem hides the tops of his tooled deerskin leggings and brushes his knitted silk garters. "Do as I say."

Abuelito plans to face potential gunfire with a jacket meant to stop arrows? Even Don Alonso Quixote, the madman in one of his books, would have better sense. If those garters were *riata* loops, I'd keep him from going anywhere.

I fold my arms against my chest. The curves of my blossoming breasts rest against my white calico sleeves. I may be disobedient, but my childhood has passed.

"If you consider me insolent," I say, careful to use the formal and respectful form of you, "flog me. Or make me sit in the corner next Sunday afternoon while you and the rest of our family eat *la comida*. But we greet the riders together."

He mouths words in silence.

"Then at least put some shoes on," he says. "I don't want friends—or enemies—to claim I've raised a barefoot savage who lacks good judgment and social graces."

I'm getting my way, despite his biting comment. I hurry back to the front door before he changes his mind. My silk stockings probably lie wadded at the foot of my bed. Instead, I grab my *botas*—the deerskin riding leggings won in a bet from my thirteen-year-old brother. But there is no time for fussy leather tubes and instep slings. I put my shoes on, leave my ankles uncovered, then drape the scarlet leggings over one arm.

Abuelito opens the front door to let me pass, then presses a narrow and weighted object into my free hand. A small dagger with an ornate silver hilt. My grandmother's dagger!

Didn't Abuelita María use this knife once to fend off a drunken pirate? My skin stings where my crucifix rests. Maybe a bad omen. What will happen when the riders arrive? My grandfather's pistol lies hidden inside his jacket's pocket. I conceal the knife within one of my leggings.

Outside, I walk across the low, wide porch, then duck under the inverted bouquets of dried red peppers hanging from the hand-hewn beams. That graveled voice returns, the one I heard earlier in the courtyard but couldn't understand. Whose voice? And coming from where? Is the cryptic message about intruders?

The voice speaks a familiar word, one the old vaquero taught me. *Suletu.* His people's word for flight...and flies.

3. The Bitter Taste of Truth

THE RIDERS ADVANCE at a trot along the dusty trail, weaving their way around scrub oaks and greasewood toward my home. I stand beside Abuelito in the courtyard, pressing my arms against my sides. My folded scarlet leggings hang from my hands, like stirrups from a saddle. Abuelita's knife hides within one. Holy Mother of God, may I not have to use it.

The wide brims of flat-crowned black sombreros shade the approaching horsemen's heads. Not the gray or tan rounded-top sombreros most Yankees choose. More like vaqueros or Mexican soldiers would wear. If these three men are Bear Flaggers, they come here in disguise.

Local vaqueros would be hard at work this hour. What about soldiers? No, these riders neither wear quilted leather military jackets nor carry lances, sabers or shields. Odd. Perhaps they're travelers seeking fresh horses and supplies. If so, selecting this rancho, the smallest in the region, makes little sense. That strange taste in my mouth from before returns, a hundred times as bitter as parsley. The twisted olive tree in the courtyard shades me from the sun but not from some unknown and unpleasant truth.

"No Andalusians," Abuelito mumbles. "But trouble rides to us nonetheless."

So, he feels it too. How fast can I pull the knife from my legging if needed? I clench my toes and feel the contours of pebbles and dry adobe soil through the calfskin soles of my suede shoes. A dagger is such a small weapon. If only Papi and his men stood beside us. Still, I must not show fear. And as weak as I may be, my young body has more speed and strength than Abuelito's.

The lead rider slows his horse to a walking pace at my brothers' favorite climbing tree. His two companions, wearing waist-length blue jackets, do the same. They pass the adobe corral. The strangers' foreheads glisten below the edges of black bandannas tied over their heads and worn under their hats. Their copper skin is as sun-weathered as the leather *chaparreras* they wear to shield their breeches and legs from underbrush. Crimson sashes hug their waists. Coiled rawhide *riatas* hang from the horns of their saddles. These vaqueros, ready to herd and rope cattle, arrive without smiles or greetings. Do their short broadcloth coats conceal guns?

One thing I do know for sure, because I always recognize our neighbors. I've never met these vaqueros before. They are not from a nearby rancho.

The lead rider reins his mount—a dun Spanish Barb with a white face and long black forelock—to standstill beside the watering trough, no more than ten horse-lengths from me. Silver spurs jut from the heels of his leather shoes. Neither his feet nor spurs press against the animal's heaving sides. At least he respects his horses.

Rage spews from the man's thin, deep-brown eyes, like sparks from a crackling fire. The fury in those narrow eyes dominates the vaquero's broad face and accentuates his thick neck and low-set hairline. All of his Indio features. Is he Costanoan, like Josefa? Maybe not. Our rancho is leagues inland, north of Misión de San José, close to the former lands of other tribes. Yet he could be Costanoan. I'll think of him as one for now. Regardless, a crimson stain soils the native man's white coarse-weave shirt, open at the neckline. Something—or someone—bloodied his left shoulder. Maybe he isn't mad at me or Abuelito.

The other two vaqueros reach the watering trough and dismount. The cheek of the older-looking one bears a jagged scar. A fly circles around him but doesn't land.

I glance toward Abuelito. He glowers over the top of his white beard, his expression sour. Then he steps in front of me and turns toward the vaqueros, as if trying to shield me. Sprawling branches of the twisted olive tree frame his stern profile.

"Welcome to our home," Abuelito says. His graveled voice betrays no hint of displeasure or alarm.

The wounded Indio nods, still seated in the saddle. Wrinkles pleat the skin near his eyes. I scan his two companions. Their thick necks and prominent ears frame flat-nosed oval faces. Coarse, straight black braids dip below the backs of their sombreros, like the tips of cats' dangling tails. Ragged black mustaches hang like mistletoe on oaks. The two resemble each other. They're probably brothers. Yet I've never met Costanoans or Spaniards with such flat noses before. Only a French trapper. Maybe these two men are *mestizos*, half Costanoan and half French. They could be the injured man's sons.

The sons might be looking for a *curandero*, a healer to tend to the older man's injuries.

"We must trouble you for water," the Costanoan says, his voice calm. "Perhaps for more."

His Spanish is more formal than I'm used to, although not flowery or old-fashioned as some from *Don Quixote* or the poem about the famous Spanish hero, El Cid. Gray streaks in his hair reflect morning sunlight. A garter—a length of braided silk cording—binds a knife to his right leg. The weapon is larger than Abuelita María's dagger. A horsefly buzzes near me. I swat the insect with my empty legging, but miss. The buzzing intensifies.

"I am Tomás," the Costanoan says. "Perhaps you have heard of me." He clears phlegm from his throat. "Is this not the rancho of Don Ygnacio Delgado?"

"It is." My grandfather squints and rubs his chin with age-spotted fingers. "Are those the horses of Don José de los Reyes Berreyesa?"

I tighten my grip on my leggings. No brands are visible on these mounts. What made Abuelito ask such a question?

The Berreyesa family lives almost as far away as General Vallejo does. Abuelito has no way to tell that ranchero's unbranded horses from another's.

"Don José de los Reyes Berreyesa no longer requires the services of horses." The Costanoan shifts in his saddle. "The white men of the Bear shot him, after they delivered the spirits of his twin nephews to our Creator."

Berreyesa murdered? A friend and harmless old man? I drop the empty legging and clutch my silver crucifix, a gift from that aging ranchero at the Feast of the Three Wise Men several Epiphanies ago. Bear Flaggers are barbarians. Someone must stop them. If only I could help.

But wait. Berreyesa's nephews were Ángelo's close friends. They often rode together. My breakfast churns in my stomach. Could harm have come to the man I dream of marrying?

Memories of Ángelo's playful green eyes and wavy black hair pour into my thoughts. His mustache, ends curved downward. His boyish smile. Then I can almost hear the crack of gunfire. A fountain of blood spurts from poor Ángelo's chest. His bright eyes dull. Close. I shudder. The scarlet legging in my left hand, the one concealing the dagger, wobbles in my grasp.

"Was anyone else—" I cup my free hand over my mouth, voice small as specks of dust.

The Costanoan, jaws set tight, turns toward me and shakes his head. "My brother was murdered. That is why I must speak to your grandfather and father. Alone."

"And your brother's name?" Abuelito fingers the side of his jacket. "I apologize if my question may bring you trouble. But I must know."

The two younger vaqueros exchange uncomfortable glances. The Costanoan tightens his hands around the reins and tilts his head upward, as if searching the pale sapphire sky. Why would the mention of his brother's name bring trouble? At least Ángelo isn't hurt. I cross myself and offer a silent prayer.

"My brother," the Costanoan says, "was Salvador Francisco de las Águilas."

"You said Salvador? Of the Eagles?" Abuelito's palsied hand trembles more than usual. The inner ends of his eyebrows pinch together above his prominent nose. "I will listen to your words on behalf of my son. For Vicente is not here."

"Then, I fear, you will need to dispatch a messenger. Request Vicente's return."

The Costanoan dismounts. He ambles with an irregular gait toward me. His legs bow outward, as if he remains astride his horse. His silver spurs jingle. Then his gaze locks on mine, tight as ropes binding steers during branding. How dare this *Indio* vaquero—no matter how well-spoken— approach me in such a bold manner? Or tell my grandfather what to do?

I step backward, half-stumbling on an uneven rock. The legging hiding the dagger dangles from my left hand. I hold the scarlet *bota* in front of me, folded end down, as if it is a knight's shield.

The two mestizos stand behind the Costanoan. Not one removes his sombrero or even tips the brim. Abuelito stands, his arms by his sides, as if powerless to speak or move.

The vaquero reaches out to me, the odors of his sweat and dirty leather *chaparreras* strong. My grandfather, who barely allowed Ángelo to get this close to me at *fiestas*, does nothing to stop this stranger. A shudder shoots through me. I deserve more respect than this. I must defend my personal honor and family reputation. So I pull out my abuelita's dagger from the legging, then unsheathe the weapon.

"Halt there." I brandish the knife in the Costanoan's direction, as if I face pirates.

He jumps clear of me, his deep-brown eyes wider than doors open on a hot summer night. He says something in a language I don't understand. Loud guffaws burst from his companions' mouths. How dare they mock me.

"Put that dagger down," Abuelito says, emphasizing each word. He shakes his head, as if reprimanding me during a reading lesson. "How ungracious to greet members of your own family at knifepoint."

My family? My arm and shoulder muscles stiffen. Mamá and Papi—all my family members—are *críollos*, Spaniards born in Alta California. None of them looks even a tiny part Costanoan or like any other native person I've seen. I must have misunderstood my grandfather's words. Or, did I? A horsefly lands on my shoulder. I flick the plump black insect away. Abuelito's face holds such an odd expression, one I can't interpret.

"Don Delgado, didn't my brother warn you?" The old Costanoan glances over his shoulder in Abuelito's direction. "Lies are serpents that return to strike when least expected." He removes his sombrero and holds it against his chest, then tucks a loose lock of his black-and-silver hair back under his bandanna. His stare bores into me. "Child, your grandfather should have told you years ago about your real mother."

Told me years ago? My real mother? What does this vaquero mean? Mamá is my real—

I utter a soft gasp as both my hands open wide. My dagger falls and clangs against a stone.

4. From Breath to Barricade

MY BREATH FLIES OUT of me, as if one of the vaqueros in front of me cinches a *lazo* around my knees and yanks me to the ground. Mamá is not my real mother? Mamá lied to me for sixteen years?

"I don't believe you." I cover my ears with my hands. "I won't believe you."

Pain radiates from Abuelito's dark cinnamon eyes— from his entire face. His thin lips pinch together, his jowls as wrinkled as crumpled paper. He does not question what the Costanoan said. He believes every word. My arms slump against my sides. My heart knows the truth my ears don't want to hear. Why has no one told me about Mamá before now?

"Come, little daughter," Mamá always said whenever disappointments overwhelmed me as a little girl. "Bring your troubles to my magic lap." Then my raven-haired mother would sit down, smooth her broadcloth skirt and pat the tops of her thick thighs. "Sit here."

Come, little daughter. Those words should have burned Mamá's tongue. A mockingbird twitters stolen songs from a twisted olive tree. A bird singing lies. Does Mamá even love me?

The injured Costanoan walks toward me. His silver spurs jingle. Blood cakes the shoulder of his cream-colored shirt. How can people of such low social status be part of my real family? I stumble sideways, trying to walk away from the old man. My shoe touches one of the scarlet leggings I dropped on the ground.

"Ride back to your home and stay there." Tears sting the corners of my eyes. They trickle like fresh blood from my wounded soul.

"Slumbering truths cannot sleep forever."

Softness grows within the man's narrow eyes. The wrinkles pleating his forehead smooth, like cloth rubbed by a servant's fingers. He stretches out one hand and cradles my damp cheek.

"Each truth has its day to awaken," he whispers.

"Who gave you the right to tell me about all this?" I snap. "About anything?"

I shove his hand away from my cheek. Abuelita's silver-handled dagger gleams on the dusty ground where I dropped it. Truth stabs deeper than any blade ever could.

"Who gave you the right to choose today?" I shove my fists against my hips and push my elbows out wide.

The man removes his sombrero, as if he prepares to apologize. Standing with his legs apart, he then presses his free hand against his wounded shoulder.

"My spilled blood gave me permission. And this day chose itself." The old vaquero turns around to face Abuelito. "I am Tomás, but I suspect you already know that. The spirit man on the black Andalusian stallion rides through the sky in our direction. Let Catalina lead my sons to your own Vicente while we still have time."

The spirit man? He rides this way so soon. What about my marriage to Ángelo?

"A proper young *señorita* should travel in the company of her father or grandfather." Abuelito squints one eye. "Besides, what makes you so certain about the spirit man?"

"I know what I know." The vaquero grins, exposing his yellowed teeth. "And you are too old for this ride."

"The day I'm too old to ride," Abuelito says, "will be my last day on Earth."

He straightens his shoulders and brushes lint off of his jacket. I tense from head to toe. The determination in Abuelito's voice does not erase the quiver in his hand.

"If my daughter's prophesy about the men of the Bear was right," Tomás says, "the last day on Earth for all of us soon approaches." He gestures toward me, his two sons and Abuelito. "Unless we act with haste."

Tomás' daughter is a seer? One who predicted the deaths of me and my family? The four men's stern expressions suggest grave concern. A shudder passes through me. Still, not all prophesies come true, and Tomás said acting with haste would help.

"What else did your daughter predict," I say, "about the Bear Flaggers?" The woman should have traveled here with her father and brothers.

The men exchange glances but avoid my stare. Tomás and his sons tilt their heads and look toward the heavens. A hawk—the symbol of a messenger from the sky—appears and circles.

Many reasons could keep the prophetess away. The war, in particular. Or being heavy with child. Yet a new uneasiness gathers in the pit of my stomach. The bitter taste in my mouth makes me want to retch. Is Tomás' daughter absent because she's my deceased mother? For whatever reason, the men are not in the mood to discuss such matters with me around. I need to talk to Papi and must obtain permission to find him.

"Please let me go," I ask Abuelito. "My father will ride back home with me—half of the journey. And these relatives will watch over me the rest of the way."

I pick up my grandmother's ornate dagger. May the winged figures on the hilt represent angels of mercy rather than angels cast out of heaven. My toes clench the leather insoles of my shoes. I stand straight and tall as I can, then slide the knife into its leather sheath.

Abuelito bows his head. He doesn't even mutter. I have never seen him this shaken before. Not ever. He's going to let me find Papi. I gather my riding leggings, drape them over one arm, then motion to Tomás.

"Your shoulder could use a *curandero's* help." My tone softens. "I'll have one of our stable hands fetch a healer from the next rancho."

Tomás nods, mystery within his eyes, his irises the color of caramelized sugar. At least his eyes—unlike Papi's all these years—suggest the presence of secrets. Many men keep mistresses, but I thought Papi was different. Did he disgrace Mamá before or after their wedding? Surely Ángelo will never do such a thing.

Mamá's eyes must harbor secrets too, but I can't demand answers from her now or in front of others. Papi has given Mamá enough sorrow already. A private confrontation with her will have to wait until I return.

#

Ready to ride, I stand beside Fandango—one of Mamá's mares—within the adobe corral and stroke the horse's velvety Roman nose. Outside the enclosure, Tomás' two sons ready the fresh mounts Abuelito offered them. Josefa hurries down the path from the work rooms but I do not see Mamá anywhere.

No doubt Mamá has learned I know the big secret, and many people's lips buzz with the prophesy of doom. Servants on this rancho have ears like coyotes. Gossip travels fast.

What remains unrevealed, though, concerns me more. I still don't know all the reasons for fetching Papi from the southwest pasture, where he went to herd his stray stock away from cattle-thieving Yankees.

Perhaps these vaqueros seek revenge for the murder of that person—Salvador de las Águilas. They plan to fight Bear Flaggers and expect Papi to join them. Don José Berreyesa— may his departed soul dwell with saints in paradise—was Papi's godfather. Honor could prompt Papi to join the vaqueros' quest. If so, I must find a way to lend meaningful support, even if Papi insists women belong at home.

The familiar long-horned skulls stare at me from the corral's adobe walls. Once they lived, breathed and grazed.

So final, death is for a being without a soul—according to the friars. Yet can even a human soul in Heaven smell the freshness of Earth after a spring rain or gaze into the eyes of a loved one once all flesh rots away? And who knows what really happens if the Lady of Shadows completes that fateful visit all people receive, before a friar arrives to say prayers of absolution? Something I think I read in *Don Quixote* tugs at my memory, just beyond reach. Regardless, if fate destined me and Papi to leave this earthly life soon, may the Holy Mother of God provide us with plenty of warning.

Fandango noses my shoulder, the nudge setting me off balance. The animal's hoof paws the ground. A different type of warning. The dry-mouthed mare, not accustomed to a bit, wants her usual hackamore bridle. But Tomás' two sons mount their stallions. I need to get going before Abuelito changes his mind.

"It's all right," I whisper to Fandango, my footing regained. "I won't pull your reins hard."

I wedge one foot into the stirrup, then swing my other leg over Fandango's saddle. I settle in the leather-draped seat. My shabby green skirt bunches around my thighs like mounds of sheared wool ready for bagging. There was no time to change into my good clothes. My exposed broadcloth breeches cling to the skin above my knees. Scarlet leggings hide the breeches' lower hems. Ángelo would not approve of me wearing men's pants and leggings instead of petticoats, but my chances of meeting him today are smaller than small.

"Don't you remember how to use a sidesaddle?" My grandfather rests his arms atop the fence's gate rail, his head tilted down, as if he counts splinters.

"Oh, yes, my head remembers all you taught me." My chest heaves a long sigh. "My legs don't. Please forgive them."

Abuelito mumbles. I counter with a pleading smile. My legs press against the mare's warm sides and my fingers cinch the rawhide chin-tie of my sombrero. At least he's regained his ability to speak and criticize.

The mare trots from the corral, then stops near the other two riders and nibbles on a clump of browning grass.

Abuelito closes the wooden-rail gate. Tomás stands nearby, his arms folded against his broad chest. The outer edges of his squinting eyes curve down. Surely his bloodied shoulder must hurt. Yet he hasn't rinsed the wound or requested soothing herbs and a cloth dressing. I run my hand through the coarse strands of Fandango's charcoal mane, uneven as a young girl's first piece of weaving. Perhaps my Costanoan grandfather's worries about his daughter's prediction are bigger than his concern about his wound.

"You can't ride like this," Josefa's high-pitched voice calls from behind me. She scurries from the path to my side. "Not with your breeches showing."

Josefa's short, thick fingers tug at my skirt. Then she darts from one side of Fandango to the other, smoothing wads and folds of green cloth until my skirt drapes down below both knees and hides the garment sewn for my brother. An uneasy feeling sweeps through me, as if winds from a brewing storm call my name. My real mother might be, or have been, a proud woman shamed by servitude. Does Josefa feel the same way? I should have straightened my own clothing.

But I mustn't think of myself as a Costanoan or a member of any other native people. My family belongs to the *gente de razón*, the people of reason. Respected citizens. I may be a *mestiza*, part Spaniard and probably part Costanoan, but I'm not a lowly peon.

"Now you look like a fine lady." Josefa smiles, revealing her overlapping front teeth. "A real Delgado."

A fine lady. A real Delgado. Josefa emphasized those words. She's heard the gossip about Papi and tries to make me feel better. Wait. Has Josefa known the truth about my mother all along? If so, the other household servants must have known too. Embarrassment warms my face.

"I'll clean the chamber pots for you while you're away." Josefa fingers one of her ropy braids. "Today changes nothing between us," she whispers. "Ride with God."

How sincere Josefa sounds, yet a lopsided squinting expression forms on her face. Something besides wagging tongues troubles her.

In the midst of all this, I can't help but think of my beloved Ángelo. His thick black moustache accents his suntanned skin and high cheekbones. His green eyes sparkle and bring comfort. Who cares what other people whisper about me?

Yet will I live long enough to wed him? If I do, will Ángelo want an illegitimate *mestiza* for a bride? Did Papi delay arranging my marriage to Ángelo because Don Ortega already refused his request?

I touch my crucifix, the metal cool. My shoulders and arms sag like a worn homespun sack. Today may not alter my relationship with Josefa. But it barricades the doorway between me and my dreams.

5. Jedidiah Jones

JEDIDIAH JONES RIDES the trail toward New Helvetia, the fort and ranch of John Augustus Sutter. The dust and blistering sun aren't to his liking this afternoon. Actually, any afternoon. But killing a man yesterday morning got under his skin like a bevy of ticks. Just makes the long, hot ride home worse. His mama never raised him to be a murderer.

Not that Jedidiah set out to shoot some fool Indian in the back. Hell, Indians have just as much right to live to a ripe old age as anyone else, although a lot of his own people don't cotton to that sentiment. But this crazy redskin aimed his bow-and-arrow straight for an American Army officer. Would have poked John C. Frémont in the rear of his heart or lung for sure. Jedidiah couldn't have let that go by.

Well, maybe he could have.

Jedidiah's bay stallion slows to a walk. Foam drips from the stallion's mouth. He raises his head and pricks his ears, searching for water. Time to head for a stream before the horse decides to gallop there without a rider.

The image of the dead Indian merges with that of the three other bodies: an old Mexican and a pair of younger ones who looked like twins. Jedidiah never would have pulled the trigger on that Indian if Frémont had already ordered Kit Carson to shoot Don José Berreyesa and the de Haro kids. A real bad business. Oh, there are people Jedidiah wouldn't mind seeing dead. One ranchero and his son, in particular. But wanting Emilio and Ángelo Ortega dead and taking care of the job are two different matters.

Dang dust. Jedidiah spits out a mouthful and directs his mount down a ravine. How good, to hear the sound of flowing water. The saltwater rolling onto the shore near the old mission yesterday morning sounded good too, when someone still rowed those three Mexicans to an empty beach. The gray-haired Indian with the bow and arrow hadn't arrived yet. Neither had John C. Frémont. Jedidiah had gone to the spot with a message for Frémont. The bastard held some Mexicans prisoner in John Sutter's Fort. How could Jedidiah have known Frémont had no intention of taking any additional prisoners?

The bay stallion lowers his head and drinks. Better watch his damn horse or it'll drink itself sick. Knowing when to stop ain't no instinct. Would Mexicans have shot Jedidiah if they'd found the dispatch he carried? Maybe. Probably not. Would depend who caught him.

He could use a shot of whiskey right now, but the weather is too blasted hot. Besides, he doesn't have a long ride ahead. Whiskey can wait.

Once upon a time, Jedidiah's daddy told him flies were made for spiders to eat them. Mexicans—including the Californios variety—and Indians aren't flies. Jedidiah's no spider. No matter, he helped the wrong man die yesterday morning. Whiskey would only twist the truth into a thousand lies.

6. The Spirit Man

HOOVES POUND THE TRAIL. Dust swirls upward. As I ride, I glance at my escorts, Tomás' two sons. The one with the scar on his cheek rides beside me. He's the elder. The younger trails several lengths behind. By the light of Our Lady. What drives these men to fetch Papi with such haste?

The murders of Don José Berreyesa and Salvador of the Eagles must be involved. Or the spirit man and prediction of doom. Or both. Still, some other truth waits to reveal itself, and I don't need a bitter taste on my tongue to know. Something more disturbing than the identity of my real mother.

I spit dirt from my mouth, my lips sandy as soil. The ride to the southwest pasture always coats me with grit. Today the air also cloaks my world in mystery.

"Let's slow down," the vaquero beside me says.

I give Fandango's reins a gentle tug. No need to slice her tongue. How could the stable boy have given her any spade bit, let alone one neither wrapped nor salted? What did the foolish boy think?

The horses ease into a trot. Fandango's breathing slows. Beyond a cluster of live oaks sit the open walls of a half-built hovel. A supply of pale brown adobe bricks dries in the sun. Squatters have invaded Delgado land, probably Yankees with guns and no immigration papers. Unlike the Yankee traders in Monterey—civilized merchants and sea captains—these Yankee squatters will likely fight beside Bear Flaggers and refuse to learn Spanish or convert to Catholicism. No good will come of the increasing foreign presence in Alta California. I scan the browning hillsides for the intruders. Nothing. Do they cower behind the low, misshapen walls of the hovel? No, their horses are gone.

"The Mexican government should send more soldiers to the Presidios," I mutter, head held high. "Deport immigrants without proper visas."

"Travelers in need of food and shelter may be saints in disguise." The vaquero beside me clears his throat. "Didn't your family teach you to be gracious?"

A rush of anger tingles my skin. This vaquero has impudence as well as sharp ears. Still, I shared his attitude until recent days.

"Why don't you ask the Bear Flaggers about their manners?" I bounce in the saddle as Fandango trots. "Especially the men who hold General Vallejo and his family captive?"

I don't need to mention those who murdered Tomás' brother or Berreyesa. The tone of my voice included them already.

A bend in the trail takes me to an incline. Fandango slows. Dust clouds settle. The older of the two vaqueros spurs his stallion and moves in front of me. Does he think I can't lead the way up the hill? I lean forward in my saddle as Fandango climbs the narrow path between unruly bushes and brambles, my legs hugging her sides. That briar could strip flesh from bones the way boiling water peels tomatoes. I should have worn leather *chaparreras*.

A rushing sound reaches my ears. Water. The sweet odor of lush grasses fills the air. The main creek lies ahead. The sun hangs at its highest point. My group and I have ridden over two leagues—a good distance to cover in little more than an hour—but our horses will need water soon. And I'll need to show Tomás' sons the next landmarks for finding Papi.

Tomás. The name stings my thoughts, as if I rub my wounded pride with cut limes. The news about my parentage shocked me so much. I don't even remember being

37

introduced to his two sons. An oversight Mamá would never make.

The lead vaquero signals us to stop. He has detected the creek too. He turns, then sits motionless in his saddle. His head tilts to one side as his lips pinch together. His short black braid angles between the nape of his neck and his shoulder.

"Señorita Delgado," he says.

His tone is low and respectful, as it should be.

"Which way does the creek wind?" he adds. "Where's its next bend toward this trail?"

I pat Fandango's neck and study the rugged slope. Papi always waters the horses nearby. The creek flows fast over rocks and its banks aren't steep or treacherous. Does this vaquero suggest a different place?

I point toward the valley between two adjacent rolling hills. "The creek comes from that direction. It'll bend near the trail twice before we reach the southwest pasture. But our horses need water now."

"Our horses aren't the only thirsty animals." The vaquero spurs his stallion. The mount scrambles up the rocky trail, hooves clomping and leather saddle creaking.

"What do you mean? Do you see signs of bears?" Bears often forage for berries along creeks this time of year.

A loud crack rips through the air. The sound echoes off the hills, as if Satan lashes a giant whip from the distant mountaintop. Fandango skitters. I tighten my grip on her reins. That's gunfire, I'm sure.

Perhaps the same squatters from before are hunting rabbits. Or deer. Either way, it's time to put some distance between us and the unpredictable Yankees.

"Get moving," I call to the others.

I dig my heels against Fandango's sides and jiggle the reins. The mare lunges forward, neck arching. I lurch in the opposite direction, off balance. I've ridden horses most of my life, some even bareback. How can I lose my balance now?

Another gunshot echoes. Fandango rears, hooves boxing the air. I brace my feet against the wooden stirrups. This is no time to be thrown. My knees grip the horse's sides. My hands tug the reins. I slip backward in the saddle. Fandango trumpets a terrified call to action. What has happened to Mamá's docile mare?

My hands cling to the saddle's horn. I jerk as the horse's front hooves land on the ground. Oh, no, I've dropped the reins. The mare rears again. I land even harder.

My hands let go of the horn, dart for the leather reins and yank them. Fandango bolts off the trail, leaps over a low-growing bush, then gallops as if hornets chase her. The bit hurt her mouth. I pulled too hard. My rear end smacks against the saddle. This mare is stampeding like a wild stallion. Did I sever the poor creature's tongue?

There's only one thing to do: ride this out. I lay my head and chest against Fandango's neck. My sombrero tilts. My fingers cling to her mane. Now my buttocks no longer bang against the saddle. Thick brush scrapes at my breeches. My leg burns. Thorns must have cut me. Fandango better come to her senses soon.

A third crack of gunfire reverberates off the hills. Fandango whinnies and leaps over a fallen tree. The mare will never slow down, not until she drops from exhaustion, or stumbles and falls. I can see myself with a broken leg in a thicket of poison oak.

Where are the vaqueros? They're supposed to stay with me. I don't dare sit up straight in the saddle to look for them. The wind pushes my sombrero back, pulling the tie against my throat. Did a shot wound one of my companions? Bear Flaggers don't value the lives of native peoples or us Californios.

Fandango charges onward, dodging clumps of tangled bushes. Brown dust billows from dry earth. Grit stings my eyes. I shut them. In the darkness, a wave of buzzing flies coats my body, as if I'm a fallen fawn half-eaten by a cougar. Why am I thinking about flies? I have to regain control of my horse and my fears. I open my eyes.

The ground levels out. I blink to clear my vision. Fewer brambles and poison oak clumps grow here. Hoof beats drum the earth louder than before. At least one horse gallops behind me.

Someone speeds to my rescue.

I try to glance backward, my cheek pressing against Fandango's neck. My hat bounces. The elder mestizo must be the one coming to my aid. Wouldn't that be his responsibility?

A horse with a lofty gallop races beside mine, as if he charges into battle. This animal is larger than Fandango, over a full hand higher, and black as obsidian. I blink over and over. My eyes water. An abundant ebony mane flows over the horse's arched neck. The forelock whips between well-placed ears. *Madre de Dios*. This horse is no common mustang, no Spanish barb. It is an Andalusian, like the one in the prophesy.

A man leans out of the Andalusian's saddle, his arm stretched out. The wind billows his white sleeve. Fingers hidden by short, black leather gloves grab Fandango's reins. His exposed wrists are as pale as those of the dead.

Fandango slows down. Fragments of a saying I once heard or read to Abuelito slide into my memory. Something about being full of life and then meeting death. A shudder starts within me and works its way from my bones to my skin.

The spirit man has arrived sooner than expected. I'm not ready to die.

7. Hoof Prints

I SIT UP in the saddle, my heart beating hard. As Spirit Man's black Andalusian halts, so does Fandango. I dare not look at his face, despite his chivalry. Not yet. What if a hollow-eyed skull with a macabre grin stares back?

More hoof beats. Tomás' two sons approach us on horseback. I need to acknowledge Spirit Man, if only to express my gratitude and make introductions. Is not bravery a virtue? Besides, no stench of death or dank earth comes from the stranger. He gives off no odor of any sort. Tilting my chin upward, I turn in his direction.

"Thank you, for—"

What is this? Whiskers bunch on the stranger's ruddy jowls, like wool on a half-sheared lamb. Sunburned skin peels on his nose and beardless chin. Hair the color of reddish-brown sand pokes from under his gray narrow-brimmed sombrero. This man is no spirit. In fact, he is neither Mexican nor Spaniard. He is a Yankee!

"A thousand pardons, *señorita*," he says in mispronounced Spanish. He tilts the brim of his hat in my direction. "My friends chased away a bear. We meant no harm to you or your servants."

"Meant no harm?" The words race from my mouth before I can stop them. "Shooting here and there, even as rumors of war buzz around like flies on a bloody carcass? I could have been killed." And how dare he assume that *mestizos* must be servants! I'm not one.

I put my sombrero back on my head and reclaim Fandango's reins. The vaquero with the scar edges his mount between me and the Yankee, as if this stranger is a calf to cut from the herd and brand. An odd multi-colored light gleams within the stranger's irises. Just as quickly, it's gone. I must have imagined the glow.

"My friends," the Yankee says in a low voice, "were unaware of your presence."

"Well, my vaqueros could offer you some fine lessons on controlling bears." I smile with all the sweetness of unripe fruit. "They rope them. For sport." My fingers push a loose strand of black hair away from my eyes. "And these men are not my servants, kind sir. Does a chaste young woman ride unchaperoned? These are members of my dear family."

There. I'll let the Yankee chew on those words and try to digest them. A breeze whispers in my ear. Should I try harder to digest my own words?

"Lessons would be better another time, señorita." The Yankee's mouth curves in a tentative grin. No wrinkles form on his face. "Today I resume my journey to Monterey."

He appears younger than my father and now, somewhat familiar. Yet I've never seen him at my rancho or at Misión de San José. When I traveled to Monterey Harbor with Papi last year, I bartered cowhides and tallow for dressmaking cloth. Did I see this man while there?

A flash of opalescent light from the stranger's eyes makes my hands tremble. No expressions of alarm cross the vaqueros' solemn faces. They did not notice. I must end this unsettling meeting.

"Thank you for your help," I say, voice faltering.

The Yankee nods his head and jiggles his mount's reins. Just for a moment, the man's eyes turn golden. The black Andalusian stallion he rides trots in the direction of the stream. Dust puffs from the dry ground, like spilled flour swept hard with a broom. Foreigner and horse disappear from sight down a wooded ravine.

Does the man live in Monterey? My breakfast of beans and tortillas begs to return to my mouth. I don't let it. I will not ask Papi to take me to Monterey this autumn, even if I need fabric for a bridal gown.

I must not dwell upon matters of marriage right now. The vaqueros wait, their mustaches glistening with sweat. Time to head for water, then find Papi. He will have some explaining to do, and not just about my real mother. Yet I don't think I'll ask him to explain eyes that flash light.

"The ravine where the stranger went," I say to the vaqueros. "It has water this time of year."

"Bad luck, using this part of the ravine," the younger-looking vaquero says. "Let me show you something."

He rubs the back of his neck, then leads me to the ravine's edge. He points in the direction the stranger took. No, he points straight down toward the ground ahead. Then I realize what's on his mind. I see no hoof prints, as if the Andalusian's four hooves touched only air.

#

Fandango ambles up the eroded trail as I lead the vaqueros toward the crest of another hill. The horse's uneven movements jostle me in the saddle. Right now, I could use Spirit Man's stallion, the horse whose hooves don't have to touch the ground. How dry my mouth turns, as if my jest is blasphemy. At least we found a safe part of the ravine to water the horses.

A few wild blackberries would refresh my mouth, but mazes of thorns and poison oak guard all the plump, ripe fruit nearby. Hard to tell where temptation ends and punishment begins. A breeze tugs at my sombrero and shifts direction. A divine instruction meant for me? Yes, I need to shift, to leave spirit horses for the spirits, even in my thoughts.

Clomps of hooves quicken behind me. Soon the vaquero with the scared cheek rides beside me again, the high collar of his blue waist-length jacket darkened with sweat. He turns toward me. I study his deep-brown eyes and tilt of his head. His eyebrows pinch together as he clamps his jaw. Something disturbs him.

43

"Let me lead, until I see the path down," the vaquero says. "My father, he lost his brother. He's not prepared to lose a granddaughter too."

I glance away. Granddaughter. So that truly is my relationship to Tomás. I run my fingers through Fandango's mane. How degrading, being the granddaughter of a Costanoan.

"Don Ygnacio Delgado is my grandfather."

"A hare wishing to fly, changes not into an owl," the vaquero replies. "Don Delgado is only your Spanish abuelito."

I rub one of my shoulders, my cheeks warm again. This man's odd statements leave me ashamed of being ashamed. At least I am a Delgado. I'll find a way to cope with the rest.

"Then take the lead, my dear Costanoan uncle." My reply repeats in my mind. How strange to address a vaquero as family. And he might be from a different tribe.

"I am half *Oljon*, Catalina. It would please me and our ancestors if you refer to our correct name, the one we all recognize. Or simply acknowledge we come from the peoples of the west, family of Tomás Tomás."

So now I've insulted him? And why is his father's given name identical to his surname?

"Do you not know your family name?"

"The priests and friars, they hid away my family name generations ago. Look to the sky, then to the earth. That is my family."

A puffy white cloud bears the shape of Spirit Man's pale hand. On the ground, golden poppies reflect one of the colors within Spirit Man's mystical eyes. Is Spirit Man part of my family, or the key to discovering their identity? At the hill's crest, I peer at distant mountains capped with a blue haze. The life I knew before this morning dwells equally far away.

I must not let such concerns distract me from what is most important. Finding Papi.

The sun hangs more than a little beyond its highest point. The early hours of the afternoon slip away too fast. In the valley below lies the southwest pasture. Fandango picks her way down the rocky, uneven slope. I lean forward, pulled by gravity, and rock from one buttock to the other. The wind gains strength. My calico cloth skirt puffs up like a sprouting mushroom cap, exposing the breeches underneath. I press my narrow-brimmed sombrero against my head. The sleeves of my white blouse flutter.

No sign of Papi or his cattle yet.

Deep ruts border the path down the adobe hillside. Mire lies where late spring rainwater has pooled and flowed. Patches of lush green grasses flourish in the muck. Soon I see them, the cattle grazing in the valley, a broad strip of flat land wrinkled by shallow ravines. There could be four hundred longhorns here, or more. I can't see Papi yet, but he has to be around somewhere.

"Hurry," I call to my elder uncle, who rides several feet ahead of me. "We're here."

He halts his horse and looks back at me. "Only a foolish fox leaps off a cliff to speed his way to the river."

"Why should I listen to—to vaqueros?" The pain in the man's eyes makes me glance down at my scraped leggings. That was a cruel remark. My Oljon uncles were only trying to help keep me safe. May God forgive me. "Besides, I don't even know your names."

"Jesús," my older uncle says.

"You should not take our Lord's name in vain," I scold, "just because I didn't pay attention when Tomás introduced you."

"Jesús is my name. The one my mother gave me." The vaquero smiles and scratches the side of his neck. "I'm Jesús María of the Wolves."

What a foolish mistake. Surely my cheeks turn red as Mamá's salsa. Tomás and his wife must be good Catholics to have given their son such pious first and middle names. Perhaps this side of my family includes people of reason, after all.

"Why are you a wolf?" I say, my tone of voice softer. "Your father's brother was an eagle. Is it because the priests and friars kept your real family name a secret?"

45

"My abuelita, she chose sacred names to protect us. She always worried something bad would happen to us. Wanted us each to have a different guiding power." He gestures toward his brother, behind me up the hill. "Each name holds magic."

"What was your sister's name?" Was my real mother a wolf too?

"Speaking a name of the dead won't bring trouble after all these years. But it is not yet time for you to know."

So, my natural mother truly is dead. I have no memory of her. I picture Mamá's broad smile and raven-black hair. What will Mamá say when I ask for information?

"We should move along," I say.

The path widens. Jesús and I ride side-by-side. Earlier today, my grandfather apologized to Tomás when asking about Salvador of the Eagles. Maybe recently departed spirits can hear their names and make mischief.

"Why did your abuelita always think bad things would happen?" I clutch the reins with one hand.

"Because many years have passed since Creation Time." Jesús María's eyes appear deep, as if they are liquid pools of wisdom. "Ever since Creation, the good part of the world has faded like dyed clothes in the sun. Or, so her stories claimed."

"Do you believe as she did?"

Jesús María shrugs. "Most of the time."

Mamá taught me about the six days of creation. I don't recall anything about dyed clothes, though. According to Mamá, Adam and Eve wore nothing at all. Did two creations happen? How could the world have been formed twice? Jesús María's grandmother must have added her own opinions to the story.

"Tell me more," I say.

Jesús María smiles. "My grandmother, she claimed grass was more beautiful long ago. I ignored what she said for years. But one day, I realized what she meant. Spaniards filled Alta California's hillsides with herds of cattle. I don't know why it is so, but cattle changed the grasses and the land." He sits up straight in the saddle. "I respect the words of elders. The old ones speak of truths they once lived."

How hard to imagine more beautiful grasses growing around here, at least when they are green. I scan the landscape and squint. Amber blotches mar the hillsides, a typical sight by late June. Did those other grasses stay green longer, like the ones thriving in still-damp adobe muck? When did his grandmother first notice a difference? The change, unlike the one in my life today, couldn't have happened all at once. How could anyone be so observant?

Dust clouds puff up off the ground in the distance. Riders approach from the north end of the valley. Only three. Not enough to be Papi and all my brothers, or our vaqueros. Bear Flaggers would likely travel in a larger group. Another unexpected horsemen puzzle.

Jesús María again maneuvers his chestnut stallion ahead of Fandango. His brother catches up and joins him. The trail curves to the left. Jesús reaches down the side of his hide legging. His fingertips brush the silver hilt of his dagger, as if he needs to know the weapon remains strapped in place. These vaqueros are good uncles, concerned for my safety.

The approaching riders are now easier to see. Two appear much smaller than the third. Wind billows the loose sleeves of their open-necked white shirts. Red ribbons lace the sides of their breeches, ribbons I threaded through eyelets just this morning. Diego and Gabriel! My ten-year-old brothers. Their companion is much slimmer than Papi.

Fandango reaches the valley floor. I spur the mare's sides. A *caballero* rides behind my youngest brothers. His low-crowned sombrero, canted in a stylish manner, obscures his face. His gilt hatband sparkles in the sunlight, while many silver buttons decorate the legs of his black velveteen *calzoneras*. Only a fine gentleman would wear such expensive long pantaloons instead of ordinary breeches. Yet Papi and my other brothers are nowhere in sight. Did something happen to them?

Jesús María signals for me to slow down. Both vaqueros rein their horses to a walking pace. They place themselves on either side of me.

"Catalina?" the caballero calls.

Ángelo's voice. My beloved. May saints be praised.

My heartbeat quickens, like castanets clicking when I dance in circles. The backs of my hands tingle. Why did I not recognize him? Because I did not expect to see him? Yet here I am, wearing men's pants instead of women's petticoats. And my old skirt better suited for cleaning chamber pots. Diego and Gabriel squeal welcoming greetings. Grins spread across their cherubic faces. My uncles and I rein our horses to a standstill. Ángelo does the same.

He removes his sombrero and stares at me with wide gray-green eyes, his rosy lips parted. His eyebrows raise faster than a startled porcupine's quills. Even the narrow band of whiskers along his jawline seems to stiffen. His drooping black moustache twitches.

"Who are you?" He glares at my uncles, the expression in his eyes cold and hard as hailstones. "What are you doing with Señorita Delgado?"

I glance down at my dusty arms and hands. My scraped leggings. After that wild ride through brambles, I look as if I rolled on the ground. No reputable young Spanish woman would ride with vaqueros and no chaperone. Ángelo imagines the worst.

"Señorita Delgado takes us to find her father," Jesús María says.

"These are my uncles," I add.

My stomach twists. Warmth surges to my face. The words escaped my mouth far too fast. Anyone can see my uncles are part Costanoan. Oljon, I need to remember that word. Do most Californios even pay attention to the names of various groups of native peoples or the differences between them?

Regardless, how will Ángelo feel about me being a *mestiza*? A fly lands on the back of my hand and rattles, as if it were trapped inside of a glass jar.

8. The Promise

ÁNGELO'S GLARE burns into me. He returns his sombrero to his head, then clutches his horse's reins. His bronze hands tighten into fists. I expected news of my Oljon lineage to shock, even repulse him. I didn't anticipate wrath.

"These are your relatives?" Ángelo emphasizes every word and gestures toward my two uncles. His upper lip curls.

Jesús María and Santiago edge their chestnut stallions across trampled grass and in front of Fandango. They sit straight in the saddle, waist-length jackets tight on their lean frames, and form a barrier between Ángelo and me. Fandango whinnies and skitters. Her hooves raise puffs of dust from a bald stretch of the valley floor. I stroke the mare's neck, the taste of grit and misery inescapable.

Why did I admit that Jesús María and Santiago are my relatives? Couldn't I have explained their presence in a better way? But, wait. Ángelo always treats his papi's servants with respect, an attitude not expressed by several of the men in his family. Might disbelief of my words prompt the dark, furious expression filling his face? Does he think these men are not related to me? If so, he probably accuses me of lying. Of scandalous and dishonorable behavior. Only several horse-lengths separate me from my heart's desire. The distance might as well be leagues.

I need to speak. Do something. My insides shudder. My cheeks warm. Why can't I talk? And why does Ángelo not say anything else?

"Abuelito Ygnacio sent us to find Papi."

49

I flash an uncertain smile, then fidget with the horn of Fandango's saddle. My uncles speak well and are good Catholics. If they aren't actually *gente de razón*, they must rest pretty close to the mark. I should not feel ashamed to introduce them.

"Bear Flaggers have murdered Don José Berreyesa. My honorable uncles—Jesús María and Santiago—brought the news."

Ángelo looks down. His glare dissolves into nothingness. His arms and shoulders sag as much as a ship's sail on a windless day. Now he believes me. Yet does he only want a pure Spanish wife?

Ángelo removes his black, flat-crowned sombrero and clutches it against his chest. "I already told your father about Don José de los Reyes Berreyesa. And about Berreyesa's two nephews." He takes a slow, deep breath and exhales. The corners of his eyes glisten. "I saw them die. Don José, Francisco. Ramón. All three of them."

"You were—"

A rush of bile stings my throat. I swallow hard. My hands cover my mouth. Ángelo witnessed the murder? They could have shot him too.

"I could do nothing," Ángelo says. "Nothing!"

What does he mean he could do nothing? Did the Yankees hold him back? No, those horrid men simply would have killed him. An expression of helplessness freezes on his face. Did helplessness cause his inaction yesterday? Did fear keep him from defending his friends?

A putrid taste coats my tongue, one having nothing to do with bile or butchered longhorns. Is Ángelo a coward? My very thoughts burn my tongue.

No! I've seen Ángelo's bravery with bulls during *fiestas*. How grand he looks when he maneuvers a red cape as a horned beast charges. Ángelo, at eighteen, is shorter than his four older brothers, and probably not as strong. But he's no coward. Yesterday, with Berreyesa, surely he barely escaped death. My poor, dear love.

"I rowed the three of them to the beach," Ángelo says. "Near Point San Quintín. Don José Berreyesa was anxious to reach his son in Sonoma. With the arrest of Maríano Vallejo, and all the turmoil, the old man feared for his son's life."

Ángelo appears to scrutinize Jesús María and Santiago. His lips pinch together. Does he worry about confiding in vaqueros?

"It's all right to speak. These are trusted men. My natural mother's brothers." There, I spoke the whole truth. What will happen now?

My twin younger brothers, wearing matching breeches and gray felt sombreros, sit on their mounts behind Ángelo. I almost forgot the boys were there. Puzzled expressions fill their faces. Yet Ángelo nods, as if the news about my real mother does not disturb him at all.

Ángelo must truly care for me. Does he love me with great passion? Dare I even think such a glorious thought in the middle of this wretched tale? My heart throbs so.

I listen, floating on Ángelo's every word. He speaks about Berreyesa's nephews. Yesterday, Francisco carried a sealed military message in his shoe. As the four men removed saddles from the rowboat near *Misión San Rafael*, Ángelo noticed a stranger standing on top of the hill. He thought the man to be a trapper. I clench my stomach muscles, preparing for the dreadful words to come.

"I did not know the content of the military communication Francisco carried." Ángelo's voice sounds hoarse, as if emotion pinches his throat shut. "But I did know of his plan to plant false messages for the Bear Flaggers to discover. I could not risk someone borrowing the boat we might need for escape. So, I pushed off from the beach to conceal the vessel somewhere else and left my friends. Then other men joined the one on top of the hill."

Another deep flush reddens Ángelo's light bronze cheeks. If only I dared to jiggle the reins and maneuver Fandango toward him. Grasp his hand. Do the solemn expressions on my uncles' faces warn me not to try? My uncles would disapprove of such forward behavior. And Diego and Gabriel would tell Mamá.

"Those cowardly Yankees." Ángelo spits upon the ground. "They feared to challenge us to a fair fight. May the devil take them."

His expression softens, eyes pleading. He turns and smiles toward Diego and Gabriel, then faces me.

"Oh, my dearest." His voice lowers. "We were totally unarmed. If only I had brought one of Papi's muskets and could have returned fire." Dampness softens the color of his irises, as if they melt. "How will heaven ever forgive me when I can't forgive myself?"

My dearest? How sweet—wonderful—those two words sounded. Yet pain lines Ángelo's face. What bitter anguish he must feel. I twist a stray wisp of my black hair around my finger. Ángelo couldn't have known what would happen. He mustn't blame himself.

"You did not murder your friends," I say. "Bear Flaggers did."

Ángelo edges his stallion between Jesús María and Santiago. Jesús holds his own horse steady and mutters a gruff, guttural sound. His face grows stern, as if he knows my deepest desires. The inner ends of his eyebrows almost knit together. How I want to prompt Fandango forward and within reach of Ángelo.

Were Berreyesa's nephews married or engaged? If so, two unlucky young women will never see the handsome gentlemen they love again. I should be content that Ángelo is here and safe. I lean forward in the saddle. Ángelo might feel better if he talks more about things.

"And the false messages?"

"I planted them with several Indios. Not Costanoans, but ones living farther north. I pray they've been intercepted already."

Indios. Costanoans. Again, those words come without mention of what the peoples call themselves.

"I dare not reveal more." Ángelo fingers the black sombrero in his hands.

I can keep a military secret. Jesús María and Santiago probably can too. War makes for dangerous circumstances, though. I shan't request additional information. But, in all this, I forgot to ask about Papi. He must be safe, or Ángelo—distraught or not—would have mentioned something.

"Where is my father?" I try not to stare at Ángelo. If only we could share a few minutes alone. How can such a tiny amount of time ruin anyone's reputation? "Papi is needed at home to discuss what we must do to defend ourselves."

"Your father and other brothers are taking spare horses north. Mexican soldiers gather to cross—" Ángelo raises his head skyward. A hawk spreads its wings and glides across the pale sapphire sky. "I must ride to the rancho of Comandante José Castro. To volunteer my services to México."

"To enlist?" I almost gasp the words. Of course, military enlistment is honorable. If I were a man, I'd enlist too. But what might happen to Ángelo? To my dreams of marrying him? Will Bear Flaggers kill him? Will cannon fire rip away his limbs?

"I am a man and capable of determining my own future." Ángelo prompts his stallion closer to me. Jesús María and Santiago steer their own mounts to the side, letting him pass.

Oh, my wonderful uncles! Ángelo is little more than an arm's length away. I can almost feel the warmth of his breath. Will Diego and Gabriel tattle to Mamá and Papi? My legs tense against Fandango's sides. I'll bribe my brothers to keep their mouths shut.

If only I could touch Ángelo. Even brushing my fingertips against the soft nap of his velveteen jacket would bring indescribable joy.

"If I serve my country as a soldier," Ángelo says, "my father can't refuse—"

What can't his father refuse? To arrange a marriage? To me? That must be what Ángelo is talking about. He has disclosed deep feelings for me already. He is probably reluctant to say more in front of my uncles and brothers. Marriage! My head lightens, as if I ate no breakfast at all.

I must offer Ángelo something to remember me by in the long, dangerous days ahead. Don José Berreyesa gave me a silver crucifix. Perhaps the holy symbol—often kissed with my own lips—will protect my dear love in battle. A strand of rawhide secures the cross around my neck. I untie the knot.

"Wear this, please." I clasp the crucifix and extend my arm toward Ángelo. "May the saints watch over you."

Ángelo hangs his sombrero on the horn of his saddle. He unlaces the neck of his white linen shirt. His own crucifix, on a magnificent silver chain, rests against the dark hair on his chest. Does he even want to wear my common rawhide cord? Besides, it might be too short.

Ángelo removes the cross and figure of Christ from around his thick neck. He accepts my gift, then presses his own crucifix and chain into my open palm. The touch of his fingers is as hot and sweet as the finest breakfast chocolate. My heart races. I can hardly breathe. He releases my hand. Elation lingers.

"We will be man and wife," he whispers. "In Heaven, if not on Earth. I vow."

"And I will wait for you until the end of time." I keep my voice low and slip the silver chain around my neck. The warmth of Ángelo's crucifix presses against my breast. "Never doubt my love or loyalty."

Ángelo's full lips curve into a smile. Oh, the fire of passion in his eyes.

9. To Change the Color of the Sky

I OPEN the main work room door. What will I do if Mamá tarries inside? Demand the truth about my natural mother? Or embrace Mamá and confide in her about Ángelo Ortega? "We will be man and wife," Ángelo vowed. Surely those words have the power to carry me to the stars. If only I could let my love for Ángelo burst free from the secret chambers of my heart.

Odors of leather, fabrics and wool yarns invite me to step inside the one-story structure. How I love those aromas and the memories of sewing dresses for my rag doll. Evening shadows fill the dirt-floored room. The ride home with Jesús María and my two youngest brothers took a long time.

No brown hands lay cowhide pattern pieces on top of uncut cloth on the rough-hewn cutting table. No seamstresses linger here at all. The servants have finished sewing for the day. They've returned to their families and hovels. Mamá often enjoys a little solitude after the other women have gone. Perhaps she remains nearby.

"Mamá." I finger Ángelo's silver crucifix and chain through the fabric of my blouse.

Part of me aches to sit on Mamá's broad lap, the way I used to as a child, and to inhale her sweet fragrance—mixed aromas of soap, yarns and corn meal. Mamá thinks Ángelo is handsome and well-mannered. Surely his pledge of love to me will please her. And Ángelo doesn't care I have Oljon blood.

His father will, but Mamá and I can plan how to win Don Ortega's approval.

Maybe Mamá is in the other work room, better for sewing in the late afternoon. I step outside and open the door to the west annex. Waning daylight trickles through a window in the thick wall. A young servant woman sits on the packed earth floor with her handloom, her tan calico dress and skirt soiled. Beside her, a gray-haired seamstress tugs at a bone needle, her face more wrinkled than dried apples. She forces the implement through the shoulder of Papi's velveteen jacket. Excitement flushes through me. When Ángelo returns from fighting the Bear Flaggers, these women will help sew my magnificent wedding gown.

"Where is Mamá?"

The two seamstresses share an uncomfortable look. I recall this morning's events. Mamá did not see me off. Didn't wish me Godspeed on my way to find Papi. Mamá isn't my real mother. She fears to face me.

A swish of petticoats prompts me to turn. Mamá stands beyond the curved arch of the adjacent storage area, her raven hair hanging loose and free. Her swollen waist less prominent than her eyes, reddened with sadness. She has been crying.

"Papi travels north. I didn't find him." Has my other uncle found Papi by now? Santiago claimed to know the trails leading to the north bay where Papi headed. My teeth press against my lip. "We need to talk."

Mamá is already upset. The gossip has reached her with the speed of stampeding stallions. It would be inconsiderate and unwise to ask her about my birth mother in front of the servants.

"Please come outside," I say.

Mamá nods, then retrieves her silk *rabozo* from a worktable. She tilts her double chin upward, as if praying for guidance. Petticoats rustle beneath her blue skirt as she walks toward me and the open doorway. Once outside, I stand under the spreading branches of an oak. Insects buzz around me and the remnants of daylight filter through the boughs, creating patterns on Mamá's face. How fair her skin is compared to mine. She wraps the rabozo around her shoulders. Her sturdy fingers fidget with the crimson shawl.

"I know I'm part Oljon," I say, voice almost quivering. "And you're not my—" The bite of tears stings my eyes. I didn't plan to cry.

"If you look toward the heavens," Mamá says, "you'll see where tonight's crescent moon will soon shine. God made the moon both beautiful and blemished." She casts her glance downward. "He created your father too."

"You should have told me." I brush moisture from my cheeks. "Is this why you have me do servant's work? Because you think I am one?"

"To respect the hard work of others, you must learn to work hard." Mamá's top front teeth press against her plump lower lip. "The gente de razón raise too many spoiled, arrogant daughters."

"What about a daughter clouded by mixed blood and shame?"

"Mixed blood and shame?" Mamá gestures with her hands, fingers spread. "Do you think the dons of Alta California and their wives are all of some ancient pure Castilian lineage? The Moors invaded or controlled parts of Spain for hundreds of years. *Madre de Dios.* Our history mixed our blood long before our family sailed to this new world. Furthermore, the Conquistadors didn't sail off with their Spanish wives and sweethearts to explore México. Look at our own governor, his grandmother a *mulata.* If there was hopeless shame to mixed blood, would his countrymen have chosen him?"

The situation with Governor Pico is different than mine. He owns much land and wealth. My family doesn't. My fingertips feel the dirt on my soiled skirt.

"You were born a week before my own first child—a daughter lost within hours of birth." A distant longing fills Mamá's eyes. "My labor was long. Two days. I became delirious with fever and hovered in the arms of saints. Your papi and abuelito put you in my deceased daughter's basket. Your cries for love gave me the strength to live."

"And my real mother?"

"Her name was Rain Falling. A beautiful woman with expressive eyes, the color of polished amber. She became your wet nurse. She died from influenza when you were three." Mamá spreads her hands against her swollen belly. "I did not know you were not my own until seven years after the saints took her away."

I was ten years old, the same age Diego and Gabriel are now, when Mamá learned the truth. Fresh tears flood my eyes. Abuelito arranged Papi's marriage. Mamá and Papi met only once beforehand, barely knew each other. It will not be this way with me and Ángelo. We're in love, and we make our own choices. Ángelo will never be unfaithful, will never be like Papi. Don Ortega must grant Ángelo permission to wed me.

"Mamá, I beg you for your help." I step closer to her and clasp her pudgy fingers. "We need to make Don Ortega like me better, so he will allow Ángelo to marry me. Could you talk with him, gain his favor on my behalf?"

"Don Ortega grows a little deaf," Mamá says. She presses her lips together, forming a bittersweet smile. "And there is no worse deaf person than the one who does not wish to hear."

"Somehow we will wed." A surge of happiness spreads through me. I must share. "Today we exchanged our crucifixes and—"

"You were with Ángelo?" Mamá steps backward, her brows arched and eyes wide. "Today? When you were supposed to find your father?"

"Ángelo was riding to San José, to enlist in Comandante José Castro's army." This time Mamá, not me, has leaped onto the head of a wrong conclusion. "Ángelo wants to fight the Bear Flaggers. To prove he is no longer a child."

"Ángelo always will be a child to Don Ortega." Mamá massages the sides of her temples, then folds her hands, thumbs under her chin. "Don Ortega has sent for a young woman in Spain. The daughter of a distant cousin."

"Ángelo won't marry her," I snap. How could Don Ortega be so wretched? "Even if he's disowned."

Mamá stretches out her arms and rests her palms on my shoulders. "Would you truly wish Don Emilio Ortega to disown Ángelo? To leave him—the man you claim to love— without any inheritance of cattle or land?"

"Ángelo and I can find another place to live." Blood warms my cheeks. My eyes sting. Doesn't she understand? "My Oljon grandfather and uncles will help if Papi won't."

"Your papi and I would celebrate your marriage to Ángelo. But mortals can't change the color of the sky."

Mamá's arms encircle me. I sag against her softness, her breasts and pregnant belly. I can't—mustn't—accept Don Ortega's plans for Ángelo. That strange gruff voice whispers into my ear, the old vaquero's words for sky and rainbow. God changes the color of the sky at every sunrise and sunset. He places rainbows there after storms. Heaven permitted Ángelo and me to exchange crucifixes today. Somehow, the angels will allow us to wed.

My eyes close. An image of Mamá's blue-and-yellow pottery tureen fills my mind. The vision must have come to me for a reason.

"When Papi returns in a day or so, I must serve the men dinner," I say. "To change the color of the sky."

II. Encounters and Escape

10. Pottery and Plans

THE BLUE-AND-YELLOW pottery tureen, Papi's favorite, sits on the wide window ledge. No visible cracks mar the vessel's surface, despite the fact Josefa dropped the dish last month. Good. I need this tureen tonight. Papi and the older two of my younger brothers—Vincentius and Jorge—have returned home. Abuelito, Papi and my Oljon relatives, across the courtyard in the main room of the house, discuss matters of war. I don't have their permission to leave the kitchen and join them. Not yet. But a clever woman can clear paths around all manner of obstacles.

I lift the empty tureen by both handles and set it on the nearby kitchen table. The serving vessel can hold enough beef and *frijoles* for Papi and the other men. Josefa often swears the tureen's clay houses a disgruntled spirit of the land, and for that reason, has refused to touch the blue handles on several occasions. I grin. What a perfect excuse to bring dinner to Papi myself.

Papi! The man who dishonored and deceived Mamá. And me. Many married men let their attention drift toward other women. But during the same week as their wedding vows? Waning sunlight, filtered by the olive tree in the courtyard outside the kitchen, casts a mottled shadow beside the flowered tureen. The shadow's pattern shifts, as if a spirit lingers within to watch my every move. My forefinger rubs the sleeve of my calico blouse. The breeze plays with the leaves of the olive tree and my imagination.

A sizzle. The aroma of cooking beef. Steam seeps from under the lid of the cast iron pot hanging in the fireplace. Liquid drips onto red-hot coals. I step around the tortilla oven and stand in the kitchen doorway, the threshold between the one-room adobe structure—separate from the house—and the courtyard. Josefa sits outside on a stool, her hands mixing corn masa for tortillas. Hard to believe the stool was once part of a whale's backbone. The responsibility pressing upon my shoulders feels as heavy as an entire whale.

"The pot's boiling," I say. "Where's your mother?"

"Gone to draw more wine from the cask," Josefa says. "The men are talking themselves dry."

Yes, tonight each of the men will want more than the usual cup. I have to tend the stew for now. I turn and reach for the long-handled bone ladle and cowhide potholders on the wall. Ángelo's sister never does any of the servants' chores. But she is neither a product of infidelity nor is her father's land grant small. No matter. I know how to use menial duties to my advantage.

Infidelity. Oljon blood in my veins. Still, I must honor Papi as best I can. Based on what Mamá said, Ángelo will need to marry me without his father's permission. We will live on this rancho, subservient to Papi and Abuelito. Tonight, when others are around, I'll confront Papi only with my eyes. More obvious rancor will generate gossip among the servants and humiliate Mamá. I stir the mixture of beef, chiles and beans, a dish usually prepared for mid-afternoon meals. I must lend support to Mamá—the woman who raised me, who loves me and always will.

"You should bake the tortillas soon," I call to Josefa. She is still outside. "The meat and beans are tender."

Josefa steps into the kitchen and groans. Her shoulders slump. Her full lips part. The servant girl points at the tureen, her braids jiggling as she shakes her head.

I make a buzzing sound and shrug. "Flies do not enter a closed mouth. You have no need to worry. I intend to personally serve the beef and *frijoles* to the men. You carry the basket of tortillas."

"What about later?" Josefa flashes a tentative smile, exposing her protruding front teeth.

I gesture toward the covered cast iron pots in the fireplace. Josefa dropped the fancy tureen last month and has burned her hands on the handles several times. She'll be happy to serve Mamá and my brothers in the courtyard if she can ladle from an iron cauldron. First, I'll serve Papi a dose of my questioning stare.

#

I wait in the entryway of the house, my arms against my sides. Several *varas* away in the main room, the pottery tureen rests on the warming brazier—in turn, supported by a metal base. Stones rim that portable heater on the tile floor. A little while earlier, I helped Josefa's mother place the serving dish there. I can hear the men continue their conversation around the long oak table. A mere dozen paces separate them from the brazier. More distance lies between them and me. I'm not in their line of sight. All is well, so far.

The deep throaty voice, like a bullfrog gargling gravel, is Abuelito Ygnacio's. The smooth, mellow one is Papi's. The voices of Tomás and my two uncles are less distinct and blend together.

"A black Andalusian stallion?" Papi asks. Then he whispers words I can't decipher.

"Death caused by false bears," another voice mumbles.

Did he refer to the Bear Flaggers? And did my uncles tell Papi about me meeting the Yankee, and then Ángelo, on the trail several days ago? A muffled reference to Rain Falling, my natural mother, follows. Jesús María? I need to move closer. I'll get ready to serve the stew and have a better place to eavesdrop from there.

My leather slippers make a soft padding noise against the floor. I reach out, potholders in both hands, and grasp the tureen. Now I'll stand motionless and listen. The lid shifts with a rattle, as if on its own. Might a spirit haunt this vessel, as Josefa believes?

The men's conversation fades into silence. Papi, Abuelito, Tomás, Jesús María and Santiago become as quiet as robins on a branch when a hawk soars above. They can see me. I must pretend I only intend to serve dinner. This "light" meal at the end of the day grows as heavy as boulders.

Steam and the aroma of beef cooked with chili peppers rises from the tureen I carry to the oak table. Papi glances my way. Does guilt tug the corners of his mouth into that uncertain smile? A candle on the table flickers, as if in reply. Yes, Papi knows I've learned about his unfaithfulness to Mamá.

I set the tureen down at the end of the table, next to a stack of pottery bowls. Five pairs of solemn eyes watch me dip the ladle into the thick, savory stew. Five sets of jaws clamp tight, as if nailed shut. I give the full bowls of beef and *frijoles* to the men. How loud, each clunk of pottery against wood. No waiting mouths deliver a single word of thanks, to me or to Heaven. The men act as if I've served them pork fat and worms.

I stare at Papi hard, at his drooping mustache and black bushy eyebrows, the brown and amber striations within his irises. His expression reflects neither anger nor remorse. His eyes study me, as if he has never really done so before. Perhaps something more than my parentage and love for Ángelo troubles him—troubles all these men.

"I hope you are very hungry." Josefa's musical laughter fills the room.

I turn. Josefa walks barefoot across the tile floor with her usual mixture of graceful steps and a shy, awkward smile. She uses the formal form of "you," as she always does when serving. Josefa reserves the informal "you" for private conversations with her parents and me. Her dark-skinned hands clutch the brimming basket of tortillas against the waist of her two-piece muslin dress. Tomás acknowledges Josefa's offering with polite words of gratitude. The other men nod.

I bow my head. "May we prove worthy of tonight's bounty. Use this nourishment that the saints and the Almighty have graciously provided to do their will." I clear my throat, the way Mamá would have, and nod with approval at the mumbled prayers the men offer in response.

The odors of corn and chili entice me. I ate little during our main midday meal. It will be good to enjoy dinner soon with my brothers and Mamá.

"Do you wish for anything else?" I stand beside Josefa and wait for dismissal. I'll talk to Papi alone tomorrow. "Should I refill the wine jug?"

Tomás fingers the bandage on his shoulder, encrusted with dried blood. Abuelito scratches the gray whiskers on his chin. Papi sips red wine then coughs.

"Sit down with us," Abuelito says. "Josefa, bring her a spoon, cup and bowl."

Sit down with the men? Eat with them at the dinner table? Warmth flashes across my cheeks. I must have misheard, yet, Jesús and Santiago make room for me on the end of one bench. Josefa nudges me forward then hurries from the room. I sit down, my body rigid, as if they had instructed me to sit in a patch of poison oak.

The tureen. A sulking spirit of the land must actually dwell there and has affected the men's wits. "Lunatic. Sanity. Madness..." A man's voice—not the one of the old vaquero—speaks a jumble of words inside of my head. His words remind me of something I read in *Don Quixote*. Using that book, Abuelito taught me to read. Yet I've never understood much of the story's meaning. When Josefa brings the bowl, I better serve my own helping of chili stew. The spirits—including the author of *Don Quixote*—might make Josefa drop the blue-and-yellow pottery cover.

#

I chew the last piece of beef, my bowl finally empty. Abuelito, Papi and the other men already finished theirs, have waited for me. Abuelito raises his wine cup and motions for the rest of us to do the same. My wine remains untouched. Reputable young ladies don't gather with a group of men and drink wine or brandy. My fingers touch the hidden silver chain of Ángelo's crucifix. We clasped hands several days ago. Am I still a reputable lady?

Maybe drinking with family is different. I sip the heavy but pleasant wine. Tomás, sitting across from me, rubs the side of his nose and smiles.

"In the old times," he says, "Coyote stole dried fish from my people's tule huts." Dark circles shadow the skin below his narrow eyes. Three thick, white candles flicker on the dinner table. "Now Coyote has asked our family to fish for rocks."

"Rocks?" I squint. Josefa has told me stories about Coyote, the trickster spirit. Nothing about fishing for rocks though.

"These are special stones. Small but with great power." Jesús María, on my left, cants his head. The candle glow and vanishing daylight soften the appearance of his scarred cheek. "Water spirits flushed them down from the mountains. Nuggets, Catalina. Gold."

Gold? I straighten my spine. Alta California can't have gold. Spanish soldiers and Catholic priests would have discovered the treasure long ago. What sort of nonsense is this? Coyote—if such a spirit exists—has played a trick on Jesús María. But I mustn't insult guests, particularly members of my family.

I take a second sip of wine. "I am only a young señorita. Not as wise as many. Kindly rearrange your words so that I comprehend them better."

Abuelito, sitting diagonally from me, chuckles. Papi, seated on his right, also laughs. Their shoulders relax. My response has pleased them.

"It started with your wet nurse's dream." Papi winces and leans forward. "Pardon. Your natural mother's dream."

His eyelids lower, as they should.

"Rain Falling," Jesús María says. "She was only a child when Coyote traveled with her in her sleep, revealed his plans to steal her first baby, a daughter."

"The baby would be returned to her." Santiago, larger boned than Jesús María, places his sun-browned hands, palms down, on the table. "Returned when the gold was retrieved."

"When the gold was hidden," Tomás says.

"From Yankees and Mexicanos," Papi says.

"From all," Abuelito adds.

Now the men speak all at once, to me and each other. The gold will appear when a false bear flutters in the wind and murders a brother, they claim. When a man on a black Andalusian stallion rides a thunder cloud. What does all this mean?

An unexpected chill hits my shoulders, then races down my spine. I rub my arms through the calico fabric of my blouse. I'm so cold. Papi and Abuelito—not a spirit—took me from Rain Falling, my mother. And, anyway, what use does this Coyote creature have for gold? I, made out of flesh and blood—of Adam's rib and God's breath—would have much use for gold though. The precious metal could help Mamá and Papi, plus provide me with a dowry to marry Ángelo. I could even use gold to build a little adobe house for Josefa's parents so they won't have to sleep in a leaky hut with Mamá's seamstresses anymore.

The men stop talking and turn their faces toward me, waiting for me to do something, to say something. I close my eyes and take several slow breaths. Most people have use for gold. Hardly a revelation. Profound thoughts play games with me, remaining beyond reach. I shiver, raising one eyelid. The candles on the table flicker. An odd draft.

But wait, gold in Alta California's rivers will attract more than honest rancheros. Mineral riches will lure the best and the worst of men. Legions of miners will crawl over the land, as numerous as flies on a bloated corpse. They'll steal horses and cattle, hoist their bear flags, cut down trees faster than Heaven can replenish the growth. A plague of two-legged flies will transform lush meadows and hillsides into wastelands.

My eyes pop wide open, gazing toward the end of the table, toward the cobalt blue flower in the tureen's glaze. A false bear—a bear on a flag fluttering in the wind—oversaw the murder of Tomás' brother. When I met the Yankee on the black Andalusian stallion, nearby gunfire sounded as loud as thunder. The prophecies my family discussed a few minutes ago have come to pass.

I study each man's face, searching for secrets in their wrinkled, weathered skin. If the men's story about Coyote is true, the gold will appear in rivers soon. Yet the holy friar at the mission claimed Coyote is a superstition and belief in him, sacrilege.

Papi folds his hands in his lap and his entire body sags. "I cannot ask you to travel with Tomás and the others." Even his black mustache droops more than usual.

"This is no task for any decent señorita." The creases around Abuelito's eyes deepen. "Least of all the granddaughter I cherish."

My head throbs, perhaps from the wine. Papi and Abuelito believe the Oljons' tale. Heresy. This is heresy. Abuelito and Papi rarely attend mass, but always say their prayers in our chapel at home. How can they believe in Coyote? How can I, a good Catholic, ever believe? Still, a prophesy has come true, and I believe in spirits of the dead. The old vaquero has spoken to me since his death, and didn't a vision of Moses and Elijah appear to *Jesucristo* in a Bible story?

Tomás, across from me, stands up from the table. He places both hands on the tureen's cover, his veins prominent. His stare penetrates my being. If Coyote exists, how long will it take to find and hide his gold? Who will help Mamá around the house and read to Abuelito?

My headache intensifies. Warmth radiates from the silver crucifix against my breast. Ángelo. Pending war. What if my dear love sustains wounds in battle and sends for me? How could I do Coyote's work instead? Besides, those Bear Flaggers remain a threat to my people. If rebellious Yankees have no respect for the great General Vallejo, how will they treat a young *mestiza* and her Oljon traveling companions? I can't go with Tomás.

"I need to think. To pray." My fingertips massage my temples. "Pardon me please, but I must take leave of your company for the night."

11. The Vision

I COVER MY HAIR with my shawl, then cross myself and enter the family chapel. The odors of candlewax and lilies grow strong. Following the way of Coyote is sacrilege. How will I purify myself once I complete his task? I kneel and bow my head in front of the altar, within a pool of candlelight on the packed dirt floor. I ought to close my eyes in prayer, but don't.

A sketch of our Lady of Guadalupe stares down at me from the wall. I need not raise my head to see the image. Soot flecks the yellowed parchment. In Spain, inquisitors burned heretics at the stake to save misguided souls from Hell. My stomach churns. The sour taste of bile coats my tongue. Hail María, full of grace. Will fire provide my only path to salvation?

Wilted poppies lie on the lace altar cloth, near a vase containing three lilies. Always close to death, life is. Only a couple days ago, Spirit Man could have carried me away. Yet, he did not. Is he a devil who will claim me only if I serve Coyote? If so, he isn't a very impressive disciple of Satan. His Spanish is horrible, would prompt me to laugh if this situation were less serious. Still, everyone knows the Virgin of Guadalupe appeared to a Mexican native a long way south of Alta California many years ago. Did that honored man ever pray to Coyote or the spirits of the land? If so, he received forgiveness without fire.

I finger the crucifix Ángelo gave me. "Holy María, Mother of God, pray for us sinners, now and at the hour of our death. Amen."

What if the spirits of the land are actually voices of God's angels? No, the friar who comes to speak at the mission—born in Mexico City and educated in Zacatecas—would teach us so. But Papi often claims Friar Fernandoco doesn't know everything. A fly buzzes near my ear. I brush the insect away. I don't want two-legged flies—the Bear Flaggers—to destroy Alta California, God's beautiful, bountiful land. May the Holy Mother forgive me for planning to serve Coyote. I cross myself and stand.

"Mistress Catalina," Josefa's soft voice hovers behind me. "Have I done something to distress you?"

I turn. How long has Josefa been there? The servant—no, friend—bows her head, like a child awaiting due punishment. Does Josefa actually believe she is to blame for my unrest?

"Many things make my heart ache tonight." I don't dare reveal the secret of Coyote's gold.

I clasp Josefa's chilly hands and peer into her dark, uncertain eyes. She is pledged to Manuel, the blacksmith's older son. If Don Emilio Ortega grants Ángelo permission to marry me, I'll need to leave her behind. I want Josefa's company for as long as possible. Too bad we can't search for Coyote's gold together.

"Trouble gathers like rainclouds waiting for thunder," Josefa says. "I'm part of it. I'm certain. My tongue tastes a bitterness that won't wash away."

"Each of us must follow our own destiny. That is the bitterness, nothing more."

I bow toward the altar one more time, then pick up my tin lantern. Josefa and I hold hands and stroll back toward our room. Mamá will be waiting to lock us in for the night. The reputations of señoritas are important. Appointed tasks are too. Josefa has some knowledge about Coyote. I should ask her for information.

"Part of my destiny is to talk with Coyote. Where might I find him?"

"I'm not sure," Josefa says. "My mother doesn't say much about him anymore. She claims we are good Catholics now. Weren't we always? I think it's all because of Manuel's father.

He prays his Rosary twice a day and she wants to impress him."

"What about all that singing and dancing?" When she was six years old, Josefa loved to wave feathers around and pretend to sing the chants of her ancestors.

"Actually, the men did most of those things." Josefa chews on her thumbnail. "I think they used to fast first, or at least not eat any meat."

No meat? Lent has passed. Mamá will think I'm sick if I refuse to eat beef. For sure, she'll summon a *curandero*.

"What about offerings?" I often place flowers on the altar in the chapel and light candles.

"Hmmm." Josefa crosses her arms against her chest. "Tobacco? My grandfather had a special pipe decorated with feathers. I don't know if a pipe is necessary though. Once he dropped a pinch of tobacco into the cook-fire when Mamá wasn't looking."

Papi and Abuelito smoke sometimes. When they do, they leave ashes and bits of tobacco on the main room floor or patio and I sweep those places every day. Tobacco will be easy to find.

"Then what should I do?"

"Wait for a vision." The lamplight accentuates Josefa's frown. "Oh, I think I forgot something important. Receiving a vision is more complicated than that. You might have to go somewhere at night and stay there alone. Or, maybe that was for something else. I wish I could remember."

Go somewhere at night, alone? Young women have only one reason for such a disreputable action—to meet a lover. If anyone finds out what I'm doing, gossip will sprout wings and fly everywhere. Ángelo and his father will hear. I must never venture alone from the rancho grounds after dark, even if I manage to get out of my room.

I groan. Maybe I should speak to my Oljon grandfather and uncles about visions. No, they're as protective as Mamá, Papi and Abuelito. I couldn't have a vision with them stationed a mere fifteen or twenty *varas* away. A burning sensation flashes from my stomach to my chest.

"Even in bad times," that man's voice I've heard in my head lately says, "fortune will keep a door cracked open. Look for it."

The scent of wild mint beckons me to the side of the path. Mint disguises bitter tastes and strengthens weak stomachs. I pull a sprig from the ground. How refreshing to chew the leaves. Fortune. An open door. Seeking a vision in solitude is my responsibility. A grove of oaks stands on the knoll beyond Mamá's work rooms, a good place to sit on the ground and search the night for inspiration. A bold voice and taste unfurl a bold idea.

"I must discover how to pick our bedroom lock," I say. "So I can have a vision tomorrow night."

"You don't have to pick any lock." Josefa looks away from me. "Manuel. He made a key to your room. When I started sleeping there."

"He did what?" Blood carries heat to my face.

"He gave me the key right away," Josefa says, "to show me he could have visited me at night but didn't because he respects my honor."

The son of a Costanoan blacksmith made a key to my bedroom? Papi should flog him for such an offense. My hands clench into fists. No, I should beat Manuel myself.

Fortune. An open door in bad times. I exhale. Manuel only meant to prove he is worthy of Josefa's favor. Indeed, he's a man of good character, like my uncles. I could never grow angry if Ángelo made a key to my bedroom. I trust him. However, embarrassment would paint my face red. My shoulders and arms relax. Well, if I ever need a key of any sort made, at least I know a trustworthy blacksmith.

#

A hooting owl interrupts the chirping of crickets. Too bad I don't speak either of their languages. Will Coyote send me a signal I'll recognize? Wearing a hooded wool cloak over my muslin nightgown, I slip out of my bedroom and lock the door. The pebbled ground under my shoes feels more uneven than usual. I clench my fist and bite one knuckle. This transgression—going out into the night alone—is greater than any I've ever committed. May God forgive my sin against Mamá and Papi. More than that. May he forgive me for planning to beckon Coyote. For not trusting solely in the power of the Holy Virgin, the Trinity, and Santa Catalina de Siena, my saint.

May God also forgive Papi and Abuelito for their belief in Coyote.

Still, what if Coyote is a saint God gave to this land's tribal peoples? There may be ideas the friars don't want ordinary people to know.

I grip the handle of my tin lantern and step away from the house. It is possible the book Abuelito refuses to let me read contains such information. Those words I saw a year ago when I brought him his afternoon hot chocolate and glanced down at a page. "Flies are born to be eaten by spiders."

The words meant nothing then, but they do now. Bear Flaggers are the flies and I must become one of the spiders, eating away at potential Yankee victories before they happen. Like making sure Bear Flaggers don't discover the gold I learned about last night.

Clouds obscure the moon and most of the stars. Just as well. Any servant man out for a breath of fresh air won't notice me. Nevertheless, I walk toward my destination with much care. The single candle in my lantern is better than nothing, but not by much. A good thing I measured the distances earlier: One hundred and forty steps and turn right—then three hundred and seventy more. I cross a rutted path. I shiver as I reach the stand of live and tanbark oaks. The night, colder than anticipated, saps my warmth. How foolish of me not to bring a blanket.

Regardless, I must find a place to wait for a vision. Leaves crunch under my feet. I slip a dry, spiny leaf into my cloak's pocket. Several trees in, I place my lantern on the ground and sit down. The leaves here are damp.

I unwrap my handkerchief, where I put all the tobacco shreds I could find. The lantern's warm door opens with reluctance and a metallic squeak. The flame flickers. I rub tobacco bits between my fingers and sprinkle the powder onto the dry leaf. Then, I feed the leaf to the flame.

"Señor Coyote, I hope you enjoy this tobacco. It's Papi's favorite."

The flame swells, then subsides. Time to close the lantern. Does Coyote wait close by? Perhaps I should spit out my request now, in case I have his attention.

"If I am to help you hide your gold," I say, "so foreigners don't ruin your lands, please tell me where I should ride and when."

Closing my eyes might help me communicate better with mystical forces. I don't know any Oljon chants, dances or prayers. Even if I did, would the Holy Virgin, the Trinity or my saint block all messages from Coyote? The silver crucifix from Ángelo warms my chilly hand. Best to start my prayers in the way Mamá taught me.

"Hail María, full of grace, the Lord is with thee. Blessed art thou among women, and blessed is the fruit of thy womb, Jesús." I take a deep breath. "Holy María, Mother of God, please allow Coyote to bring me knowledge so I can help my Spanish and Oljon peoples. Amen."

I draw my cloak closer. Why didn't I keep on my daytime clothing? No, too risky. I'll make less noise when I return to my room and climb into bed if I'm already wearing my nightgown.

So twisted, the oaks near me. Some are so close to each other, I doubt a rider could pass between them. Those trees could be giants, the way their entwining branches obscure whatever sky the clouds haven't. If I still believed in giants. Regardless, I dare not venture any deeper into this grove.

At least I hear crickets chirping. The old vaquero once claimed the familiar sound comes from rubbing their wings together. They chirp to tell the world all is well. So, why do I feel more dread than comfort right now? Then I realize something is changing. The crickets grow quiet. Does the approach of a predator interrupt their song?

A beating rhythm, quick and hard, as if from a drum, a heart, or a dance, grows louder with each passing second. I hear hoofbeats: the hoofbeats of a horse in full gallop. A messenger bringing news about the Bear Flaggers' war against my people? What will the man think if he discovers me here?

I grab my lantern and hide behind a broad oak. If a courier approaches, he ought to turn toward the main house soon. I'll hurry back to my bedroom while he delivers the news to Papi. This rider has ruined my plans to have a vision tonight. With luck, I'll still have a chance to save my reputation.

Over and over, my slow, shallow breaths bring air into my lungs. I must wait for the hoofbeats to fade. They don't. If anything, the pounding grows stronger, as if the rider heads toward me. But that doesn't make sense. Only a fool rides at full gallop into a dense stand of trees on a cloudy night. Unless—

A shiver darts down my back. Unless the rider isn't a person.

Can Coyote ride a horse? Can he gallop like one? Dare I move from behind this tree and find out?

I step from my hiding place. Beyond the trees' shelter, a shaft of lightning angles across the sky. Lightning without a rainstorm! The dark shadowy form of a figure on horseback speeds into the grove. I jump backward. A long arm reaches down and plucks me from the ground, as if I weigh nothing. Something rips the lantern from my grasp. The odor of leather grows strong. This creature is not Coyote.

"No!" I cry.

I twist my body. I can't break free. My legs dangle. My arms flail. Long hair whips against my face. My locks are braided. This coarse hair doesn't have the texture of my own. A hard surface presses against my stomach. With the next bolt of lightning, I find myself lying face-down between a man in a saddle and his steed's flowing mane. The wild mane belongs to an Andalusian. Trees don't slow the animal down.

Spirit Man has kidnapped me. The old vaquero's prophecy has come true.

Abducted! The chill of the air cuts through my nightclothes and cloak. My reputation, my chances for an honorable marriage to Ángelo or anyone else, is about to dissolve like sugar in hot water. I'm ruined for the rest of my life—if I don't die first.

I need to escape, to somehow roll to the ground without the animal trampling me. Maybe if I pound my fists against the horse's side? My mind screams for my hands to take action. My hands refuse to obey. Worse, my legs stop kicking. My shoulders can't even shrug. Spirit Man controls my every move. What am I going to do now?

An eerie sound plays in my ears. No, with my ears. For, in reality, I hear no sound at all. No crunching of twigs or leaves—no hoofbeats. Horse, rider and I race forward in silence. The animal's feet make no contact with the ground.

Lightning tears across the sky. The heavens should have ripped in half. The black stallion leaps upward as if trying to reach the fiery bolt. So high, the Andalusian rises. More lightning flashes. Illuminated treetops sway below me in the wind. How can this be? Does an angel or a devil claim me? Spirit Man's hand presses against my back, his icy touch like death's fingers.

"Holy Mother of God," I whisper. "Pray for us sinners."

12. False Light and the Trickster's Gold

I KNEEL BESIDE a river. Shallow water tumbles over smooth, gray rocks, the foam as delicate as lace. How thirsty the terrifying horseback ride with Spirit Man has left me. I dip my cupped hands into the flowing liquid, then drink. Cool and refreshing. Behind me, Spirit Man's black Andalusian snorts, as real as the river. If only my abductor and his horse were a mere vision sent by the great trickster, Coyote. A vision was all I wanted when I offered that tobacco.

"Señorita Delgado, have you quenched your thirst?"

Such perfect Spanish pronunciation and he used no English. Not like the first time I met him. Why the difference? Can I trust him at all? I need more time to gather my thoughts and make sense of this situation.

"I'm working on the quenching, Señor Spirit Man." It is best to sound polite.

I drink more. The front of my woolen cloak parts and reveals my frilly nightdress. I dare not turn toward the man until my hands are free to close the outer garment. Never again will I leave my bedroom without being properly clothed. May the holy saints protect my modesty and honor. I can't depend on Coyote's help tonight.

I lift my chin. Yes, this must be night, despite the pale amber gleam enveloping the river, bushes and trees—as if I were seeing them through Mamá's transparent healing stone after sunrise. Do not the heavens still bear hints of stars and the outline of the quarter moon? Plus no sun hangs in the sky.

I press my lips together. The earlier thunderstorm without rain has passed but tonight's strangeness has not.

"You would satisfy your thirst faster," Spirit Man says, "if you would drink more and ponder less."

"Sí, Señor Spirit Man." He has guessed I'm stalling.

I swallow more water, then bow my head. A power beyond my understanding has brought a false dawn. My wet fingers touch the chain on my crucifix as if it were a rosary. Hail, María, Mother of God. I thirst most for a big, fat cup of comprehension.

Flecks sparkle on the palms of my damp hands. This river I drank from carries false gold, not what Coyote wants me to find. Papi has always claimed real gold hides in bedrock. Too bad. What will Papi think when Mamá finds me missing at sunrise? They, Josefa, Abuelito and my Oljon relatives don't need any more worries.

I scan the riverbanks. Irregular brush clings to their slopes. Here and there, clusters of three leaves thrive. Poison oak. I could be in any one of a hundred or more Alta California locations. How can I find my way home tonight should Spirit Man refuse to take me back? Can I even escape if I try?

"Enough contemplation," Spirit Man says. "We only have an hour or so to do our work."

I grip my cloak, still on my knees, and turn toward the sound of the man's deep, throaty voice. Spirit Man stands a mere *vara* away from me beside the river, a distance half his height. When he dismounted, I did not hear the creak of leather or jingle of spurs.

"I'm done drinking." At least I'm not yet undone.

He stretches out his leather-gloved hand and helps me up. I avoid his stare. Why did he choose this particular spot for getting water? Because the terrain holding Coyote's gold lies nearby? Finding the treasure is my destiny and duty. I accepted that fate when praying in the chapel.

I clench my toes. There's the little ruffle on the bodice of my nightdress again. I glance up. Spirit Man grins. *Madre de Dios.* Coyote himself should visit me. No, Coyote has a reputation for lusty behavior, according to Josefa. I'm better off working with this foreigner.

"You haven't explained." My lip quivers. "What you want me to do."

"Greet the river. Say good day to Señor Río. Say good night. Introduce yourself."

"¿*Buenos dias y buenas noches* Señor Río?" This flesh-and-blood spirit *hombre* is *loco*—crazy—as well as a threat. "¿*Me llamo* Catalina Delgado?"

"Spirits of our earth reside in the river," the man says. "Treat them with respect. No sarcasm."

Spirit Man has just spoken the way my Oljon uncles would instead of like a foreigner. Still, he is neither a member of my family nor trustworthy. Better to keep company with a swarm of horseflies than with him.

"Do you treat river spirits with respect?" I say. "You've not greeted them or given them your name."

The man steps toward me, the expression in his eyes unreadable. He has no odor. None at all. Yet he's close, too close, to me. If I try to get away, any step back will deliver my feet, and the rest of me if I trip, into the watery hands of Señor Río.

I edge to the side, away from him. He grips the front of my shoulders, then pushes hard. I stumble backward. My foot slips on a wet rock. I fall with a splash into moving water. The river closes in. I sink, kick and gasp for air. How can this water be so deep? It looked shallow from the shore. Why did that horrible man push me?

The current carries me. I'm not a strong swimmer. Yet all rivers have places for standing and washing clothes, don't they? I must keep my head above the surface until I find such a spot. The weight of my cloak tugs at me. I kick harder. My knee bangs against submerged rocks. Maybe this section of the river isn't so deep, after all.

Ahead the river channel slides around a huge gray boulder. Thank God for false daylight. I'll stop there and maneuver toward the calmer shallows. Rushing water roars behind me. I cling to the face of the boulder and turn my

head. A wall of churning water and foam—as tall as me—
tumbles in my direction. Oh, dearest Lord.

The wall of water slams my back, thrusting my chest
against the boulder. My lungs suck in air. The next wave
attacks. One force pins me against rock. Another tries to
shove me back into the channel's own maelstrom. How long
can I hold on?

I mustn't—cannot—die, cannot leave my family and
Ángelo in grief.

Bit by bit I edge toward the shore. This roiling funnel of
water, this whirlpool, arose from calm shallows no more than
the length of my arm away. Why is Señor Río trying to drown
me when I'm supposed to safeguard Coyote's gold?

"Introduce yourself," Spirit Man shouts from the shore.

Didn't I do that already?

"I'm Catalina," I sputter, kicking to keep my head above
water. "Delgado." Angry water hammers the side of my face.
"Daughter of Rain Falling."

Waves stop pounding me. The whirlpool vanishes. Calm
water laps against the back of my waist. I pant, my lungs and
muscles sore. The boulder supports me. Oh, dearest saints
and blessed joy. I straighten myself. Shallow rapids hurry
around my knees, pushing and tugging at my skirts.

"*Gracias*," I whisper. "Thank you, Señor Río. Santa
Catalina. Holy María, Mother of God."

I slosh toward shore at an angle, heading back upstream.
Spirit Man waits on the riverbank, his arms folded against
his chest. The river only carried me a short distance. How
strange. Spirit Man's black clothing remains dry as dust. His
face bears the same unsettling grin as before. Surely every
curve of my body shows through my sopping garments. He
doesn't glance away or look embarrassed. And he doesn't
extend a hand to help me onto dry ground. How dare he treat
me with such disrespect?

"I could have drowned," I yell. "And you did nothing.
Nothing! You are as worthless as the Bear Flaggers."

"You would have drowned," he replies, "if you weren't the true daughter of Rain Falling." He shrugs. "And if you hadn't introduced yourself to the spirits of the river."

"And just what am I supposed to do now? Shake myself dry like a dog?"

"Empty the pockets of your cloak."

My pockets. I placed the key to my room in one. What if the river claimed it for a prize? I won't be able to sneak back to bed unnoticed. Then I remember. True dawn will arrive before I reach home. No way exists to return to my room before Mamá or Papi discovers my absence. The room key no longer is the key to saving my good name. Not tonight.

I shove my hands into my pockets. The key is there. But something else is too, bearing the gritty texture of dirt. I pull wet sludge out of my pockets. Golden bits dot dripping sand. False gold? No, the men always claim false gold sparkles. This doesn't. The color is distinctive though. Can this be real gold?

"Now, I'll show you where to hide this treasure." Spirit Man scratches one of his bushy muttonchops. "For Coyote."

"May I go home after?" Gold or no gold, I've done more than enough riding, flying and swimming in my nightgown for one night.

"Each week or so, we'll ride by night. Maybe more often at first."

"So you can push me into another river?"

"So spirits of the water," he says, "can entrust you with gold washed down from the mountains and hills."

Gold really can wash out of rock. For how long will I have to gather such nuggets? Until I marry Ángelo? Or as long as I live? Ángelo will never permit me to ride away with this man, especially during the middle of the night. Nor will I want to trade Ángelo's loving embrace for a cold bath. Yet there is the prospect of Yankees and other foreigners overrunning Alta California if they learn about the gold. Sometimes there are no good choices.

"I want to go home as soon as this gold is safe," I say. "By way of an ordinary road."

"Yankees will learn our secret."

"But you're a Yankee." Even if the inside of his head isn't.

"Don't believe all your eyes tell you."

The Andalusian stallion snorts as if to punctuate his master's words. The animal approaches me, lowers his head and nickers. Such a long mane, coarse yet somehow soft to touch. And full eyelashes—like those of a flirting señorita. The old vaquero once told me Andalusians understand people.

I stroke the horse's arched neck. "What is the truth about your master?" I whisper into the steed's ear. If Spirit Man's horse understands my question, he doesn't give me an answer.

Cold air whips across my back. My Oljon abuelito and uncles led me to believe they, as family members, would journey with me to find Coyote's gold and carry the treasure to a secret place. A young woman of good name and virtue should travel with a chaperone. I must request a proper one now.

I open my mouth to speak. Spirit Man's yellow eyes shoot me a glare that could freeze fire. In the false light, his presence radiates more than ever. A pale, translucent worm-like creature crawls from between his parted lips.

Madre de Dios. A worm! My stomach twists. Blood pounds its way through my head. Only rotting bodies issue worms from their mouths. Why do my eyes show me the impossible? Besides, Spirit Man has no odor of death, has no odor at all. Something is even more wrong than before.

Two worms join the first. Dearest God, this must not be. Crickets chirp. An owl hoots over and over. The three worm heads sway back and forth. Surely my stomach drops to my toes. My mouth fills with saliva, then turns dry. I see two spirit men and six worms—double vision.

Abduction, unnatural daylight, an enchanted river—and now dancing worms.

"El Diablo," I whisper. Spirit Man, he must be a servant of Satan.

I shriek, turn, then tear away from man, worms and river. The false daylight disappears. Only the dim glow from the quarter moon remains to guide my feet.

The ground grows so uneven. I must have strayed from the path. I stumble through darkness. My ankle turns, I pitch forward, and my arms flail. Somehow, I recover my balance.

No hooves pound the ground behind me. No road to follow lies in sight. Where am I? Surely Spirit Man will decide to pursue. In what direction should I flee?

A series of high-pitched whoops sound in the distance. A coyote. Night music I've listened to from the safety of my bedroom a thousand times. Josefa often says coyotes laugh to fill their enemies with dread. A second coyote—louder and closer—joins the first. Perhaps the great trickster trots in my direction.

This may not be a good time to encounter him.

13. Jedidiah Jones and a Message

JEDIDIAH JONES BLINKS as he sets down the iron pot of soup in the middle of the unfurnished room. That prisoner on the bare wooden floor—one of four seated within pissing distance. Are Jedidiah's eyes seeing the same person his brain figures they do? Yup, the Mexican has the same wavy black hair. Long curved sideburns. The goddamned poise of a diplomat. Jedidiah's tongue pushes the tobacco plug between his cheek and gum. That's General Vallejo, all right. Holy tarnation! What the Sam Hill's going on? If surprise could make Jedidiah shit gold, he'd be a wealthy man.

The general gestures a request for a spoon. Jedidiah shrugs and raises the pot's lid, releasing the rich aromas of beef and beans. Nobody gave him spoons or tortillas to deliver. Not up to him to ask the guards on duty here at Sutter's Fort for such stuff, neither. Not unless he hankers to get arrested like these unlucky four. If the general and his company are hungry enough, they'll figure out how to move the soup from the pot to their stomachs. Hell, Sutter makes his Indian workers lap their supper out of a hog's feeding trough. Regardless, Jedidiah flashes a sympathetic look in the general's direction, the least he can do for someone who once sent a rescue party to pull him out of a Sierra snowpack.

"*Gracias,*" general Vallejo says, his eyes as penetrating as two lighthouse search lamps. "Thank you, Señor Jones."

Jedidiah nods. Crap. Did the guard overhear Vallejo? Guilt by association isn't what Jedidiah wants. What if crazy Captain Frémont arrests him too?

Heck. Crazy isn't a strong enough word to describe the Captain's maverick actions. For years, General Vallejo has supported an American takeover of Alta California, while some other rancheros—sick of being México's second-class step-child—have favored the British or French. If Frémont owned even half-a-brain, he'd praise Vallejo. Then lock up Don Emilio Ortega instead, a filthy-rich grandee and Yank-hater who stockpiles muskets in his spare work rooms.

Besides, Jedidiah has a score to settle with Ortega. Would love nothing better than to see that puffed-up patriarch put in irons. Jedidiah would be working his own land-grant rancho right now if Don Ortega didn't petition against him two years ago. Cow chips in a frying pan! Even John Sutter, a cheat and swindler who ran out on his wife and kids, received a big fat land grant from Mexico. Although Jedidiah got a mite too friendly with Ortega's unmarried daughter—hell, he only held her hand—nothing he ever did approached Sutter's shenanigans. Well, so far.

"Enough talking with the enemy, ya hear?" Frémont's uniformed, boot-licking guard says to Jedidiah. "Come back later and collect the pot."

"Sure," Jedidiah says.

"Sir's the correct word."

"I ain't never been in the military. So I don't know the proper lingo."

The hell Jedidiah doesn't know. Furthermore, he sure as heck knows which one of Don Ortega's sons caught him sweet-talking seventeen-year-old Epifania Ortega last year and then totally exaggerated the situation. Ángelo, that's the one. A pup who barely realizes his willy might be useful for needs beyond pissing. Jedidiah heads downstairs. His fingers brush the hilt of the sheathed long-knife strapped to his thigh. Both Ángelo and his blasted father will reap the bushel of thorns they deserve when the day of reckoning comes. With any luck, some other disgruntled fellow will take care of the whole matter on his own. Better for Jedidiah to remain in Epifania's good graces.

#

One of John Sutter's lady friends peers down her pretty brown nose and delivers a folded document into Jedidiah's waiting hand. He shifts his lantern to get a better look at the seal. The blob of wax bears an unfamiliar insignia. Probably Captain Frémont's. Crap. Why does Jedidiah have to play the role of dispatch courier, just because Frémont is short of staff? Far better to risk an Indian's hide. Jedidiah burps, revisiting the taste of chili stew. And why did Sutter send this Hawaiian gal to their usual meeting place behind the stable instead of showing up himself?

Still, if the Americans win them skirmishes against México, Jedidiah might wind up with that fine piece of land he coveted. All good things come with a price.

"What lucky man is to get this?" Jedidiah slips Captain Frémont's communication into his buckskin coat pocket.

"A second courier," the woman says. Her sweet face pinches up and turns extra serious.

A light breeze tickles his whiskers. Why is it so all-fired important to rendezvous with another courier? Let someone else carry the document to its final destination? Jedidiah's toes practically curl against the innards of his leather boots. The identity of that recipient must be a thundering big secret.

"Captain Frémont is of a mind that no circumstance should interfere with the delivery of the communication I gave you." The woman smiles and shifts position. Night and her hooded cloak make it hard to interpret her eyes. "Mister Sutter is not of that same opinion. But if you tell anyone I claimed so, Sutter will see you hanged or shot."

"Then I'm of a mind to keep my mouth shut when I should."

Frémont must be spying on Sutter. That's why the old fox sent this gal in his place. Sutter ought to make loyalty worth Jedidiah's while. He always does. Still, what's that huckster plotting this time? Frémont has practically taken over Sutter's fortress and home. Orders Sutter about like he's some half-wit servant. Threatens to confiscate his belongings. Let Sutter deal with the situation in his own way. No sense in Jedidiah's curiosity interfering with his own breathing.

"Where do I take Frémont's dispatch and when should I get it there?"

"Mission Carmel." The woman smooths the front of her cloak. "Midnight tomorrow."

Well, that's a long, hard ride. Wonder if Frémont and Sutter have different plans for the dispatch's fate? And how will Jedidiah recognize the courier he's supposed to meet?

"A red-haired American riding a black Andalusian stallion," the woman says, as if she's reading Jedidiah's mind. "Give the document only to him."

"Yes, ma'am."

Andalusians ain't usually used for deliveries when time's short and distances long. Damn fine pieces of horseflesh, though, with them flowing manes and tails. Jedidiah scratches his shoulder and turns to leave. Jumping Jehoshaphat. Bet that secret courier isn't going to travel far once Jedidiah hands him the papers.

"One more thing," the woman says. "Don't come back here for a week or more. When you do, look like you've been in a fight for your life."

"And then," Jedidiah replies, "come straight to Sutter, right?" He chuckles.

He walks to the front of the stable where guards and his saddled mustang wait. A mare? Maybe the stable hand meant this as an insult. No matter. Jedidiah isn't no Mexican fella. A horse is a horse.

He mounts and aims the pinto toward the fort's open gate. Carmel's near Monterey. That town has some sweet-smelling gals with shiny black hair and tarnished reputations. Some give away unwanted presents, though, and there's no way of guessing beforehand which ones are unclean. Too bad Señorita Epifania Ortega lives so far north of Monterey Bay. Would be nice to pay her a secret visit once his dispatch delivering is through. Soft, luscious curves. A head savvy enough to leave reading and money matters to men. A man could see fit to hitch up and raise a family with a woman like that.

Beyond the fort, the dusty road splits. Jedidiah checks the position of navigational stars and veers southwest toward Monterey. Dang, his guts hurt all of a sudden. He'll need to relieve himself soon. The way the scanty moon keeps ducking behind them clouds, he better light his lantern before settling his innards off the trail.

14. Escape

I RACE THROUGH darkness on some sort of path, my heart pumping, my feet thumping. I pull air into my lungs, expel hard, then inhale again. Does Spirit Man pursue me? The path angles downward. It's a miracle I don't trip. Either angels guide my feet or my shoes have eyes of their own.

The night air carries no sound of approaching hoof beats, but then again, Spirit Man's stallion can gallop through the sky. The two might swoop down at any moment and capture me. To make matters worse, those worms could be covering him from head to toe by now. Bad enough he pushed me into a river enchanted with spirits. Or maybe he bewitched the river himself. If Spirit Man isn't a disciple of El Diablo, he's accomplished at acting the part.

My next breaths bring my nose a new odor, a musky animal smell. A coyote? Or a gray wolf on the prowl? Something else to worry about. Oh, how my chest aches. Sharp pains stab my sides. My panic likely disappoints "The Coyote." What does he expect? What would Papi, Abuelito and my Oljon family expect if they were here? To become a heroine and remain a reputable señorita, I need a well-behaved spirit man I can trust.

A horse whinnies from somewhere. The black Andalusian, so soon? I halt. Which way should I flee?

Light flickers ahead of me from the side of the trail, like a lantern would. Not a false dawn. Perhaps a messenger, not Spirit Man, halted his mount to rest. If so, I can find out where I am, even get a ride home before dawn. But the horseman may be a Bear Flagger, or another such man without honor. I listen to the night and to my own deep breaths.

A coyote yips in the distance, as if warning me. Maybe walking alone to the nearest rancho will be better than approaching this stranger. I should move off the trail until the rider leaves. He won't notice me if I crouch near a bush.

No, I need to return home on four legs, not two. I creep closer to the light. The horse snorts. Its shadowy outline shows no sign of its master. Unlikely that someone abandoned the mount though. The lantern flickers several horse-lengths away from the animal. Maybe a pinto. Certainly not black. This isn't Spirit Man's horse. The lamplight vanishes. Has all the tallow burned? No, there it is, moving away from the horse and the path.

I edge closer. The pinto's lead rope is draped over a bush. No hobble around the legs that I can tell. The rider plans to return soon. Divine providence left this horse unattended just for me. All I have to do is—

What am I thinking? It's one thing to trade a tired mount for a fresh mustang in a ranchero's herd. Or to cut a horse out of a herd and settle later with the owner. But to take a horse practically from underneath a rider's nose isn't proper, especially in the middle of the night. I'm no *bandida*. Yet Spirit Man might arrive any minute. I have to escape.

I reach the pinto. Clouds let more moonlight through, but not enough. My hands tell me what my eyes cannot. This saddle horn wasn't made for working cattle. It's a military saddle. I step away from the horse and squint. This animal is a mare.

A Mexican dragoon—any Mexican man—would choose a stallion. And the long gun hitched across the saddle's back is no Spanish musket. The rider must belong to the cavalry of Los Estados Unidos. That settles the matter. I'll steal the foreigner's horse for the honor of México. Ángelo and my family will be proud of me.

"Who's there?" a man's gruff voice shouts in English.

The soldier is returning. I better clear out. I mount, then jiggle the pinto's reins and press my heels against its sides. The horse takes off at a canter.

The crack of gunfire echoes. The pinto whinnies and breaks into a gallop. The path is too uneven to travel so fast at night. The mare could sink her hoof in a hole. No searing pain, though. The soldier missed. I let the horse run for a while longer.

A gentle tug on the reins slows the mare down. Thank the saints this pinto is more manageable around gunfire than Fandango would be. Peril remains, however. The soldier might be on his way to rejoin his company. It is dangerous getting caught with stolen military property. What would Papi or Abuelito suggest? Probably that I find a sidesaddle.

Well, I won't find any saddle on this path. The old vaquero taught me to ride bareback when I was five, even ride without a bridle, although not very fast or far. "Move with the horse," he always advised. "Someday you'll need to." How did he know?

I rein the pinto to a halt. "We have a job to do, little wise one," I say.

I dismount. The mare presses her nuzzle against my bosom and nickers. Trained for a woman. Soon the saddle, bridle and rifle rest upon the ground. I dig my teeth against my lower lip. If later caught, I'll claim I mistook this horse for a runaway.

Still, military men can carry important messages. My country is at war.

"Stay steady, little wise one."

I kneel on the ground. A flat bundle, the size of a tobacco tin and wrapped in scratchy fabric, sits in one of the leather saddlebags. A little rawhide purse with a drawstring sits in the other. I pull the purse out. The contents jingle. Coins. Mamá taught me never, ever, to steal money, even from a bad person. I place the purse under the soldier's saddle, stand, then stuff the flat bundle into the inner pocket of my cloak.

"We have a long ride ahead." I stroke the mare's neck.

My feet push off the ground while my arms pull myself upward. The clumsy vault lands me astride the pinto's bare back. I can almost hear the old vaquero chuckle. The horse steps to the side with a jerky motion and snorts. I lean forward.

"Good girl," I say. "I'm not as graceful as you."

The mare steadies. What now? I lean forward and wrap my arms around her neck. Bear Flaggers murdered Berreyesa and his nephews for carrying a message. If I get caught, I expect someone will force me and then kill me. If I'm lucky, death will happen first. Wherever I am now, heading west to the coastal ranchos ought to be safer than going any other direction. How will I be able to tell one direction from another before sunrise? Not that it matters. Without a bridle, I've little control over the mare or our direction.

"Which way toward the sea, little wise one?"

The pinto continues at a walking pace along the same path we were using. The night breeze brings a strong whiff of urine. Ahead, a pair of yellow-green eyes glow. A coyote marks the way. If the mare rears, I'll tumble off and bust my neck.

Stupid of me to leave that saddle and bridle behind. What was I thinking? The horse breaks into a trot, then a gallop. How am I even staying on? Then something changes. I no longer hear the sound of hoof beats. I clutch my horse's mane tighter, a long, dark, flowing mane—wild in the wind. The mane of an Andalusian. The pinto has vanished.

I'm not riding with Spirit Man. I fly where I must, without any being I can trust.

#

Dawn's first light brings the sight of a two-story adobe building. A row of twisted olive trees and a low wall border a spacious courtyard, a familiar place. Soon I'll be near enough to see dew glistening on the red roof tiles. I tighten my grip on my horse's mane, the pinto's very ordinary mane. Every hoof beat drives dust into the air, even at a walking pace. No doubt about it, I'm riding that cavalryman's mare again, on the

95

ground. And I approach the hacienda of Don Emilio Ortega, Ángelo's father.

I stare down at my bare legs, at the bunched fabric of my still-wet nightclothes and soiled cloak. Don Ortega's! Of all the places to end up right now, and without a chaperone. I groan. I mustn't stop here, even if Epifania Ortega—Ángelo's sister—is one of my close friends. Besides, home is only a few hours away.

"Little wise one," I say, "please don't stop here."

The horse lifts her head and whinnies. Her plodding pace transforms into a gallop, straight toward the hacienda. I cling to the racing mare's neck, my buttocks numb from the long ride. Maybe if I jump off I'll die and won't have to face my fate.

The pinto leaps over a wall and lands with a spine-jarring thud in the Ortega family courtyard. Only the power of Heaven keeps me on the mare's back. The horse prances across dirt and bricks to a watering trough, then lowers her head and drinks. There's no separating a thirsty horse from water. Like Fandango, this mare has more than a streak of spirit.

Several servants gather around me, women with thick black braids and ankle-length calico dresses. Women with arched eyebrows. Women I know. Even if I escape this very minute, their tongues will wag for weeks. Yet if I say the right things and can borrow some clothes from Ángelo's sister before Don Ortega sees me, I might save my good name—and future with Ángelo.

"Is Señorita Epifania all right?" I say to the servants. "I awakened from a terrible nightmare about her and rode here as fast as I could."

Better they think me impulsive and misguided, than without virtue. What if someone asks me how I escaped my locked bedroom? What if my mare bears a foreign brand? I touch one of the pockets of my cloak. The flat bundle. I try not to think about what the package contains.

III. Gold, Legends and Lies

15. The Lie

EPIFANIA AND I walk side-by-side toward the main house on the Ortega rancho. Dew, struck by sunlight, glistens. Morning songbirds welcome God's new day. Already a messenger rides out to summon Papi. Consequences cloud beauty and song.

The messenger will need three hours to reach my home, and an equal amount of time to return. In six hours, Papi's wrath will explode in my direction like a full powder horn lit on fire. Mortifying. I'll dissolve in a puddle of my own tears. All by siesta time, unless the gossip about my scandalous arrival has already reached the ears of Don Emilio Ortega. In that case, death from embarrassment will strike me long before noon.

Epifania opens the massive front door. The size of this grand door and entryway always makes me feel smaller than my friend, even though she and I are of a similar height and frame. From somewhere a clock chimes. Epifania clasps my hand and leads me upstairs.

"I still can't believe you rode all the way here," Epifania says, "just because you worried about my well-being." She hugs me at the top of the landing, despite my wet clothing. "You're a true friend."

Prickles poke at my stomach, short little cramps. How dishonorable to lie to Ángelo's family. But what else could I do? Besides, I might—no, will—try to ride here if I ever have such a nightmare about Epifania. I've never forgotten the month we spent together at her uncle's hacienda when I was ten. We pretended the suit of armor in his main room was El Cid. Of all the young women in the local *gente de razón*, Epifania has always been the most fun and treated me with respect.

"Let me find you some dry clothes," she says. "I'll have the servants hang yours in a warm place."

The bandanna wrapped around mud and gold in my cloak's outer pocket. The unknown bundle I stole from the soldier. I mustn't let Ángelo's sister—or anyone else here—see them.

"My cloak will dry well enough, if I hang it near your window." I point toward a wrought iron sconce on the wall.

"Then I insist, you at least put on one of my dresses. You will get a chill—even a fever—wearing damp clothes until your papi arrives and takes you home."

What about Ángelo's crucifix hiding underneath my cloak? His older sister will recognize the sacred jewelry. Ángelo might not want Epifania to know he gave it to me. Plus she's eighteen, pursued by suitors and anxious for her father to arrange the match she prefers. We haven't seen much of each other in recent years. Informing Don Ortega about Ángelo's gift would be an act of dutiful obedience. Put her in his good graces.

"I'll be fine." I clutch my cloak against my chest.

"No you won't." Epifania stamps her foot on the wooden floor. "What will Ángelo think of me if I don't take good care of you?" She whispers, "Please let me help."

I heave a heavy sigh. Epifania's not going to let me have my way.

"I'll change my clothes if you promise not to tell anyone what I'm wearing."

"You're wearing a night dress." Epifania laughs. "Everyone already knows that. The fabric shows when you walk."

"But there's something you can't yet see," I whisper. "Promise."

"I vow."

"Shut the bedroom door."

Epifania turns and closes the door. I unfasten my wet cloak, then drape it over one arm. At least the garment no longer drips water. Ángelo's sister swivels to face me. Her eyes widen. Even her curly lashes express surprise.

"Oh, blessed saints." Her hand flies to her mouth as if it has wings. "When? How?" she utters in a soft voice. "Oh, my dearest sister."

I press my finger against my lips. Epifania reaches out and touches my wrist.

"Your secret about the crucifix is safe with me," she whispers. "You must wear my yellow dress. It comes all the way to the neck."

Her yellow dress? Her favorite? What an honor. Epifania opens the large clothes trunk on the floor. The scent of cedar grows strong. She pulls out the frilly, yellow garment she loves to wear to *fiestas* and fandango dance gatherings. So fancy with all the ruffles and lace.

Don Ortega is wealthy enough to afford many vaqueros as well as excellent seamstresses. He spends his days at home instead of with his cattle. How can I escape his watchful eye for the next six hours?

"What will your father say when he sees me in this?"

"He's away," Epifania says, "chasing after Ángelo to keep him from enlisting with Comandante José Castro's forces." She giggles. "Or so he thinks."

"What do you mean?"

"Ángelo stopped here the day the Bear Flaggers murdered Don Berreyesa and his nephews. He assured me that Castro's dragoons are on the move."

Epifania lays the yellow dress on her bed, one with a thick feather mattress instead of the hide sling I have to use. She slept on hides in the old days.

"If my dearest brother was right," she adds, "Papi rides in the wrong direction."

"Your father will be furious when he finds out."

"He's already furious." Epifania presses her teeth against her lower lip. "I dearly love Papi and my worries about Ángelo tear my heart into pieces. But Ángelo loved Francisco and

Ramon de Haro like they were his own brothers. Honor calls him to respond. He's no longer a child."

Honor—yes, of course. I nod. But Ángelo told me he also is enlisting to prove he is a man. To show his father he's old enough to make decisions for himself. Including his decision to marry me. Will Don Ortega disown his son as Mamá claimed? Me showing up here in my nightgown won't help matters.

Epifania takes the cloak. I step behind the shoulder-high dressing screen and remove the rest of my wet clothes. Epifania hangs them on the sconces, on either side of the glass window. How elegant to have windowpanes. Even the Ortegas didn't have any until last year.

"Your cloak's so heavy." Epifania opens the window a little and lets the morning breeze through. "What do you have in your pockets? Secret messages tied to rocks? Remember when we used to do that? Leave special messages for each other?"

"I remember." Epifania is closer to the truth about the cloak's pockets than she will ever know.

"You should have ridden with a saddle tonight." She fingers one of the tortoise shell combs holding her up-swept tresses in place on top of her head. "Then you wouldn't have fallen into a stream. Just because you think you know how to do something doesn't mean you should try."

"I fell into the water," I say, "because I tripped." It's time to end this particular direction of our conversation. "I should put on some clothes now."

I dry my skin with a linen towel, then slip into a spare set of Epifania's undergarments. Such soft fabric. A luxury, indeed. She's Don Ortega's only daughter. Well, the only one that survived infancy. He has the money to spoil her and does.

Epifania carries the dress over to me. "First, step into it. That always works well for me."

The yellow dress waits, with its high waistline, puffy short sleeves and sleek sleeve extensions. A long row of shell buttons graces the back. How many servants like Josefa worked to make this frock? Surely more than will ever sew my future wedding gown. I glance down at my borrowed petticoat and pantalettes. I gather them against me and step into the skirt, then slide my arms down the sleeves and attached extensions.

"My lady will look stunning," Epifania says with a false high-pitched voice. She curtsies.

"Oh, Epifania." Warmth rushes to my cheeks. I cannot even pretend my well-born friend is my servant. "I'll take good care of this for you. Bring it back here as soon as possible."

She laughs "No, *mi hermanita pequeña*, my little sister. The dress must be yours. Forever."

"But—"

"Hush." Epifania moves behind me and buttons the back of the neckline. "But you must act only like a proper Spanish lady when you wear this. We look so much alike from a distance. People will mistake us and I'll get the blame."

"I promise."

Do I look that much like Ángelo's sister? I don't need a bevy of suitors mistaking me for my friend. Especially the Bear Flagger, the one with an odd name who expressed interest in Epifania last year. Not the sort of attention I need.

"Breathe out," Epifania says.

I exhale. The dress fits loose at my waist but tight under my breasts. I've never worn such a stylish garment before. What if a button pops out of place?

"If you wear this to Misión de San José, all the Bear Flaggers will pretend they're Catholics and flock to mass." Epifania winks.

Is Spirit Man a Catholic? He isn't a Bear Flagger. No matter. I better not wear this dress when he rides in my direction, regardless of how he rigs his saddle to seat me. Even if I don't have to greet Señor Río. The skirt and blouse I wear to clean chamber pots will do for keeping company with Spirit Man. Why invite trouble?

The clock chimes. An hour has passed. Five more to go until doom. Papi, not Spirit Man, will deliver the next round of trouble. Praise the saints for Don Ortega's absence. At least

I won't have to confront Ángelo's papi and my own at the same time.

Too bad today's gossip will linger at this rancho like the odor of skunk on an unlucky burro. Don Ortega will learn it all when he returns home. Then he'll be even less willing to accept me as a daughter-in-law.

16. A Different Route

JEDIDIAH JONES spits out a string of words he'd never speak in front of a lady. No ladies around, though. Not even the pinto mare. Dang the horse thief who made off with her and the dispatch from John C. Frémont. All while Jedidiah was sick as a poisoned hound.

He retrieves his musket from the side of the road. Looks all right, at least in the dawn's light. His purse, canteen and ammo bag are still full too. Odd, the way his most valuable possessions got dumped here, just a ways down the trail from the crime. The varmint's probably some Indian who don't wish to be caught with stolen goods and lynched.

Well, nothing to be done about any of that. Not now. It's time to find himself a horse and he's not likely to find one with a rope attached. He'll just have to sweet-talk the critter into being caught without a lasso. Won't be the first time. Might even be able to meet up with that *hombre* riding the black Andalusian stallion. Jedidiah owes Mr. Sutter that much, to reveal the status of the stolen dispatch. Or does he? Sutter, according to one of his lady friends, doesn't seem to care if the message from Frémont gets through or not.

Jedidiah rigs his saddle and other possessions, then hefts the load onto his shoulder. Sweat runs down the sides of his cheeks and temples. His nose aches for a whiff of the sea. He did a stint at whaling in his youth. A rough two years, but the pay got him to California. When he ran out of money, John Sutter took him on as a hired hand.

An uncomfortable feeling now lumps in Jedidiah's stomach. Not the same sort as twisting his guts inside-out last night. That sickness didn't likely come from a hard ride, neither. Sutter wasn't anxious for Jedidiah's speedy return to the fort, might not want him back there at all. In fact, it might be safer to just keep moving on after he meets up with the red-headed American in Carmel.

Maybe even before he reaches Carmel?

A split in the trail lies ahead. One route heads south through the inland valley. The other eventually snakes through the western hills to the coast. That winding trail will lead him to Monterey and Mission Carmel, where his contact waits. Then he could backtrack north in the direction of Epifania Ortega. If he's still alive. Dang it all. He just doesn't know if Sutter is double-dealing to get back at Frémont and if he's to become skunk bait in the process.

The dispatch was stolen. What the hell does Monterey or Carmel matter? Jedidiah's main mission should be finding a horse. He shifts his possessions to his other shoulder, then plods in the inland direction. Eventually, he'll hit another fork in the road and lean toward Indian territory. Guess a man has the right to choose what type of trouble he prefers.

17. Secrets

THE SUN IS STILL high when Papi arrives at the Ortega's hacienda. He says little to me as we face each other in the entryway of the main house. Just as well. His glowering, dark eyes already say far more than my ears wish to hear. Soon I perch in my sidesaddle and taste the dust of the trail as we ride side-by-side homeward. My reckless behavior has created a scandal.

"How did you get out of your bedroom?" Papi says. "Josefa would not say. All she did was weep and beg me to forgive you."

I can't tell Papi about the key Manuel gave to Josefa. He will punish both of them, even though they meant no harm. But how can I lie to him? That will be a sin against God.

"Truth. Stretch it out fine. Not necessarily broken." Again that strange voice speaks inside of my head. The idea about truth could have—must have—come from *Don Quixote*, although the author's choice of words in my mind are easier to understand than the ones in his book. Does the spirit of Señor Cervantes try to give me advice? What an honor.

"Coyote wanted me to get out," I tell Papi, "so I did."

"Then you did not have a nightmare about Epifania?" Fresh anger rises in his voice. "You lied to the Ortega family?"

"The truth was not for them to know."

At least I didn't lie to Don Ortega. Only because he was away, hoping to stop Ángelo from enlisting in the Mexican army. Had my dearest love succeeded? Regardless, concerns about Ángelo and our future together will have to wait their turn.

"Is the truth," Papi says, "for me to know?"

What is the full truth? I brush dirt off of my riding cloak, now mostly dry. The sand in the pocket probably remains damp. And the gold? Are the nuggets real or imaginary?

"Coyote gave me a vision about his gold. But it was more than that."

"What happened?"

"I'm not sure." I stare down at the yellow ruffle on the dress Epifania gave me. "May we stop for a few minutes?"

Papi helps me down from Fandango's saddle, as he has done many times before. I hurt him today, but he has hurt me too. And Mamá.

"Please remove your neck bandanna," I say.

Papi squints one eye and rubs his mustache with his bent finger. He unties the scarlet kerchief around his neck.

"Now cup it in your hand," I say. "I need to put some damp sand in it."

"Catalina—"

"Please, Papi."

Either the gold is in my pocket, or it isn't. And what about the bundle in my other pocket, the package I stole from the soldier? That surprise will come next.

I dig one hand into my cloak pocket and remove all the sand I can, careful to leave behind the key to my room. I transfer the damp grainy sludge, without looking at it, into the bandanna in Papi's cupped hands. My lungs suck in a full breath. What will I say if the gold isn't there, if I imagined what the river gave me?

"*Madre de Dios*," Papi says.

If his eyes open any wider, they will fall out of their sockets. A favorable sign. Yes, the same small nuggets I saw the night before now rest upon the bandanna Papi holds. I exhale, feeling my grin spread across my face.

"There is more," I say.

I fold the bandanna around the sand and gold and stuff it back into one of my cloak's pockets. I extract the flat burlap bundle from the opposite pocket. The contents might be of little or no importance to México. Letters from the soldier's wife. Identity papers. An ordinary map.

"And what is in there?"

"Maybe a secret," I reply. "Or nothing. A Yankee carried it."

A flat leather pouch lies beneath the coarse fabric. Someone tucked a folded sheet of parchment within the pouch. A blob of embossed wax seals the document.

"Don't disturb the wax," Papi says. "The marks can reveal who sent this if the words inside don't."

"What if it's in English?"

"Your Abuelito might be able to read some of its secrets," Papi says.

"What secrets have you not told me?" The words leap from my mouth before I can stop them.

"I am a man. That is no secret. I saw a woman and I wanted her and I'd drunk too much brandy. The rest was inevitable."

"Did you force her?"

"What should that matter to you? If that night hadn't happened you wouldn't be here."

"Did you—"

"We shall speak no more about this," Papi says. "Ever."

How can he suggest this isn't important?

"Then we'd best hurry home."

I return the folded parchment to the leather pouch, wrap the pouch in the burlap, then wedge it back into my cloak pocket. Why did the soldier risk losing the document by leaving it unattended in a saddlebag? Perhaps the content is of no military importance, after all. Of course, the soldier didn't know that a young woman might discover the letter as she ran to escape from a spirit man with worms in his mouth.

#

Abuelito passes his knife blade through a flame, then eases the metal tip under the crimson wax seal. I barely breathe as he works. Will he damage the markings made by the sender's signet ring? Tension pinches the facial expressions of Jesús María and his brother, Santiago, who stand nearby. Only Tomás, seated in a chair, appears relaxed.

"It is almost impossible," Abuelito says, "to open a sealed document without leaving evidence of tampering." He grins. "Far easier to simply preserve the integrity of both the seal and parchment."

Within minutes, the document lies unfolded on the table in the main room of our house. Once again, Abuelito's former military duties have served him well. The letter, written in black ink, isn't in Spanish.

"What does it say, Abuelito? Can you tell?"

Abuelito traces his forefinger along a line of writing. He mouths silent words. Crinkles deepen along the sides of his mouth and the corners of his eyes.

"Tomás, come over here," he says. "I think this is French."

Tomás scratches the side of his nose as he studies the dispatch. "It's in French, all right. But I've read little French for years."

"Can you figure anything out?" I say. This message has to be important. Why else would the writer use a language few in California know?

"There are the obvious words we all use," Tomás says, "such as *the* and *he*. There are names we might expect in a military communication. Frémont. Vallejo. Castro. There is talk of guns and ammunition."

Tomás steps back from the table. He runs his hand through the top of his thinning hair. He walks to the opposite end of the table and pours himself a cup of water.

"Do you have any idea," Tomás says to me, "where you were when you stole this and that soldier's horse?"

I went through all of this earlier with Papi—everything except the part about Josefa's key. I confessed how Spirit Man rode away with me. How I fell into the river, found gold in my pocket and worms in Spirit Man's mouth. I have no idea where that river was, other than we traveled there in little time at all, but I rode until dawn to reach Don Ortega's rancho.

"There was moving water," I explain. "Up to my knees, at least in one place. Wider than any body of water around here. There were trees. Oak and willow for sure. I don't recall smelling pine but I might have. I was distraught."

"Is that all?"

"I'm tired. I haven't slept since the night before last."

"This is important."

"I know, I know." I rest my face against my palms. Oh, to just curl up on this floor and sleep for a while. Even an hour.

"You said there was a false light," Tomás says. "How did the amber light make things look?"

"Things sparkled."

"What things?"

"The water, I think." Yes, the water. Now I remember. "There was false gold in the water."

"Ah," Tomás says. "False gold may be the clue we need to solve the mystery. I don't know how far or fast a spirit man and his horse can travel, but you may have been somewhere near General Vallejo and his captors."

Tomás returns to the secret document. His finger follows line after line. Sometimes going forward. Other times in reverse.

"Some words have been written backwards," Tomás says. His stare locks on to me. "Three of them are Don Emilio Ortega."

Don Ortega? Ángelo's father? I gasp a half breath. Do Bear Flaggers plan to capture him as they did General Vallejo? Murder him as they did Don Berreyesa? They—I—have to stop such an atrocity from happening. But how?

18. Coyote's Gold

BEFORE I DO anything else, I have to put Coyote's gold in a safe place. Spirit Man tried to show me the proper location, but the worms in his mouth kindled pure panic. How foolish. He's a mystical being. He can fly through the sky, or at least make me feel that happens. Maybe he is really a huge bird who eats worms all the time. Life and religion have grown so strange these days.

I transfer the river sand and gold nuggets to a rawhide pouch, pull the drawstrings tight, then stuff the pouch into an old stocking. The resulting bundle fits into the carved wooden box containing my mementos and a thin book of prayers. Dear Manuel, Josefa's betrothed, is already on his way to the Ortega's rancho to warn them of danger. Now I can sleep while the men in my family decide what to do next.

With a yawn, I lie down on my bed, cattle hides stretched across a wooden frame like a piece of weaving on a horizontal handloom. Epifania Ortega's bed has a feather mattress, but her father possesses much wealth. In my home, even Abuelito takes his rest on hides. How magnificent to have great riches. I never will, for Don Ortega will disown Ángelo because of me. My chest heaves a deep sigh. Could the little bit of gold the river gave me purchase a bed such as Epifania's? What a shameful thought. My face warms. I didn't even dare to steal money from an enemy soldier. A river will drown me if I claim Coyote's property for myself.

My eyelids lower, so heavy, then shoot back up. What if the Bear Flaggers succeed in capturing Don Ortega? If I need to spend Coyote's gold to rescue him? No! I must never do such a thing. Ownership is ownership. Plus, if the foreigners discover the presence of the precious ore in California, they will unleash new horrors upon Californios and the native peoples of every tribe. I curl up in the middle of my bed and close my eyes. Better to trade my virtue and what's left of my reputation to save Ángelo's father, than to offer what isn't mine to give.

#

Loud voices come from the courtyard beyond the bedroom window. I rise and stretch. Papi and Jesús María gesture at each other with raised arms and open palms. Why are they arguing? I wrap my cloak around me to hide my nightdress, then step out the bedroom door and onto the brick path.

"Catalina must ride with us," Jesús María insists. "She is the one who found the military dispatch from Frémont."

"Take my virtuous and only daughter to a camp full of Mexican dragoons?" Papi folds his arms against his chest. The breeze ripples his shirt's cream-colored sleeves. "She will be safer at home."

"No place this close to the Ortega rancho is safe right now." Jesús María has already strapped his hunting knife to his leg. "That's why my father and brother plan to stay here and keep watch while we're gone."

They don't even notice me. I go back to my room. Their argument is a familiar one. What is best for my reputation? Not what is best for the future of Mexican Alta California? I glance at my clothes chest and the ruffled yellow dress Epifania gave me. As much as I loathe riding side-saddle, I'll dress and ride like a proper señorita today, if needed. I lay the frock across my arm and return to the courtyard.

"If you please, Papi," I say, walking toward the men. "I would love to ride with you. I am rested now. Additional details about my encounter last night may come to mind as we travel."

I gather the dress in front of me and curtsy. Jesús María smiles. Papi doesn't.

"Then," Papi says, "you will not wear fancy clothing I could never afford to pay for." He tilts his chin down. "Wear your plain blue skirt—not the shabby green one—and a modest blouse."

"Sí Papi." He gave in so easily? Hail María, full of grace. "I wish to please and honor you."

I'm still keeping one secret from Papi. Beneath cloak and nightdress, Ángelo's crucifix presses against my breast. I only have one old blouse that might hide it well. May the Holy Virgin permit me to see my love if he has succeeded in enlisting. Even to view him from a distance will be enough. I did not lie, though. I wish to please and honor Papi. Too bad wishing isn't doing.

19. Meeting with the Soldiers

I'VE SEEN MEXICAN soldiers before. Lancers. Dragoons. Mostly in Monterey, where Papi barters cowhides for finished goods every year. Once a small company of leatherjackets stopped at the Delgado Rancho for water and supplies. Tonight is different though.

The seven soldiers who stand and greet me wear no padded jackets to stop arrows. Nor do they wear the plumed hats and embroidered coats of important officers. Two wear dark, ill-fitting coats with double rows of brass buttons. Perhaps the coats fit better in the men's younger years. The other five wear the multicolored serapes of ordinary rancheros. In fact, I've met all seven of these gentlemen at annual roundups. Do any of them recognize me as the girl who once roped cattle better than boys her own age? Warmth spreads across my face and the back of my neck.

"My daughter," Papi says, "chanced across a military dispatch written in coded French. Perhaps by John Frémont. According to a friend of mine, from a family of French trappers, the message discusses confiscating muskets and shot from our fellow ranchero Don Emilio Ortega."

The officers exchange mumbled comments and surprised glances. If Papi told the entire story, the men's expressions would reflect total shock. Papi hands them the document. They gather around the unfolded dispatch.

"The seal is Frémont's," one of the uniformed officers says. He turns toward me. "Señorita Delgado, where did you find this? And when?"

I knew this question would come. Answering truthfully could ruin what's left of my good name. If I lie, vital information might be misinterpreted. Some of my countrymen may die. My hands tense at my sides.

"I found an unattended horse on a trail," I say. "The night before last. Maybe around midnight. The horse had a military saddle. The dispatch was in one of the saddlebags."

Foreheads wrinkle and eyebrows raise. None of the men say a word.

"Midnight?" one of the officers asks. "Were you returning home with your family from a fandango?"

How can I say this?

"No, I was running away from someone who abducted me. This is a family matter. My honor remains intact. Once I realized that the pinto must belong to an enemy soldier, I claimed the horse for México and rode to safety."

"Do you have the horse now?"

I explain how I left the horse at Don Emilio Ortega's rancho and lied to his family.

"You must understand, Ángelo Ortega and I hope to obtain his father's permission to marry. I chose to create a small scandal instead of a large one."

"And where had you been taken, when you escaped?"

"By a river. Deeper than any stream near my home. The man tried to drown me but I escaped. He had a light, though. And the water sparkled as if it contained false gold."

"Pyrite?" another officer asks.

"I am not familiar with that name," I say.

"Her abuelito," Papi says, "calls pyrite false gold."

"How many hours," one of the serape men asks, "did it take you to reach the Ortega rancho?"

"I arrived close to dawn."

"And how did you and your horse find your way in the dark, if you did not know where you were?"

"I prayed to the Holy Virgin, and to the saints."

"Her prayers were answered," Papi says. "Catalina is a devout woman."

"Who can ride astride and rope cattle." The serape man grins.

"Catalina is of great help to both me and her *madre*," Papi says, accentuating each word. "She also is not afraid to read and entertains her abuelito with *Don Quixote*."

I stare down at my shoes. Some of these gentlemen's daughters refuse to read for fear of discouraging suitors. At least one of these fathers doesn't permit his daughters to learn how. And reading is not the same as understanding the confusing things an author thought when writing. Time to change the subject.

"Is the Ortega family in danger?" I ask. "They are all dear to me, even Don Emilio."

"It could be a diversion," one of the uniformed officers says.

"I agree," Jesús María says. "Yet if false, why did Frémont make the dispatch so difficult to read? Why use the language spoken by his father and write important words backwards?"

"How do you know his father spoke French?" one of the serape men says.

Jesús María gives the officer a polite nod. "I know many things. My father is a wise man."

Uncle shrugs, as if expecting the officers not to believe him. A grin spreads wide and he rubs the back of his neck. He is up to something.

"John Frémont," Jesús María says, "was involved in the murder of my father's brother." He shifts his weight from one foot to the other. "When someone orders the back of your uncle's head blown off, you search out that someone's history to learn his strengths and weaknesses well."

One of the officers clears his throat. Another one coughs. From somewhere, a clock ticks. My turn to speak has come.

"Don Berreyesa and his nephews were not the only honorable men murdered on the twenty-eighth of June. The message I found may be true or not. But we must plan appropriate action for either situation. Soon."

20. Supper and a Song

I RAISE THE HOOD on my cloak and step out of the officer's tent. Papi slips his arm around mine. Jesús María will follow us and keep watch for trouble on the way home. I don't need an encounter with Spirit Man or a disgruntled enemy soldier.

A group of men, a total of at least thirty, gather around the campfire in a clearing. It is too dark now to recognize Ángelo if I see him. Too bad.

None of the men wear uniforms. Hardly a surprise, based on their leaders' attire. I should have stolen both the money and gun from that messenger. This company of Mexican soldiers could use the donation.

Papi and I reach our horses. He helps me into Fandango's saddle. Crickets chirp their repetitive tune. Papi mounts his roan stallion, who paws the ground over and over. More crickets' chirps. Now impatience fills me too. Why is Jesús María taking so long?

"Catalina," a voice whispers.

A man wearing a serape emerges from the shadows. Moonbeams dance upon his cheeks and forehead. Ángelo. My love. My everything. How my hand aches to touch his.

Ángelo bows his head. "*Buenos noches*, Señor Delgado. Thank you for warning my family of possible danger. The son of the French-speaking Costanoan just told me why you're here." Now his back straightens and his chin tilts upward. "That's all, sir. I must return to my duties. Please excuse me— both you and the kind señorita."

Ángelo is not bold enough to wink at me, but that's all right. Most likely his enlistment infuriates Don Ortega. He is too wise to anger my papi too.

My beloved disappears into the night. Jesús María emerges from the shadows. Time to return home. What will happen next?

#

I pat tortillas in the kitchen. Josefa stirs the beef and green chili stew, while her mamá darts back and forth to the main house, making sure the entire household will be fed their third meal of the day on time, although not all at once. Another night. Another dinner. As if the past several days—Spirit Man, the messenger and the meeting with army officers—never happened.

Still, elation fills me. And not just because I saw Ángelo last night, and Don Ortega didn't drag him back home to their rancho. I personally took action against John C. Frémont. Frémont must have wanted his forces to confiscate Don Ortega's muskets and cannon shot, and the directive didn't get through. I helped thwart the Bear Flaggers. That's even better than roping cattle.

"Manuel and I thank you again, for not telling your papi about the key," Josefa says in a low voice.

"And I thank you, for weeping instead of saying words we would both regret."

I grasp Josefa's warm hand. How different this closeness is as compared with my friends from other ranchos. Epifania Ortega gave me her frilly yellow dress. But Epifania has many lovely clothes. What is one dress to her? If Josefa owned just a single fancy dress, she would give it to me if I needed it. No matter. Sharing loyalty has far more value than sharing garments.

"Here comes Mamá again." Josefa giggles. "Keep patting those tortillas or she'll run back and forth faster than ever."

Josefa is right. The cook has always taken care of the way she reprimands me, and is even more careful now that I've reached marriageable age. Even though subservient to my parents and Abuelito, I'm old enough to demand obedience from household servants. Rather than confronting me, the cook will scold Josefa. Or even try to do my work herself.

"I can imagine your mamá running between here, the main house, the wine cellar and the pantry. Patting balls of masa into tortillas while shouting orders to herself."

"Even Papi teases her. Once he threatened to rope her like a steer to slow her down."

I smile. All this conversation is pleasant, but I need to ask Josefa the big question that bothers me. Too many distractions keep happening. Now's the time to tidy up the matter.

"Did you know before I did, about me being part Oljon?"

"I knew Señora Delgado did not give birth to you," Josefa says. "I didn't know who did. Mamá was careful to keep that information away from my ears."

"Oh." How embarrassing, being the last to learn the truth.

"Will you fault me," Josefa says, "If I tell you something?"

"I shall try not to." That's the best I can offer right now.

"I used to pray you were my half-sister. That was before I understood how babies are made." Her front teeth dig into her lower lip. "I suppose that was impudent of me."

"I suppose it was. But I guess it's not now." After all, Josefa and I have shared both secrets and work. Sorrows and joys. "I do wish, though, that Mamá gave birth to me."

Josefa tilts the cast iron cover on the stew pot hanging over the coals. Steam escapes and floats away from her. The beef smells so inviting. She sets the lid down on bricks, then stirs the simmering food with a long-handled wooden spoon.

"Señora Delgado loves you as her own," Josefa says. "I think the angels have made a mystical bond between the two of you. She has become your natural mother."

"Did your mamá tell you that? About the angels?"

"No. My heart did."

#

I help Josefa carry the tortillas and savory stew to the men's dinner table. This last meal of the day is never a big one, but Mamá likes to make it special. There will be no secret meeting tonight about prophesies and Coyote's gold. Or military dispatches. With luck, there won't be any chats about avoiding scandals, either. I spoon the stew into pottery bowls, then serve Papi, Abuelito, and my Oljon relatives food and gracious smiles. How good it will be to enjoy dinner in the company of my brothers and Mamá. Maybe it won't be such a bad thing if Ángelo and I have to live at this rancho after our marriage. I'll miss my family and Josefa if I move away.

"Gracias," Abuelito says when I turn to leave the room. "For finding that dispatch as well as serving dinner."

"You are welcome," I reply, using the formal form of you to prove I remember good manners. "Please excuse me now."

As soon as Abuelito nods, I scurry out of the main house. Josefa soon joins me. My empty stomach gurgles. Time to eat at last. No doubt Josefa is hungry too, but the vaqueros and servants always eat dinner after Mamá and her children finish. That's the way things are, and I have no power to change them.

Mamá and all four of my brothers have already gathered at one of the two long tables on the patio. A pleasant breeze has arisen, a relief from working in the kitchen.

"Catalina loves Ángelo," little Diego says in a teasing sing-song manner. His grin takes over his face.

"Hush," Mamá says.

"So tell me about your ride the other day with Papi," I say to my brothers. That ought to shift the conversation away from my private thoughts. "Did any of you get to rope a longhorn? I miss doing that."

"Vincentius did," Diego says. "You should have seen him. He snared the animal's legs on the run, just the way a vaquero would do."

"Next time I'll sail my *lazo* over a steer's head and horns."

"Muy bien." I clap my hands. "I won't be able to beat you at roping anymore."

"But you were able to meet with real soldiers," my brother Vincentius says. "Someday I'm going to be one of those."

"The war will be over by then," Gabriel says. "Why didn't the Bear Flaggers wait until I'm old enough to fight?"

How little my brothers understand about war. I exhale a heavy sigh. There's the bravery and the camaraderie, of course. But war injures soldiers. Men lose arms or legs. Even die. Vincentius, Jorge, Diego and Gabriel should be grateful that the Bear Flaggers did not wait. Of course, the Berreyesa family doesn't think that way. Nor do the Vallejos, whose beloved Papi Mariano probably faces torture this very minute.

"Tending to cattle," I say, "is better than mending from battle."

"The men fight when duty and honor calls." Mamá sips water. "But we all pray the call won't come."

I spoon a chunk of beef into my mouth and chew. Not tough at all. The chili peppers add a perfect tang. Ángelo would love this stew. When will I see him again?

#

The music from Papi's guitar floats through the evening air. I smile. Vincentius, not Papi, strums the strings. Still, the oldest of my younger brothers plays well. The men remain in the main house, discussing whatever men discuss in times of war. Too bad. Vincentius' fingerwork, although he hasn't yet learned flamenco, would make Papi proud.

Vincentius' high-pitched voice sings a ballad about the Spanish hero, El Cid, often called El Campeador, or outstanding warrior. A thin book from General Vallejo containing a poem about El Cid resides in the trunk with the two other books Abuelito owns. Even in death, El Cid rode with his knights and defeated enemies. Hundreds of years ago, that happened. Right now, my own people in Alta California could use El Cid.

"The loyal warhorse, Babieca," Vincentius sings.

My eyelids lower. The melancholy music and my satisfied stomach relax my entire body. I can almost see the tall, stern-faced hero from medieval Castile, riding his white Andalusian stallion into battle against the Bear Flaggers. How the enemy would flee in terror. They would never return to Alta California. My people could live in peace.

The song ends with El Cid's burial. A closing chapter for mortal bodies. Now, after hundreds of years, even his bones will have turned to dust. Dust can't ride into battle and protect Mexican California. Untrained soldiers such as Ángelo Ortega will have to do the job.

I stand and yawn. I hug Mamá and my two youngest brothers goodnight. Mamá will lock me in my room later. Vincentius stops playing Papi's guitar. He sets it on the table, then stretches his arms around me, his mouth near my ear.

"Did the spirit man," he says, "take you from your room to find that military dispatch? Whispers buzz like flies around here. No one will tell me a thing."

How can I answer that? I mustn't tell any of my brothers—not even Mamá—about finding Coyote's gold. I made a vow.

"I found the message through God's grace," I say. "When the saints give you a task to perform in the middle of the night, they make sure you get out of your room."

"Is the spirit man a saint?" Vincentius says.

"I know not what he is."

"Well, I might." Vincentius backs away from me. His stare burns into my eyes. "El Cid has returned."

But such is impossible. El Cid died during the siege of Valencia, way back in 1099—one of the few historical dates I know. His officers propped his corpse astride his warhorse. Surely there is nothing left of those remains to prop up. The ballad Vincentius sang tonight has stretched his imagination too far.

No, wait. Spirit Man's red hair and his stern appearance, his straight back and height in the saddle. El Cid had such features. Pieces of images float together within my mind. Worms wiggled inside his mouth. Perhaps the tips of grave worms? And those strange words he spoke: Things aren't always as you see.

Is the return of El Cid possible? Did I really ride with him?

21. Like Shattered Glass

THE BANTER OF servants and crickets blend as I walk toward the main house and my room. Josefa has not yet finished her kitchen duties. Once Mamá locks my door at night, she doesn't open it until the cock crows. I mustn't risk Mamá learning about Manuel's key. Josefa will have to sleep in her family's one-room hovel if she doesn't finish washing pots soon. Not good. A comfortable place to sleep is the least I can do for her.

Fandango whinnies from her corral three times. Did something spook her? I veer in that direction, my boxy little tin lantern raised. Won't take long to check. A coiled riata hangs from one of the longhorn skulls. My youngest brothers probably left it there. Diego and Gabriel love to practice roping the top row of skulls. Josefa's mother gets angry when they try to rope her milk goat or the chickens.

Am I still capable of roping a steer or a horse? Many months have passed since I last tried. I enter the corral, close the gate behind me, hang the candle lantern on a longhorn skull, then retrieve the riata. The knot's good and my eyes have adjusted to the meager light. I get the feel of the rope in my grasp—the weight and balance of the braided strands of rawhide. Fandango perks her ears up and prances in a circle. She senses a game. When my brothers try to rope her, she never cooperates.

"Come on, Fandango." I hold the loop at arm's length from my body. "It's dark. Give me a chance."

I twirl the loop, the rawhide stiff enough to stay open. She dodges, but I'm ready for her next move and cast the loop. It sails around her head. What a perfect landing. I pull the rope taut and laugh.

"Now come here and I'll take that off of you." Papi taught me never to leave a *lazo* around the neck of an untethered horse.

She walks over. I kiss her nose. She's a good mare. Well, most of the time. There was that day with the spade bit, the day I first met Spirit Man. Not her fault.

I slip the rope off her and leave it hanging where I found it. The candle in my lantern flickers and goes out, the way it probably did the night Spirit man abducted me and it fell to the ground. Moonlight plays tricks with one of the dead longhorn's eye sockets. The skull appears to wink. Does the spirit of the old vaquero still watch me? When I was five, he pulled me out of the path of an unbroken mustang. Perhaps it is more correct to wonder if he still watches over me. I bid him and Fandango good night.

I edge my way to my room, open the door and step inside. It's even darker in here. I fumble for my ceramic lamp and tinder box. A quick strike of a flint against a piece of torchwood, and a glow fills my bedroom. How nice, not having to rub two sticks together, the way Josefa's mamá makes me do in the kitchen.

"Someday you won't have a flint, or a little stick coated with wax and sulfur," the cook always says. "Then what will you do?"

Obviously, I will rub two sticks together. I've had enough practice to last a hundred years.

I lift the lid of my clothing trunk and remove my linen nightdress. Such soil on the garment and the resulting odor grows more unpleasant with each passing day. Tomorrow I'll leave it on my bed to air. War makes us women nervous about traveling to the river to do laundry. If we wait much longer, our collective stink will attract buzzards.

The key turns in the lock behind me. On the other side of the closed door, Mamá bids me to rest well. I'll miss chatting with Josefa before falling asleep. Cleaning up after tonight's dinner takes her longer than usual. Mamá wanted that special pepper sauce prepared in honor of Papi. His favorite. Mamá always has ways of calming turbulent waters. Food and prayers work miracles, she often claims.

Prayers. I should read from the little prayer book Papi's sister sent me at Epiphany. Just this once, it won't hurt to burn a little extra tallow, will it? Then I'll undress and put on my night clothes.

The breeze blows in through the paneless window. The fresh air smells good. Well, except for that whiff of dung. Thick glass covers many of the windows in Don Ortega's house. Probably because having more servants means more latrines. There are drawbacks to wealth. Bet Epifania Ortega does not even know how to rub two sticks together and start a fire. She certainly couldn't rope a longhorn or a horse. And heaven help her if she ever has to clean her rancho's chamber pots.

I sit at my desk and open my book of prayers. *Renew within me a resolute spirit.* Do I have a weak-willed spirit? Well, sometimes. Everyone does.

There's a low-pitched noise behind me. What makes it? I turn, the legs of my chair scraping against tile. Spirit Man faces me. *Madre de Dios.* How has he entered my locked room?

"What are you doing here?" The real El Cid would never force his way into my bedroom. "You have no right—"

But what is this? His skin appears darker, more olive, than before. His golden eyes turn the color of a stagnant pond. And his hair, now black as midnight, gleams like polished boots. Who is he? El Cid is no longer a possibility.

"You've changed your appearance," I say. "Are you a devil after all?"

"I'm neither angel nor devil," he says. "And I have a right to have come here. As I recall, you ran away with some nuggets of Coyote's gold."

"Oh." My face grows warm. "I ran away from you, as I recall. Besides, the gold is safe. Do you want me to show you?"

I study his face again. Is he my earlier visitor? "I will show you, if you can prove you are the same spirit man I was with several days ago."

"I am the same and I am not the same." He reaches his hand toward the candle. The flame flares, giving off a thin column of black smoke. "Air and tiny cinders flow like the mane on my black stallion, do they not?"

"Sí," I whisper, as if he reduces me to the size of a mouse.

"And you found the dispatch," he adds, "I had plans for."

"What do you mean?"

"The courier had instructions to meet me at *Misión San Carlos Borromeo de Carmelo*. He failed to show up at the rendezvous point. Hardly a surprise."

"What makes you think I stole anyone's horse or message?"

"Ah, a slip of the tongue." He laughs. "I mentioned nothing about stealing a horse, now did I?"

More than a slip of the tongue. More like a tumble off a cliff. A green glow outlines his form, as if an enchanted candle burns behind him. Not good. Now what am I going to do?

"What did you do with it?" the man says. "The dispatch, I mean."

"What did you plan to do with it?" If he is an imposter, I don't want to reveal secret information.

Spirit Man cups his hand around his chin and beard. Now his pupils resemble darting emerald flames. The hard expression of El Cid returns to his face.

"You play a game with me, Señorita Delgado. But I am not a man accustomed to playing games I don't choose."

He places his hands upon my shoulders. They press against me like two huge adobe bricks. This man is not the same one who visited me before. He's an imposter. He wants gold that belongs to Coyote and military secrets that belong to my people.

"All you have to do," I say, "is to appear in the form you took the other day. Then I'll gladly give you both gold and information."

I back away from him. My glare challenges his. "And that, Señor Spirit Man, is no game."

The candle lamp's base explodes with a crack. Pottery shards spew everywhere. How can pottery shatter like glass? I shield my face, pressing my hands against my nose, cheeks, mouth and closed eyes. Pottery slivers pierce the backs of my hands. The candle, wherever it is, goes out.

I scream. My own hands muffle the noise. The man's laugh echoes, as if from a cave of many chambers.

#

The Black Andalusian gallops into the wind. Perhaps on ground. Perhaps not. Right now, my body tenses and my eyes remain closed. My upper body faces forward, but I'm not ready to see where I am or where I'm going.

Spirit Man has wedged me into the front of his stallion's saddle, the underside of one of my knees hooked around the saddle's horn, my other leg against the horse's side. This is the way a bride might ride with her groom. The comparison leaves an acid taste in my mouth. His arm tightens around my waist. I'm not ready for that, either.

When Spirit Man One abducted me, I feared most for my reputation and honor. True, he tossed me into a river, but only after preventing me from falling off runaway Fandango. The worst panic came when I saw worms in his mouth.

Spirit Man Two, on the other hand, is a bully with a nasty temper. And so unpredictable. He might even toss me off of this horse on a whim. Yes, tonight the stakes for me climb to the height of a jagged mountain peak. Forget mere loss of good name and purity. I also fear for my life.

"Hang on tighter to the mane," Spirit Man Two shouts. "He won't mind."

Ouch. Clutching anything hurts. I must have bits of that lamp base embedded in my hands.

"Lock your legs into the saddle."

"Sí, Señor Spirit Man," I mumble.

"Do you carry pebbles in your mouth?"

"No, Señor Spirit Man." My voice is loud and clear.

I get a better grip on the stallion's mane, despite my discomfort, then twitch in the saddle. Victory for a sliver of ceramic. Spirit Man Two chuckles. How dare he do so when I'm hurt? He's worse than dangerous. He is annoying and dangerous.

"Brace yourself," Spirit Man says.

The stallion's hooves hit the ground hard. I jolt upward. My eyes pop open. Only Spirit Man's grip keeps me from tumbling off. Darkness and shadows surround me, broken by the man's milky green glow. The waxing moon hangs in the starry sky. Far better than traveling in total blackness.

What happened mere moments ago? Did the Andalusian jump over a fallen tree, or did he land after flying high above living oaks and evergreens? My stomach twists as if giant hands braid my innards into twine. Whether we jumped or flew, the feeling isn't good.

The horse slows to a near standstill and picks his way up a steep incline. Shod hooves click against rock. The air smells of pines. I lean forward and brace my dangling left leg in the sash stirrup. The sound of rushing water grows louder yet I see no cascade. Cool spray dampens my face. Wherever I am, I'm not near home.

"Where are we going?"

"Where you're going to hide Coyote's gold."

"I didn't bring the gold. Remember?"

"I meant in the future."

That's one of the most ridiculous things anyone's ever told me. How can I return to a place without knowing which trail to take? Spirit Man Two is dangerous, annoying and speaks nonsense.

Water smacks my face. Cold. No, icy. Now water showers me as if someone upended a brimming-full horse trough over my head. My hair. My blouse and skirt. Shoes. The waterfall sops everything.

"You did that on purpose." My voice echoes. Strange.

The green aura around Spirit Man Two quavers in the corners of my vision. Darkness closes in around me. No moon or stars and the air smells damp and moldy. We've entered a cave.

"You could have warned me about the waterfall."

"I could have thrown you into a river, like I did the last time."

"That wasn't you. That was Spirit Man One."

"Can't a questionable hero with a dark streak, have an even darker side?" Again comes his disturbing laugh.

"A soul can be good and evil." My shoulders shiver. "But God gives each person a unique appearance that doesn't change every few days. No one soul can live in two people."

"Why do you think I'm two people?" Spirit Man Two reins his stallion to a halt. "Didn't I already mention? Eyes don't always tell the truth."

"Neither do mouths."

I glance over my shoulder. His eyes turn from green to yellow to crimson. Perhaps I made too biting of a remark. Time to change the subject.

"So, this is where you want me to bring Coyote's gold. What I've already collected and what I collect in the future. I'll need to find this tunnel again. What's its name and where is it?"

"The Tunnel of the Twin Falls." He coughs. "No map or chart marks its location and none ever will."

"Oh?" Water drips from the ceiling of the cavern, joining a narrow rivulet on the rock floor. Such an unpleasant edge, his voice has. "I only notice one waterfall."

"For that, you should be most grateful."

"I'd be most grateful if I understood what you're talking about."

Spirit Man Two dismounts, then helps me down from the saddle. The aura around him retains a crimson glow, like blood flowing from mystical wounds. I've offended him.

"I spoke with haste before." Locks of my hair dangle in my face. I push them back. "Both my parents and Abuelito taught me decent manners. Please accept my apology."

"But, of course, Señorita." The glow around him softens. Sometimes violet. Sometimes gold.

"Tell me about this cavern," I say. The formation might be as tall as Don Ortega's two-story adobe main house, but not nearly as long. Why has no one but Spirit Man discovered it? "And what makes you think gold will be safe here?"

"Those who enter the Tunnel of the Twin Falls alive," he replies, "do not leave that way."

Spirit Man's hand moves toward the side of his leg. Dear God, he reaches for his knife. Murder! He plans to murder me.

I scream. I must escape. I jerk backwards. My ankle slips and twists. I crash hard onto wet stone.

"Tell me where you hid Coyote's gold," he demands. "And who now has the dispatch I was supposed to receive."

Spirit Man Two moves toward me, the knife in his grasp. His scarlet eyes glare. To save my life, I must tell him what he wants. No, I must tell him nothing and save my soul. His pale lips form words. My arms shield my face, my cries too loud for me to hear anything else he says.

22. Don Julio and a Suit of Armor

JEDIDIAH JONES bites into the soft tortilla and savors the flavor of corn. The aroma of roasted beef lingers in the air. Sure beats hardtack and dried fish, but then, rancheros are known for their generous hospitality to strangers—as long as them visitors leave the señoritas alone. Jedidiah leans back against his chair at the supper table, delivering another round of smiles and compliments to his hosts: Don Julio Pacheco and his buxom wife. His mouth might as well be gracious while his mind bashes good old Julio's brother-in-law up north. If Don Emilio Ortega was a fly on a nearby wall, his wings would rattle.

"And that's a magnificent suit of armor," Jedidiah adds, gesturing toward the imposing antique in the main room's corner. "Did you bring that over when you moved from Spain?"

"I purchased it off a ship docked in Monterey. The broadsword too." Julio's eyes glimmer, like those of a fox wandering into a chicken coop. "You are brave to have traveled the inland trail. An uncivilized foreigner shot a couple Indios earlier this year. Tribal anger simmers like beef-and-chili stew over hot coals."

"Bad business." Jedidiah's guts twitch. "Hope the fool *hombre* gets what he deserves." As long as Jedidiah doesn't get a serving of the same vengeance chowder. "Are you getting by all right? Up north, the Bear Flaggers have been causing plenty of trouble."

"Less trouble here," Julio replies. "Maybe things are worse along the coast or in the City of the Angels. Nothing as bad as General Vallejo or Emilio have seen."

Jedidiah knows about Vallejo. Doesn't everyone in Alta California by now? The news about Emilio Ortega, however, comes as a total surprise.

"What's happened to Don Ortega?"

"The Bear Flaggers planned to take over his rancho. But an important dispatch was intercepted by our people. According to everything I've heard, the Bears abandoned their plan."

"A dispatch?" This story sounds too familiar.

"Sí," Julio replies. "Rumors claim Frémont himself sent it, but we don't really know."

"Guess I've stayed off the main trails too much this week." Jedidiah pushes back the gritty lock of hair hanging in his eyes. "Haven't heard a single word."

And that's the truth. Not "one" word on the subject. His brain now announces a barrel full, all adding up to one obvious conclusion. Someone set him up, like a dealer stacking a crooked deck. He was poisoned, tracked, robbed and humiliated out of a job. Is Sutter responsible for his plight? Frémont? Some other confounded weasel? The best Jedidiah can do for a while is keep drifting and hope nobody dresses him up in a rope necktie or casts lots for his scalp.

Well, there's one more thing to wish for, that Don Emilio will ship Epifania south to this serene place. Not likely, but it would sure be sweet to see her pretty little shape in her ruffled yellow dress again. Ain't nobody who looks so comely in frills.

23. Gold, Magic and a Name

I SIT ON the floor of the cave. My hands tremble. No, all of me trembles: inside and out. Spirit Man returns his knife to its sheath. He tosses me his canteen. I drink. The cold water tastes of minerals.

"Congratulations," Spirit Man says. "You have passed the trial of Spirit Waker Cave. It is only a matter of time before the Yankees discover gold in Alta California. We must hold off the inevitable as long as we can. I needed to be sure about you. Too much is as stake."

"Does that mean—" What sort of place wakes up spirits? "—I'll leave this cave alive?"

Spirit Man crouches and picks up a pebble. He turns the small stone over in the palm of his hand. The surface appears shiny, as if wet. Then he stands.

"Keep this with you," he says, "at all times. Its magic will allow you to leave and reenter unharmed."

He places the stone in my hand and closes my fingers around it.

"As long as you return with offerings of gold, the magic will renew."

How will I know where to find the gold or how to get back here? Why can't he do those tasks himself?

"And if I find none?"

"Wherever my horse takes you, there will always be gold to find."

"What's your horse's name?" Papi always names his special horses.

"He answers to no name," Spirit Man says. "Call him what you will."

"So," I say, "What You Will shall find me whenever you wish."

"Whenever Coyote wishes."

What if Mamá needs my help? The baby might come early or be turned the wrong way. I'll have to ride to the next rancho for their highly-skilled midwife. Putting aside such family duties could lead to disaster. Will this happen for the rest of my life? The smooth stone feels rough in my grasp.

"You know, I could fall ill with a plague," I say, "or break both arms and legs."

"You will ride when called, until the waterfall protecting the front of this cave runs red with blood."

To have blood color the barrier of clear water, a battle would have to take place above this very cave. Yet no map shows the way here. Will Bear Flaggers follow me, and the spilled blood include my own?

I slip the stone into my skirt pocket and button the flap. The pebble might not be magic. All of what Spirit Man just said could even be an untruth meant to frighten me, to persuade me to do as told.

"May I return home now?" At this very moment, my family probably worries about me.

"As you wish."

Spirit Man whistles to the Andalusian. The horse's coat glitters, as if tiny stars hide within, his hooves clicking against rock. Air from below the cave rushes upward through the animal's mane. He whinnies. Spirit Man gestures toward me, his golden irises glowing in the dim light. He removes the stirrup sash, the band of cloth that allowed me to ride sidesaddle in front of him.

"You will not need me with you," he says. "This time."

Of course, the Andalusian knows the way. I mount astride the stallion. My feet slip into the regular stirrups. A perfect length. When did Spirit Man adjust them?

"What You Will." I lean forward in the saddle. "Please return me to the rancho of Don Ygnacio Delgado.

The horse makes no effort to move, let alone head for the cave's mouth. But then, had not Spirit Man claimed the animal answers to no name?

"All right, No Name. Home. *¡Andale!*"

The Andalusian bolts forward. My buttocks bang against the leather saddle. I lean forward and cling to the animal's neck. At least I know now what this horse agrees to be called.

#

"*Gracias*, No Name." I run my hand down the black Andalusian's nose and tell him good night. My ceramic lamp base broke hours ago and the candle went out, yet a glow shines through my bedroom window. I step from the courtyard and into my room with care. Candlelight flickers beside my bed. The heavy ceramic lamp base and its lone candle rest undisturbed on my little square table, as if tonight's violent abduction never happened.

But it did happen. I rode to the cave of no return, and then returned. The magical stone, the one I must keep with me. Is it still in my skirt pocket? I feel for the lump of rock through the broadcloth. There it is. I extract the stone from its hiding place. The rock smells damp and shimmers with a blue-green luminescence, like the ocean after twilight. Tonight was real, more than just a vision. Why isn't the ceramic base in a thousand pieces on my bedroom floor? I set my bedroom key next to the lit lamp.

"You have not prepared for bed?" Josefa asks from behind me.

I turn. My friend steps into the room, the candle in her own metal lantern flickering beneath thin plates of sheet mica.

"I am sorry for being so late." She sets down her lantern and yawns. "There were extra dishes to wash. Plus we put tomorrow's beans in to soak."

"You have good reason to be tired." So do I, but I'm wide awake.

Best to feign sleepiness. I stretch, rub my eyes, set out my night clothes, then remove my shoes. Exhaustion from my latest encounter with Spirit Man should hit me from head to toe. It doesn't, as if time is an ever-flowing stream and I've stepped upon the shore to watch.

There must be an explanation for all this. I slip the magical stone into the pocket of my nightdress. No sense in taking needless chances. For now, I'll accept what Spirit Man claimed about my fate, and sew the stone into my undergarment tomorrow.

I climb into my cowhide bed. Josefa unrolls her sleeping mat and blanket on the floor. Oh, to confide in my friend. To share the details of tonight's adventure. But that cannot be. Not now. Maybe not ever.

"And Josefa, would you use your key to lock the door now? Mamá already came by."

24. The Letter

THE NEEDLE SLIDES through the linen one last time, then I knot the thread. There, all finished. I've sewn the luminescent pebble from Spirit Waker Cave into the lower hem of my chemise. From now on, the stone will accompany me by day and reside near my bed at night. I've also fashioned a hidden pocket in my wool cloak for Coyote's gold. My treasures are safe.

Mid-morning sunlight shines through my bedroom window. Time to return to my household chores. And I must pen a letter to Ángelo before the Ortega family's courier arrives. Comandante Castro keeps our soldiers on the march. After today, two weeks might pass before another opportunity to send my love a note arises.

I stand and smooth the skirt of my dress, the frilly yellow one Epifania gave me. I ought to save the garment for special occasions, but its soft, tightly-woven fabric and perfect fit make me feel so elegant. Ángelo's crucifix hides beneath the high neckline. I'll wear this dress today, then put it aside for my next visit to Misión de San José. Besides, my sackcloth apron will provide ample protection in the kitchen. What can go wrong?

I close the bedroom door behind me and head toward the kitchen. Already the odors of simmering beef and beans grow strong. No foul stink of butchery, though. The vaqueros always take care of that business well beyond the house. They keep the rendering pots at a distance too. Mamá's orders. Bravo for anything reducing the number of flies.

Flies. Odd, how they don't bother with me today. I didn't encounter them when traveling to the river and cave with Spirit Man, either. But, of course, those trips happened at night. Only mosquitoes buzz at me after sunset.

Josefa hurries in my direction. "Your mamá, she asked you to come to her work room right away."

"Did she say why?" If Mamá plans to scold me, I want some kind of warning.

"Maybe you should just go there." Josefa tilts her head to the side. "Her eyes—they are all red and swollen. I think it is important."

Mamá is crying? My chest heaves a sigh large enough to put out the flames of seven candles.

"I'll go see her."

I scurry uphill along the path to the work rooms. Mamá will think me foolish for wearing this dress. Well, let her. It belongs to me, does it not? Still, I should keep the dress in perfect condition until Ángelo can see me wearing it. I lift the bottom hem out of the dust. When will this war end and when will he come back to me?

The door creaks as I open it. Mamá is inside, her head lowered, and looking as if all of today's stitches have dissolved. She beckons me to the bright room, the one with the most daylight, then pulls a folded piece of parchment out of her pocket, the wax seal broken in half. The seal of the Ortega family.

"Manuel's mother brought this to me," Mamá says, "this morning. One of Don Ortega's vaqueros delivered it to her husband yesterday, in the south pasture."

A message from the Ortega household? Why would a vaquero make the delivery when Don Ortega's courier could have? I unfold the parchment. The scrawl has to be Epifania's. How foolish, this fear of hers—the one about improving her reading and penmanship. A man would have to flatten and bake his brain like a tortilla to resist Epifania's graciousness and beauty. Besides, her father can read and write and doesn't forbid her from doing the same. Why not take advantage of her good fortune?

I run my finger along the top lines of the writing. One word is larger than the others. Ángelo! Nearby words might be *prisionero de guerra*. Prisoner of war! Surely, I've misread. No matter how I turn the piece of parchment, an image of Ángelo—face bloodied and arms tied behind his back—looms within my mind.

"How much of this were you able to read?" I say.

"Only one sentence." Mamá moves her bowed head from side to side, her palm against her mouth. "Even one word told me more than my heart wanted."

"Prisoner." I wail. "They've taken Ángelo prisoner. What am I going to do?"

"First of all, you're going to tell me what the rest of this message says."

Mamá can't read well, even under the best of circumstances. Abuelito might be able to help decipher Epifania's scrawl. Still, Epifania didn't risk the confidence of her father's courier, the man trusted to carry letters to Ángelo wherever the Mexican Army in Alta California camps. Perhaps bringing the letter to Abuelito so soon would prove unwise.

"The dearest sister part is clear."

Epifania now considers me a member of the Ortega family. Well, that would sour Don Ortega's stomach if he knew. I can almost see his bushy eyebrows and pinched facial expression. "Catalina's behavior is impulsive and improper," he might say. Who but Heaven knows how I might embarrass the great Ortega family? Don Ortega has no idea Ángelo and I have exchanged crucifixes as tokens of our devotion and faithfulness. I can only imagine the furious don snorting bile out his nose.

I must be part of the family response to save my love.

"Oh, Mamá," I say. "Maybe Don Ortega learned about Ángelo's capture and does not wish to share the information with me."

"Read the written words. Think about the unwritten ones later."

"Papi," I read, "does not...anticipate a long war...already....
Oh, no! A bride for him will travel from Spain for a wedding
next summer."

"We have already heard the rumors," Mamá says. "Keep
going."

How can I? How can I not? Tears sting the corners of my
eyes.

"Last night." My voice quivers. "I awakened. Mamá
and *Tía* sobbing. Soft voices. The Bear Flaggers shot. Shot
Ángelo!"

My hand trembles, my knees as pliable as tree sap in
summer. Ángelo shot. I clutch his crucifix through the fabric
of my bodice.

"His very life hangs in peril." I read a few more lines in
silence before setting the letter down on the sewing table.
"Epifania implores me to use every power God has given me.
She pleads with me to rescue Ángelo now."

I lean against the worktable and rest my face in my open
palms. Rescue my beloved husband-to-be? What must I do to
accomplish such a miracle? Epifania hasn't even heard half
the magical things I've experienced these past few days. She
believes such signs come from heaven. I'm not so sure, unless
Coyote is a saint the Catholic Church refuses to recognize.

"Your papi and Ángelo's will forbid you to ride with
them," Mamá says. "What sort of *madre* will I be if I agree
when they do not? Besides, you don't have the strength to
carry an injured man and lift him onto a horse."

"But I must do something." Another day will pass before
Don Ortega receives the news about his youngest son. When
he does, the rescue party he organizes won't include me.

"Yes, you must take action," Mamá says. "To begin with,
you must pray for guidance."

I close my eyes and bow my head. Mamá will be upset
and Papi, furious, if I steal away from the rancho to find
Ángelo. Josefa will be frantic with worry. Both my abuelitos,
distraught. Riding to find Ángelo will only please me. And
Epifania, if she ever finds out.

If I clear my mind of these swirling thoughts, God may have more room to give me ideas. Yet into each small clear space rush more images of Ángelo's bloodied face, now fragmented by yellow eyes, angry rivers, and longhorn skulls. The harder I try to evict the pictures, the larger they grow.

Heaven presents all us mortals with trials on Earth, some challenges daunting and others small. A good Christian woman accepts the hardships Heaven gives her. I am Rain Falling's daughter, though. Do all my hardships come from Heaven? Which ones need I accept?

I reach out and grasp my mother's calloused hand. "Pray with me for strength. I'm afraid of praying alone right now."

Not quite true. I fear an unwanted answer.

#

The sun shone at its highest point two hours ago, and the day's heat sucks sweat from my every pore. I carry *la comida* on a serving tray to my hungry abuelitos—beef, *frijoles*, rice, tortillas and sliced apples—these two aging men will take a long siesta after eating this meal. A single rider leaving the rancho will not disturb their slumber. I press my lips together. Today, my papi and uncles help our vaqueros move more cattle to the nearby canyon. By the time they return home for dinner, I could be many leagues from here. I could find Ángelo and whisk him away to safety. Dare I try?

Abuelitos Ygnacio and Tomás sit across from each other at one end of the long dining table in the main house. Such subtle shifts of their heads as I ladle hot food into their bowls. Such fleeting glances. Few words escape their mouths but their eyes speak volumes. They can tell I'm up to something improper.

"Will you need more tortillas?" I gesture toward the platter on the table and smile.

Abuelito Ygnacio grunts.

"Maybe bring us a serving of truth about the scheme your mind weaves," Abuelito Tomás says. "Not all old men are fools."

I emit a quick little cough. Do they know about Ángelo already? Mamá wasted no time telling them about Epifania's letter. She didn't trust me to make the right decision.

"Not all young women are fools, either." My tear ducts sting. "But this one is in love and afraid."

I sit down next to Abuelito Ygnacio, without asking permission.

"Oh, Abuelito." Tears roll down my cheeks. "Tonight, the Spirit Man will want me to bring Coyote's gold to a secret cave. You, Mamá and Papi want me to preserve what is left of my reputation. But Ángelo might die at the hands of the Bear Flaggers. I don't know what to do or even in what order."

"Taking care of Coyote's gold comes first." Tomás runs his hand through his thin hair.

Abuelito Ygnacio reaches for a tortilla. He tears it in two, the resulting pieces uneven. "Work on your reputation as well. Although the fruit of divided labor can have rough edges."

"But Ángelo—" My tears practically wash my face.

"I would ask Spirit Man where Ángelo is." The voice of Abuelito Tomás is softer than before.

"If they have taken him to Sutter's Fort to be imprisoned with General Vallejo," Abuelito Ygnacio says, "it will already be too late for anything but a huge miracle."

"But if he is still on his way there, or if they take him to another place." I sniffle. "Might there be hope?"

"Then," Abuelito Tomás says, "a small miracle might suffice."

25. Dark Clouds Moving

JEDIDIAH JONES leads his bay mare to a stream and looks eastward at the mountains. That ain't the Sierra range, not after all the days he's traveled south. What they're called, he can't figure. His map is the crude sketch he made of the fancy printed one in Julio Pacheco's home. Pretty current. Maybe 1835.

The horse drinks, its shadow longer than at the last place they stopped. The afternoon grows old. He ought to start hunting for a safe place to sleep. He refills his canteens. An unsettled feeling gnaws at his innards. How many days before he's out of Alta California? Away from the craziness of his own countrymen, particularly the ones with the Bear Flag? Won't be soon enough.

Now his stomach just plain rumbles. He pulls a stick of jerky out of his saddlebag. He's got Mexican papers. Knows some Indian sign language. Speaks enough Spanish to get by. Yeah, he'll be better off out of the reach of Sutter and Frémont. Don't know what they have against him and no sense in finding out. He chews on the dried meat. Tastes good.

Of course, now there won't be any settling down and raising a family with Epifania Ortega. Too bad. How sweet it would be to take that frilly yellow outfit off of her—peek at all the beauty underneath. Pleasure each other. With a gal like that, he'd never need another. Not unusual, though, for the road between a man's fancy and reality to get washed out. His daddy taught him that. His mama taught him something even more valuable. There's no making babies when you're dead.

Water. Concealment. Potential shelter in an attack. His brain rattles through its usual list of evening-on-the-trail preparations. Should he build a fire to discourage the local predators, the hefty ones with four legs and sharp teeth? Or skip the fire, avoiding the unwanted attention of two-legged critters with a sharp aim?

Something disturbs him about camping here for the night. Maybe an instinct. Maybe not. Jedidiah always pays attention to such feelings. Like his mama's ghost watches over him. Best to ride a while longer before making camp. He glances toward the heavens. In the distance, dark clouds move in his direction. Where are they coming from so fast? In this terrain, flash floods can follow sudden rainstorms. Higher ground might not be a bad idea.

He mounts his mustang and the animal skitters.

"It's all right, gal." He speaks in a soft, steady voice, stroking the mare's neck. "You take me where I say, and we'll both be all right."

IV. Storms, Searches and Sorrow, July 1846

26. Searching for Ángelo

PALE MOONBEAMS shine through my bedroom window, my bare feet like two shadows on the floor. Hours ago, chirps of crickets replaced the buzz of flies. An owl hoots. I put on my shoes and wait for Spirit Man's arrival.

No doubt we'll seek gold tonight. After I reveal the story about Ángelo's injury and capture, I hope we'll look for him, as well.

I pat the outside of my cloak's pocket. The bulge from Papi's bandanna, the crimson cloth wrapped around Coyote's gold, is still there. So is my bedroom key. What about the magical stone? I feel the rock within the hem of my chemise. Dearest saints, I've checked for these items a dozen times since returning here after dinner. And none of them can protect me from the Bear Flaggers who've shot and stolen Ángelo. I touch his crucifix, yet find little comfort. Who needs flies to trigger unsettling thoughts?

The knife, the one that belonged to Abuelita María Delgado. I should stuff it into my coat pocket, as well. Should I first put on my *botas*, my red leather leggings? They'll protect me from underbrush.

If only Josefa could be here to discuss such matters and help me bide the time. Too much potential danger. I don't trust Spirit Man. He enjoys frightening people, I think. Josefa will fear for my life and try to follow us. What if Bear Flaggers find and harm her in the process? It would be foolish to risk the safety of my friend. No, this is my journey to prepare for and endure.

I'll sit down on my bed for a while. The stretched hide, laced to the wooden bedframe, sags under my weight. Fatigue pulls upon my eyelids. I rose at sunrise today and skipped a siesta. How nice, sleep would be. If I sleep, though, I'll not see how Spirit Man finds his way into my locked room. Does he flow in ghost-like form between the iron bars on my window? I yawn. Does it matter?

"You should have rested this afternoon," Spirit Man says from behind me.

I leap up and spin in a half circle. Did he step through the walls?

"This night will be long," he adds.

"Where did you come from this time?"

"From the ceramic base of your unbroken lamp. Or was it from under the door?" He grins. "No matter, it's time you get dressed to leave."

"I'm ready." Can't he tell?

"Wear the dress Epifania gave you. No leggings."

Ruin the only nice item of clothing I own?

"You're going to toss me into a river. Drench me with a waterfall. Make me crawl around in dirt or mud." I fold my arms against my chest. "I'm wearing what I'm wearing."

"Not if you want to find Ángelo Ortega alive."

"Ángelo?" The word squeaks out of my mouth. How does Spirit Man know the latest news about my love?

"Ah." He scratches one of his red muttonchops. "Now I have your attention. Put on Epifania's dress. You need to look like her, at least from a distance."

"Why?"

"Just do as I tell you."

"Then turn around." I'm not going to change my clothes in front of any man who isn't my husband.

Spirit Man laughs and stands in the corner, facing the wall. I slip out of my cloak, skirt and blouse, then wiggle into Epifania's frock as fast as I can. He buttons the back for me. What a relief to be covered like a decent woman should.

"I need my cloak on. The gold's in the pocket."

"That is fine. You won't need your cloak off until later this evening, when we find your dear Ángelo." Spirit Man tilts his head. "You really do look like his younger sister. Maybe it wasn't such a bad thing, you running away from me and having to stop by the Ortega's rancho before heading home."

"You had worms in your mouth."

"I told you before, that was no reason for panic. I could have captured your great-uncle's killer that night if you hadn't overreacted."

The murderer of Abuelito Tomás' brother? I press my fingertips against my lips. The digesting meal in my stomach churns.

"I'm—I'm sorry." Salvatore of the Eagles, that's what his given name was. How disappointed Abuelito Tomás will be with me when he finds out. "Next time, could you please warn me? 'Catalina, here come the worms. Catalina, my eyes will run blood.' It will help."

Spirit Man walks over to the door. He grasps the latch and opens the barrier. It's not locked. How can that be? Mamá secured the door with her key.

"Tonight will be far worse, and there will be no time for warnings. Give into fear and your great-uncle's killer will again slip from my grasp." His eyes, deep and dark as oceans, stare into my very soul. "Give into fear, and your dearest Ángelo will perish at the hands of the Bear Flaggers before sunrise."

Oh, blessed saints. Dinner turns to stone in my stomach.

#

No Name swishes his tail and waits for us in the courtyard. He paws the ground and snorts. His crimson nostrils flare. It is so easy, though, to climb upon his back, to sit in sidesaddle position with one foot in the loop of scarlet sash. Spirit Man doesn't have to help me at all. How odd. Regardless, Abuelito Ygnacio would be proud. But this is no time to laugh at my own sarcastic thoughts. Tonight I'll rescue Ángelo or watch him die. The choice is mine. A shiver speeds

151

across my shoulders and down my back. I must be brave and choose my actions with care.

"Close your eyes," Spirit Man says. "Else dust will trouble you."

After all that's happened, does he truly believe I worry about trail dust? I fret about Ángelo dying. Or me falling out of the sky. Spirit Man doesn't want me to come face-to-beak with some gliding hawk and panic. However, I don't doubt his earlier warning. I must not, under any circumstances, give into fear. I probably ought to do exactly as he directs. My eyelids lower.

No Name starts out with a bumpy trot, but soon gallops through the night, the steady clops of his hooves reassuring. Spirit Man grasps me around the waist, the way Papi did when I was small. Next, comes the sensation of the stallion leaping upward, as if he jumps over our adobe wall. No downward sensation follows, though. The pounding of his hooves has ceased. Wind whistles and moans, chilling me to my core. Dare I open my eyes? I gather my courage. Only blackness and a slab of cold, damp air.

"Didn't I tell you to close your eyes?"

"Sí." He's sitting behind me. How did he know I opened them? "But you didn't say for how long. Besides, they're shut now."

"*Está bien*, Señorita Delgado." Spirit Man tightens his arm around my waist. "Please follow all my instructions. Perhaps, then, you will yet wed Ángelo instead of his corpse."

Perhaps, then, I'll also learn to tell reality from imagination. Know for sure if we travel by land or air. I touch my cloak pocket, the lump of bandanna safe. My leg shifts. Does the magical stone still reside in my undergarment's hem? Hail María, pray for us. The prayers of Señor Coyote might come in handy too.

27. From River to Cave

FALSE DAYLIGHT returns, like a mysterious dawn in a dream. I don't know how Spirit Man manages to create the magical effect. I'm not sure I want to. In a former life, was he ever accused of witchcraft? Burned at the stake? A good thing the Spanish Inquisition has ended.

I dismount No Name. Not really. I'm freezing and my leg muscles cramp. Spirit Man has to lift me down. Once on the ground, I stumble. Oh, for the sun to rise.

"I don't see a path to the river," I say. "Not around here."

"I'd worry if you did." He laughs. "There isn't one. We'll have to make our own."

Spirit Man threads his arm around mine. We edge our way through brush and down a riverbank, following the sound of flowing water. I never like the feel of his touch: cold, damp and dead. His name is appropriate.

Spirit Man. Spirits. I've approached river spirits before; the wrong way, that is. This time I seek a friendlier reception. I introduce myself to the shadowy river and all the beings within. The rush of water tumbling over rocks grows loud. Now it's time to wade. The bottom sediment will stain poor Epifania's frilly skirt. If my action saves Ángelo's life, who cares?

Spirit Man steps into the water and motions for me to stay where I am on shore. "This is a special river. A section of it runs near Sutter's place."

"Juan Sutter's?" That's where the Bear Flaggers hold General Vallejo captive.

"He pronounces his given name John."

Near Sutter's! The night I fled from Spirit Man, the night of the worms in his mouth, I saw false gold in false daylight. I didn't run more than a mile or two before I encountered that courier's horse and the dispatch from Frémont. From what Spirit Man claimed, the courier murdered Salvatore of the Eagles. Later, my family figured I was near Sutter's place that night. If I'm going to see Ángelo, that means we could meet him and his captors on their way here. Are we anywhere near the hidden cave for Coyote's gold?

"*Por favor, Rio*, please." I bow my head. "Trust me with Coyote's gold. I'll put it in the care of those spirits of the land who wait for me this very night."

Light floods my eyes. The magical glow grows brighter. Spirit Man beckons to me. I step into the water beside him, not even removing my shoes. Chilly.

"Bend over," Spirit Man says. "Cup your hands and dip them to the bottom."

Another voice reaches my ears, a soft voice, one I don't recognize. Nor can I interpret—even reproduce—the jumble of sounds.

"Please pardon me," I whisper. "I don't understand."

Does the voice request I dig my hands into the mud? I slip them under a layer of ooze with a slippery feel, my face now against the water's surface.

"Wait there," the voice says. Or, is it Spirit Man?

How long shall I wait? I count to fifty, turn my head to the side for a fresh breath, then keep counting to one hundred. My hands grow warm. One-hundred-one, one-hundred-two... The water pushes at my ankles. I need to stand upright or I'll fall.

I straighten, hands cupped together and away from my body. Muddy water drips from between my fingers. Spirit Man unfolds another black bandanna and holds it out to me like a hammock. I empty the mud into the cloth. Several gold nuggets practically smile.

"One more time," he says. "The river will let you know when."

Will the river soon inform me when to go rescue Ángelo?

\#

We wait in the dark, Spirit Man and I, mounted on No Name, Coyote's gold safe in my cloak's pocket. I have no idea where we are. We wait for a signal—some sort of odor. Only then may we approach Spirit Waker Cave. Right now, I smell the stand of pines where we hide ourselves, not far from a granite slab. Obviously, the secret aroma doesn't involve evergreens. Was there an odor last time? I only remember being drenched by water. Something my brother, Vincentius, said to me stirs within my memory. Curiosity stirs too.

"Are you El Cid?" I say.

Spirit Man clears phlegm from his throat and spits toward the ground. "Why do you ask?"

"Abuelito Ygnacio told me El Cid was a hero. Fought for important causes. Could do magic. And one of my brothers asked me the question."

"El Cid fought for whomever he wished, sage or fool." Spirit Man sounds bitter. "Yes, he defeated many enemies in battle. But he could be defeated too."

I twist a lock of my hair around my finger. Does my question upset him? I shrug.

"So are you El Cid? Or not?"

"Sometimes I don't know who I am."

"Oh." I listen to the crickets. "Lately I don't know who I am, either."

So many things puzzle me, most importantly, how to save Ángelo from the Bear Flaggers. El Cid killed men in combat in order to defend others. Will I need to as well? I could shoot a person to protect Ángelo. Or to protect Mamá, Papi, Abuelito, my brothers or Josefa and her family. I'd fight to save Epifania. Even our vaqueros—who can take care of themselves—are dear to me. Still, *Jesucristo* asks us to love our enemies, not slaughter them. Last Epiphany, Friar Fernandoco preached not only about the gifts of the Magi, but God's gift of life.

More crickets serenade me. The noise of tumbling water—lots of it—beckons. A waterfall conceals the entrance to Spirit Waker Cave. Maybe we can't be too far away. So strange, all these mystical happenings.

Strangeness. Life. Value. What is the value of Bear Flaggers' lives, except to their families? Ragged, unwashed murderers who felled an old man and his nephews for fun. Savages with pale skin, that's what Bear Flaggers are, far worse than native tribal raiders. Abuelito Ygnacio has said hostile tribes threaten our people because Spanish Conquistadors stole their land in the old days. Just as the Yankees now try to steal Mexican land. Alta California has vast leagues of wild hills and valleys. Why don't the Bear Flaggers simply apply for land grants from the Mexican government? So much greed.

"The world is more complicated than that." Spirit Man says. "Savagery does not confine itself to the hearts of one culture or nation. It slinks to wherever it's nurtured."

I glance back over my shoulder at his vague outline. He actually can read my mind. Saints protect me. Only a holy being—or a very unholy one—knows people's thoughts. My neck itches all over, as if rubbed with poison oak.

"Don't worry," Spirit Man says. "Although I comprehend the actions and motivations of Satan, I'm not him."

"Then, are you an angel?" The itch shifts to my stomach. No lady should scratch her stomach in front of a man who's not her husband. Even in the dark.

"Not one of those, either."

Rising wind brings a sharp, metallic odor, one I sometimes smell after lightning flashes. The odor we've been waiting for? Spirit Man touches my shoulder.

"Tonight we are the spiders," Spirit Man whispers, "and the Bear Flaggers, the flies."

That's like the sentence I saw in Abuelito Ygnacio's secret book. Spirit Man must have read a copy too. Where? Or maybe he read the memory in my mind. Blessed saints. Who else, besides El Cid, has he been? The famous sorcerer, Dr. Juan Faustus? According to Abuelita María, Faustus sold his soul to the Evil One. She told me that tale nine or ten years ago, knew so many interesting stories. Spirit Man claimed he understood Satan. Does he know the Devil well? If so, my association with Spirit Man—and my hatred for the Bear Flaggers—could endanger my soul. My every muscle tenses, like drying strips of rawhide.

#

I enter the cave we sought. Spirit Man follows, leading No Name. False daylight guides my way. The Andalusian snorts and balks. He doesn't want to go in here tonight. I feel something's wrong too, and it's not the uneven ground.

My most important task is to put tonight's nuggets, and the ones I collected earlier, in a safe place. I search for a ledge, a hole, a depression—a cranny I'll be able to find in the future. A spider web guards a crevice in the main cavern's side room. Balanced on the balls of my feet, I slide Papi's scarlet bandanna into the opening, followed by Spirit Man's black one. Spiders and flies. The bandannas aren't obvious at all. Satisfied, I make a mental note, and rejoin Spirit Man.

"Do you plan to draw a treasure map? Mark that spot with an 'X'?"

"No. The rivers haven't made all the nuggets easy to find. Why should I?" Coyote is supposed to be clever. He'll know where to look. Not to mention—what use does any coyote have for gold? Josefa's claim about Coyote and tobacco makes more sense. Lots of men smoke the stuff.

I've spent enough time playing the mother hen who hides her eggs from predators. "Now, is it time to find Ángelo? Before the Bear Flaggers stow him in an impossible place to find?"

"It is time." Spirit Man rubs the back of his neck. "Are you ready and fearless?"

"Neither one."

"Good. Maybe wisdom has a chance."

The false daylight dims once I pass through the waterfall. How will wisdom help if I'm ill-prepared and scared to death?

28. The Storm

LIGHTNING STREAKS across the sky. Will a bolt hit us? I brace my foot against the stirrup sash and cling to No Name's mane. Thunder booms. The heavens crack in half. A force thrusts us upward. Next, we sink faster than my stomach wants to travel. No Name leaps upward again. We are truly flying. Only Spirit Man's firm hold and magic keep me from tumbling into the night.

It is early July, the fifth or sixth. I've lost track. To experience such a thunderstorm as this one in summer, we must be above mountains. The snow-capped Sierra? I've never seen them up close. Below lies rugged country with harsh weather, according to all I've heard, plus settlements of unfriendly tribes to avoid. I bet even the Sierra foothills take a week's ride to reach from my home. If we need to land in snow tonight, I'll freeze. Already the chilly air numbs my fingers and toes.

If my brothers were up here, they'd want to look for all the places they know: our rancho, the ocean, the Mount of the Devil. Well, I'm not them. I don't even climb my favorite oak these days. Best not to stare anywhere right now—up, down or sideways. My eyes snap shut. We drop. We climb. I shudder. God created people to walk, run and ride upon the Earth. Only birds, bats and bugs should fly. And those winged creatures probably have the good sense to avoid flying far in a storm.

"Where are we going, now?"

"The road where the Bear Flaggers travel with Ángelo."

Ángelo, at last! "Too bad we can't bring this storm with us."

Lightning rarely hits ground around my home. Another reminder that a bolt could hit us up here with ease. Those Bear Flaggers—not me and Spirit Man—are the ones who deserve to burn to ashes. I mumble yet another prayer.

"The storm intends to travel with us, Catalina."

How can a storm intend to do anything? It isn't a person. But then, how can Spirit Man's Andalusian stallion fly without wings? Once again, Abuelita María's story about the sorcerer tickles my memory. Doctor Faustus traveled by sky, not only to distant lands, but into the past. As an old man, he sold his soul to Satan in order to regain youth. I don't know if her story is true or not, but one thing's for sure: I'll never do the vile thing Doctor Juan did—refuse to believe in God.

No Name lands with a thud on the trail. The jolt almost tosses me out of the saddle. At last, his hooves pound with a regular rhythm against solid ground. If I were standing instead of riding, I'd drop to my knees and kiss a patch of dirt, even one full of flies. Kiss…. May my dearest Ángelo be nearby.

We slow to a stop. No moon or stars shine tonight, no hint of dawn beckons, and yet another branch of lightning crisscrosses the sky. Clouds hide the heavens.

Spirit Man dismounts. He reaches out his cold hand to help me down. I always find riding sidesaddle awkward. I will do it to please Ángelo, though, when we marry—that is, if he lives long enough for us to wed. But I mustn't think that way. He has to live.

"Catalina," Spirit Man says, "very soon Bear Flaggers will arrive with Ángelo. Magic I've set in place will distract them for a few minutes. Use your time well to find him and secure him on No Name's back."

"I'll need help, won't I?" Surely Spirit Man remembers Ángelo's been shot.

"Find help as you can. I must leave you, now."

"Leave me?" His words punch me hard as a fist in my gut. "Why?"

"Dear Catalina." He shakes his head from side-to-side. "What happens the rest of this night is up to you. If I interfere, what needs to happen might not. No Name will stay behind and do your bidding."

"But I need your interference, your help. When I find Ángelo, we'll need to lift him onto No Name's back. Together."

"Believe me, you are almost like a daughter, even a former comrade in arms—lost from me until recent days. I would stay with you if I could." He takes a long step backward. "Things are changing fast."

"You're the one who's changing them," I plead. "The man I love. His life is in peril. There's no room for mistakes. You must—"

"Listen, I'm becoming another, Catalina. Do you understand?" His voice, steady and low, almost cracks. "Very soon, I—I won't be here."

Won't be here?

"You've got to put it off. Delay. Please." I drop to my knees and reach in his direction. "I beg you."

Moonlight, it passes through him. The clouds have parted, revealing an almost-full moon. He's fading! Going away. Deserting me. Deserting Ángelo.

"Coyote," I cry. "Please not yet. I need him."

No Name rears, trumpeting his own cry of distress, forelegs thrashing the air. After a while the Andalusian steadies. I stand. He walks over to me and presses his nose against my breast, his nicker soft and sorrowful. I wrap my arms around his neck and weep. What am I going to do now? Where do I even begin?

#

I sniffle and brush the last tears away. Feeling sorry for myself won't help me find Ángelo, do my tasks for Coyote, or atone if God doesn't agree with my choices. There's only one place to begin: to see if No Name's saddlebags contain anything of use, such as a pistol, a dagger, or a pouch full of magical herbs, tobacco or Spanish coins. Spirit Man was, well, a spirit. I never saw him eat or drink. But he did keep a canteen around for me.

Only two objects occupy the bags. A leather pouch full of luminescent stones—like the rock he gave me and claimed was magical—and a dagger in a worn leather sheath. The cracked wooden hilt is as ancient as Noah's Ark, and the encrusted metal blade has chipped edges. The point is barely sharp at all. Not much for confronting an enemy unless I want to make him laugh to death. Maybe this is Spirit Man's dagger from his El Cid years and holds magic. It must have some purpose other than a keepsake. Oh, no! I forgot Abuelita María's dagger in my room. How could I be so careless?

My teeth press against my dry lower lip. I'm not thirsty but probably do need Spirit Man's canteen, the one he always seemed to pull out of nowhere. Seemed? I guess he did.

More lightning arrives, brighter than before. Are there riders in the distance? Far less than a league away, otherwise I wouldn't be able to see them in this weather. Thunder prevents me from hearing their approach. Their image darkens but another flash follows. Yes, riders move in this direction. Five or six. No, five. They lead a spare horse. They don't ride with haste or appear to see me. Minus this storm, they'd almost be within shouting distance. How can they be so close and not see me?

They're not meant to see me—yet.

A feeling deep down inside tells me what I most—and least—want to know. No Name has landed in a place where the Bear Flaggers and Ángelo prepare to pass. The spare horse likely carries Ángelo face down over the saddle.

Dead? Is he dead?

I blink, but don't yet see anyone slumped or tied across the spare horse. Spirit Man would tell me to stay calm. I listen to the memory of his voice. My racing heart slows. I can face this. I will face this. Fate leaves me no choice.

My fingertips brush against the saddle bag holding Spirit Man's ancient dagger. I climb onto the stallion's back.

"Pray for us sinners," I whisper, stroking his neck. Do I pray to the Virgin of Guadalupe? To Spirit Man or Coyote? I'll pray to all holy beings, accept help from any spirit who's not evil.

"We stay here," I tell No Name. "We'll let those Bear Flaggers come to us." Again my fingers touch the saddle bag. As I envision Spirit Man's dagger, my hands and arms tingle. The strength from some ancient time finds me, spreads through me. Is this why the Bear Flaggers can't tell I'm waiting for them?

The biggest streak of lightning imaginable fills the heavens. Thunder slams my ears. Yet, somehow, I manage to hear men shout—in English, I think. The Bear Flaggers. Their horses rear and whinny. Gunfire crackles. No more thunder, though—why, I do not understand.

Bathed in repetitive lightning, over a dozen riders on horseback ahead fight to control their terrified mounts. One horse grazes in the midst of this apocalypse. A figure lies like a dead body over its saddle. I would recognize this man if he were hidden inside of a giant burlap sack. Dearest Ángelo, is he still alive? No Name trots closer to him. Blood stains his hemp shirt. I'm vulnerable to attack if I dismount, but if I don't, I can't evaluate Ángelo's condition. I have to know the truth, take the chance.

I climb off No Name's back, then press my hand against the side of Ángelo's rib cage. No chest movement? He smells of sweat and his skin is cool to touch. I hear buzzing. More lightning comes. Flies gather on his face. No! Please, God, breathe life into him again.

Something whooshes past my cheek. A small musket ball? Am I meant to die too? Another whoosh follows. I can't die yet. Spirit Man—Coyote too—gave me a mission. Yet I don't want to live without Ángelo. If I do the spirits' will, maybe my dearest love will awaken. Lazarus, a friend of *Jesucristo*, returned from the dead, didn't he? That's what Friar Fernandoco often claims. A strand of rawhide still encircles Ángelo's neck. Holy Mother, he still wears my crucifix. Don't let me panic or lose faith.

I hear neither gunfire nor traveling musket balls now. Maybe the returning thunder booms too often. No lead has hit me. Still, my stomach muscles clench and my heart pounds hard.

"Who's there?" someone shouts.

I do not see the man. Where is he, and how far away?

No Name stands beside me again, his saddlebag glowing with yellow light. I need the knife. As old as it is, it's better than nothing. I refuse to be murdered without putting up a fight. The light intensifies as I unstrap the bag's closure. I reach into the pouch, withdraw and then unsheathe Spirit Man's old knife. My fingertips don't detect any encrustation. With the next bolt of lightning, the metal blade gleams—as perfect as the day a blacksmith once forged it. No Name steps backward and away from me, as if to tell me we each must perform our own given tasks. All right, No Name, I can do my share. So be it.

"I'm beside you, my love," I whisper to Ángelo. I grasp the bay's lead rope and stroke its neck. May God keep this horse calm and also permit Ángelo to feel my presence.

"Who's there?" the voice calls again.

More lightning rips the sky. A man faces me, wearing the buckskins of a foreigner. Ragged whiskers cover his cheeks and chin. His grin could outdo Satan's. He holds a pistol in his hand. Dear Lord in Heaven.

"How convenient." The man moves toward me. "I've been wanting to scalp me an Injun squaw, but a Mexican one will do me just fine."

Scalp, did he say? Scalp me? I tighten my grip on the hilt of the unsheathed dagger, the blade gleaming in front of me. I've never fought off anything with a knife, not even a swarm of flies. And this man holds a gun.

"Where did you get that knife—it is a knife, ain't it?" He lets out a guffaw. "Looks like you found it in a shipwreck or maybe buried in somebody's grave."

He doesn't see the knife—all bright and shiny—the way I do right now?

"Put the drat thing down and I promise to kill you before taking your hair."

What kind of devil does such things? I have to pretend I don't understand him, keep him talking. I have to figure out what to do.

"You say to hand it to you?" I say in Spanish. He wants to take more than my knife and hair.

"Drop it!" He points toward the ground.

"Oh, place on ground." That's it. I've thrown knives with Papi's vaqueros and my brothers. I switch my hold from the hilt to the blade, then make a downward pointing motion with my free hand.

"Hurry up," the Bear Flagger replies in Spanish. He takes a step forward and aims.

I leap to standing, pull back with my arm and hurl the ancient knife at the Yankee. Lightning strikes the ground between us, pushes me backward. I collapse, then roll. The stench of burned flesh sours my stomach. Was I hit by the bolt or a lead ball? And what about the Yankee—or Ángelo and his horse?

Thunder and lightning persist, blackening the enemy now crumpled on the ground, the knife embedded in the front of his shoulder. I did not deliver the fatal blow. The storm finished the job. The horse bearing Ángelo skitters but doesn't rear, as if an angel—or Spirit Man—calms it.

"I can't see," an unseen man shouts. "Blind! I'm blind."

His words are in English but I understand their meaning. Other men shout the same thing. The Bear Flaggers' horses, whinny, buck and throw their riders. I'm being given a chance to escape with Ángelo and better make good use of it. I pull Spirit Man's knife from the Bear Flagger's shoulder, wipe the blood on his buckskin shirt, then lead the bay carrying my love. A path of light brings me to where No Name waits. Now what do I do? I've not the strength to transfer Ángelo from one horse to another.

"Señorita Epifania," a man's voice rises above the next roll of thunder. A different voice than the others I've heard. "What in tarnation are you doing here?"

Buckskins, unkempt beard: I don't recognize this Yankee. But the power of the storm hasn't blinded him. Maybe he's not as evil as the others. He has mistaken me for my dear friend—and this is not the time to correct him.

"My brother Ángelo," I wail, in the best English I can muster, "we have to help him."

Another lightning flash comes. The stranger's expression appears uncertain.

"Please help him," I say. "Help us." I gesture toward No Name.

"Ángelo's dead, señorita," the man says. "I'm sorry, but—"

"I know it looks that way, but people can appear to be dead when they're not." Papi told me that.

"I met up with those other men." He uses mostly Spanish now. "They were going to leave him. Leave him here. The flies, thick as— Take my word for it, señorita. He was gone. Then the storm hit." He looks away from me. "Señorita, I'm real sorry."

"He's alive, I know." Isn't he? Tears sting my eyes. "I have to take him to—to a special place. Please." Spirit Waker Cave—I've got to take him there.

The man looks at me as if I'm a foolish child. There's a tenderness in his eyes though. I've heard stories about a Yankee interested in Epifania. Is he the one?

Somehow we move Ángelo to No Name's back and prop him upright—like El Cid without the armor—seated in front of this stranger. I mount astride in front of them. I don't know how we all fit. Yes, I do—by the Holy Virgin's grace alone.

A gust of wind hits. No Name steps sideways and snorts. He breaks into a gallop, then leaps.

"Close your eyes and hang onto Ángelo," I tell the man.

The ground under No Name's hooves becomes the sky. The Yankee shouts words Abuelito Ygnacio wouldn't approve of me hearing or repeating. A hole in the heavens rips wider. A black void awaits. A bolt of lightning juts across the tear, only to vanish. Thunder rumbles long and loud, then no more. The void expands, encircling us. Darkness without any gray shadows swallows us whole. No Name doesn't flinch.

"Jedidiah Jones," a deep voice booms.

Perhaps, this Yankee's name? The stranger riding behind me screams, over and over. Do I? If so, my cries never reach my ears.

29. Shelter

NO NAME paws the ground. We landed mere minutes ago and he's already impatient to get going. No surprise. Pending dawn paints the horizon with a thin bright line. Soon we won't be able to find the cave until night returns. The magic works that way. The sound of rushing, tumbling water marks the entry falls. Spirit Waker Cave ought to be a short scramble up this section of mountainside. Dearest Ángelo, may you wake up once we pass through the drenching cascade.

Jedidiah finishes tying Ángelo across No Name's back. The stallion picks his way up the steep terrain. Jedidiah follows, offering his hand to help me around the worst of the boulders.

I shake my head several times. "I have to walk this path on my own, as you must," I say in a mixture of Spanish and English. I shouldn't bring a foreigner anywhere near this cave, let alone inside. Coyote won't be pleased. If the lightning returns to strike one or both of us, its target must remain clear.

Oh, that I could have taken Ángelo to his home or mine. Epifania and I would have watched over him. Right now, his only hope for life lies within the cave. Yet what life will that be? He'll never be able to leave. We can't live in a cave—can't build a rancho there, raise children, or graze cattle.

Burning pains shoot from my head to my toes. The sound of the falls grows louder. No Name whinnies. He prompts me to hurry up.

Ahead, the rising wind catches the Andalusian's long mane. Water pours over him, over Ángelo. No Name stands where he does so I can find the entrance in the light of dawn.

"We need to hurry," I call to Jedidiah.

What did Ángelo promise me a few days ago—being wed in this world or the next? I curve through a scattering of rocks, many the size of my head. Blades of green grass grow between them. Plants farther away are desert scrub. Lightning strikes but does not hit me or the Yankee. Not yet, at least.

"I choose this world," I whisper. Then I follow No Name and Jedidiah Jones into Spirit Waker Cave.

The odor of burning pitch replaces that of flowing water. The magical torch embedded in the cave's wall flares, brighter than before. Next to it, the blurred figure of a man appears. The ridged wall behind him—I see it by staring right at his chest. No, through his chest. This is a ghost: a real one, unlike Spirit Man, who was living, dead and a sorcerer.

No change in Jedidiah's expression. He unties the rope holding Ángelo on No Name's back. The ghostly vision is for my eyes alone. The image sharpens. Wait, I know this man. Tomás—Abuelito Tomás. But he was alive a few days ago. I blink over and over. No, this isn't Tomás. He's too short and his neck is thicker. Perhaps Tomás' murdered brother? The ghost raises his arm and points his forefinger in the Bear Flagger's direction. An accusatory motion. Jedidiah murdered Salvador of the Eagles. How could I bring him to this cave, do such a stupid thing? How could Epifania want to associate with such a man?

Jedidiah lowers Ángelo to the ground. I cover my dearest with No Name's saddle blanket. I sit on the cave's floor by his side and hold his cold, wet hand between my own.

"Who are you?" Jedidiah says. "You ain't Epifania, though I thought you were before."

"Epifania gave me this dress. We're friends."

"I gather Ángelo Ortega was your friend too."

"He still is."

"Ma'am, I hate to sound disrespectful, but—"

"Ángelo is alive. He's cold, that's all."

I'm right. I have to be. I lean across his still form, try to warm his other hand. It does feel better than before. I need to remain patient.

"Listen, Ma'am, let me go for help. This ain't a good—"

A snore interrupts his sentence. Ángelo! I put my face next to his and feel his cool breath. Holy María, Mother of God. The spirit inside him awakens.

"Fried spit in Hades." Jedidiah's eyes open wider than a hungry bear's mouth. "You a blasted witch woman?"

The gleam of metal—he draws his pistol, points the gun at me.

"I'm not a witch, but you are a scoundrel and a murderer." I stand up straight as possible, glare at my opponent, and pray he interprets every word I have to say. "This day you have seen an Andalusian stallion gallop through the sky. A dead man breathe. And the most terrifying thunderstorm ever, arranged, by the way, by a higher power to mark the return of a great hero to the spirit world. If you harm me or Ángelo, my horse will trample you. If you try to ride him, he'll throw you off his back and into the ocean. If you have any scrap of wisdom at all, you'll sit quietly in this cave and behave like a gentleman in the presence of a lady."

"Yes, Ma'am." The Bear Flagger slips his gun back into its holster, then sits down on the floor of the cave, his face pallid in the torchlight, as if he witnesses his own funeral.

No doubt about it, he heard and understands every word I've just spoken. Should I tell him what will happen if he leaves this cave without magic on his side, deliver the warning Spirit Man gave to me? No Bear Flagger—especially one who points a gun at a lady after he's murdered her great uncle—deserves such a gift of mercy. Best for him to find out on his own, during whatever few moments of realization he is permitted.

No Name snorts and walks toward a side passage I haven't explored yet. He stops and half-turns, just standing there, as if waiting. His ears twitch and he snorts again. Does No Name show his displeasure of me—or of this cave's prisoner? I groan. Maybe both. I must choose my actions without panic and with greater care. I don't want to make all these decisions using partial truths for guidance. Spirit Man should be here. Ángelo coughs in his sleep. I need to tend to his wound. I can at least wash it. If only I had fresh bandages. I could ride home and fetch some. Bring back some food, though I'm too upset to be hungry at all. But what if Ángelo awakens when I'm away and steps outside? The same fate as the Bear Flagger's will befall the man I love. No, I need someone to watch him. And this wretched murderer did help me put Ángelo on horseback. Well, that was when he thought I was Epifania and didn't know what sort of ride awaited him.

I'd heard Ángelo had discouraged one of Epifania's admirers. A few Yankees do come to Don Ortega's annual cattle roundups. Festivities always follow. Last year, a fever kept me from attending most of the event. This man could have been there, met my friend then.

No Name's tail swishes back and forth. Yes, he's waiting. The false daylight returns, as if Spirit Man is still around. Except he's not. The spirit of Señor Cervantes mumbles something about heads containing empty rooms. I don't even remember reading about such a thing in *Don Quixote*. But then, it was such a long and complicated book.

Salvador of the Eagles returns, his ethereal arms crossed against his chest. At least he doesn't point a finger of blame at me. I can see better now, in more ways than one. Does this magic of false daylight belong to the Andalusian stallion, now that Spirit Man is gone? Or did it always?

"There's something you need to know." I emphasize each syllable as I speak to the Bear Flagger Jedidiah, my fingers playing with the tufted end of one braid. "Besides the fact that my great uncle's ghost is not happy with either one of us."

30. Sorting the Facts

I CAN'T RETURN home during daylight. No Name only likes to gallop through the sky at night. I don't blame him. After all, we could be mistaken for one of the horsemen of the apocalypse. A perfectly pious person might drop dead from fear.

Ángelo sleeps through the day. Once in a while he snores or shifts position. I check his injured shoulder. A gaping hole in the front and plenty of bruising, but no second wound. The musket ball remains inside him. He doesn't awaken but appears comfortable. Yesterday he was dead. Today, he's not. As long as he keeps breathing, the magic of this cave has a chance to heal him.

Jedidiah sits in the middle of the floor as I told him to last night. Sometimes he's awake yet makes no attempt to stand. Then his eyes follow my every movement. Good, the way he remains afraid of me, afraid of the magic.

"It's all right to drink water from this side of the falls," I say to him. "If Ángelo awakens, help him do the same thing. Don't pass through the falls though, or it will be the last thing you ever do. And no exploring. There could be all sorts of displeased spirits in this cave. You've heard of Coyote, I'm sure."

I've no idea if he has, but I like the ominous tone of my words.

"Bold equals dead," I add. "I want to greet you both—alive and well—upon my return."

"Yes Ma'am."

"Your last name is Jones?"

"Yes, Ma'am, like the voice in the wind said."

"How well do you know Ángelo? Might he recognize you if he awakens?"

"I'm afraid so, Ma'am."

"Because you shot him?" Our stares connect us.

"I told you, Ma'am, I'd nothing to do with all that. I'm sweet on Epifania, that's all. It offended him."

"Did you offend her?" Most Yankee men don't have enough respect for women of Spanish descent and no respect for native peoples at all.

"Ain't sure." He scratches the side of his neck and grins. "Don't think so."

I'll need to ask Epifania about that.

"You did shoot the old Costanoan, though, didn't you? The day Frémont and Kit Carson murdered Don Berreyesa and his nephews?"

Jedidiah lowers his head, as if studying the grime on his boots. Bet he thought nobody noticed his wretched deed. I won't mention Ángelo's name, though, or that of Tomás.

"The ghost of Salvador of the Eagles—my great uncle—resides in this very cave." I shrug. "I didn't notice until we came in here today. Very recently deceased, he pointed a rather accusing finger in your direction."

"He was about to deliver an arrow into Frémont's back."

"That's an excuse?" Bet Jedidiah contemplates standing and racing out of this cave, no matter what the consequences. "If you'd done nothing to stop Salvador, you'd be a hero now to Epifania—and likely to Don Ortega. You'd also have all my family on your side, including me." I tilt my head to the side. "Interesting, the way our foolish choices change the paths of our lives."

"So, what you plan to do, señorita?"

Those eyes, the way he slouches. Even the way his mustache droops. He looks like a desperado, a man happy to make sure his opponents join him if he dies. And a man happy to force a young lady. God forgive me for the lies I'm about to deliver.

"I, Señor Jedidiah Jones, plan to do nothing. I don't need to. The spirits, they watch over me and Ángelo. If you kill us, we wed then. If you don't, we wed one way or the other. The end result is the same for us." I pick dirt from underneath my fingernails and press my lips together. "Not the same for you, however."

No Name walks from one of the side chambers into the main room of the cave. He steps between me and Jedidiah and swishes his tail.

Hail María, pray for us sinners—maybe for some more than others.

31. Last Meal

JEDIDIAH JONES leans back against the uneven wall of the cave, the floor rocky and hard as hell. Damn uncomfortable. He could sure use a plug of chewing tobacco. Ten feet away, Ángelo Ortega slumbers, his breaths even, like he don't have one blasted care in this entire lousy world. If not for Ángelo, he would be courting Epifania right now. It's just plain unfair.

A flying horse without wings, a breathing corpse, and last night's crazy storm. And a beautiful, strong-willed, sarcastic señorita in charge of the entire disaster. This whole business stinks of witchcraft. No doubt about it, the Spanish Inquisition frigging failed.

Jedidiah stands and stretches, then ambles to the front of the cavern. He cups his hands and quenches his thirst. At least the water's good. His stomach rumbles. Catalina Delgado headed out on her horse right after sunset. Will she bring back some grub soon? She claimed she can only travel by night, another reason to believe she's made a pact with the Devil. Jedidiah fingers his side pocket. Two slices of jerked beef remain from his visit with Epifania's uncle. No sense starving to death with food available. Might as well eat a half slice now.

The damp air tickles at a memory as he chews. That Indian cactus, what's its name? Pyoat? Peyote? Yeah, that's it. Peyote can make a body experience all sorts of strangeness. Certainly, there are plenty of Indians working at all the ranchos in Alta California. Some medicine men and women probably have connections to the remaining local tribes.

Catalina, with her sort-of-stocky neck, looks like she could be part Indian, more so than Epifania. Only problem is, he can't recall Catalina giving him anything to eat or drink the night they met. And the storm hit before her arrival.

Jedidiah paces back-and-forth between Ángelo and the waterfall. Well, if he took some crazy medicine-woman potion, the effect has worn off. There's got to be some real clues about where he's ended up. At the edge of this cave's mouth, there's an odor of freshness, and not just due to the falls. Plus, he saw the land when the lightning flashed, before he entered. He smelled something too. Pine, or some combination of evergreen trees. He didn't smell cattle. There was a cool crispness to the air, like the time he and some other fools had trekked the wrong way through the Sierra Nevada—the snowy range. General Vallejo—bless his soul—had dispatched a rescue party through the snow once the distress message, ferried by local Indians, got through.

Snowy range—Jedidiah's up high, somewhere hard to find. Where most folks don't travel, although Americans cross illegally into Alta California all the time. Bet these mountains have places where winter snow remains on the ground all year round and snowmelt running downhill creates occasional waterfalls.

Well, that information won't help him return to civilization. John C. Frémont holds General Vallejo captive. Vallejo's Sierra rescue efforts have shut down. And Señorita Delgado predicted Jedidiah would die as soon as he crosses through this cave's waterfall.

Will he die if he takes Ángelo with him? Once Jedidiah passes the barrier alive, it won't matter what happens to his adversary. Or will it? Catalina's recent words echo inside his memory. If he didn't shoot that Indian—Catalina's great-uncle—he would be a hero to the Delgados. If he shot John C. Frémont or Kit Carson, instead, Don Ortega likely would have offered Epifania's hand in marriage as a reward. Hell, if he shot any Bear Flagger on June twenty-eighth at the San Rafael crossing, another rebel would have ended his life within minutes.

Life holds both ideals and realities. Jedidiah Jones ain't no fool, well, most of the time. He reaches into his pocket for another half-slice of jerked beef. A last meal? Only one course of action lies in front of him. May his mama, wherever her spirit floats, be proud.

32. *Truths Sweet and Bitter*

WATER TUMBLES over rocks and around boulders, froth sparkling in false daylight. I lean forward in the saddle and groan. I don't need to be gathering gold for Coyote, not yet. I need to get food, medicine and a canteen from home.

"Can't this wait?" I say.

No Name snorts, walks into the shallows, then plunges his muzzle underwater. He doesn't swallow. No surprise. Spirit Man neither ate nor drank. Why would his horse?

I introduce myself to the river, the way Spirit Man taught me.

"Am I supposed to sift through sand here?" I say to No Name, then let out a hefty sigh. "Or wade deeper?"

The Andalusian does the wading for me. When the fast-moving water reaches his belly, he stops. The current will carry me away if I dismount. Another snort tells me he doesn't agree. There's no use arguing with spirit beings.

I climb down into the river, which billows my skirt and cloak and sucks away my shoes. Dammit. The current tugs at my legs. My feet can't touch bottom. I cling to the saddle horn and one stirrup, else I follow my shoes under No Name's barrel and, with my luck, halfway to the Pacific Ocean. Somehow, I've got to work my way over to his chest.

No Name shifts a little each time I do. The current pulls less than before. My bare toes curl to clutch the sandy bottom. Saints be praised. Now the water rushes full force against my back, my head turned to the side, against No Name's neck. His forelegs support me. My hands grip his long, wet mane.

This animal knows my every need. He just pays attention to the needs that matter most. No wonder Spirit Man chose an Andalusian to ride.

"Get ready," I say to No Name. I remove my handkerchief from my pocket, then knot it around my thumb. "I'm going to try to bend over, reach the bottom with my hands."

I'll turn, one quarter-step at a time to face the foaming onslaught. Two quarter-steps later, I lose my balance. My arms cling again to No Name's forelegs. Time for a different approach.

"I'm going to kneel." I take a deep breath and shut my eyes. "Facing you."

I edge my way down, below the churning water's surface, one hand on each of my horse's forelegs. Sand swirling in the cascade bites my face. I pull my handkerchief against the palm of my cupped hand. Once on my knees, the urge to take a breath grows strong. But I mustn't stand yet, not without a handful of bottom sand.

I dig my hand into the sand, clutch my fist around the full handkerchief. My chest aches. I cling to one of No Name's legs for support as I rise. Air replaces water against my face, and I gasp for it over and over.

My handkerchief holds so little. I should carry a bandanna wherever I travel. How am I going to get to the riverbank without losing what I collected? No Name backs toward the shore. Do his withers contain a second pair of eyes? One of his forelegs continues to provide me with balance. It's as if he's human.

I climb out of the river. What a burden, the weight of my soggy clothes. The moon's face shines through the false daylight. The magic wanes. I've mined as much as I can for this time. I doubt I found much, but at least I tried. I remove my hide pouch from No Name's saddlebag, stuff my handkerchief inside, then place the rawhide pouch into my cloak's pocket. I'll pick through the sand later.

Then I see them, two familiar objects on the ground. My shoes, side-by-side, as if I set them beside my bed. A shiver runs through me, and not only because I'm sopping wet. I slip my feet into my shoes.

"Will you fly me home? I think there's still time to stop there."

The horse swishes his tail. A rising breeze plays with his mane. Does he answer with a yes? Or a no?

#

Fandango whinnies. Her front hooves land hard on the ground. I can't see her in the dark, but she must have reared on her hind legs. Not her usual behavior. But then, it's not usual for a spirit horse to stop beside her corral. I dismount from No Name's back. He gallops into the night as soon as I'm clear of him.

"Come back," I shout. What's going on?

He should stay with me, be ready to take me to Spirit Waker Cave as soon as I gather supplies. How else can I return there before dawn? Or at all? What if Ángelo awakens in my absence? And if he does, what if Jedidiah already left to hunt for food? Ángelo won't know where he is or why.

"Catalina, it that you?" That's Mamá's voice, accompanied by the glow of a candle lantern.

"Yes." She will want to know where I was the past couple of days, what has happened.

She lifts her lantern higher. The wide-eyed expression on her face does not surprise me. The fact that I see her face so well, down to every worry line, does. Dawn peers over the horizon! Why did I not realize a new day was so near? No wonder No Name deserted me as soon as I climbed off his back. The realization twists my poor stomach. Even if I want, I cannot return to the cave until tonight. No Name should have refused to bring me home, made me wait.

"I've found Ángelo," I say, "but he's unable to ride. I need to take some bandages to him. Some food." I'll gather what I can, with Mamá's help, and ready myself to ride at dusk.

179

"Not before you get permission from your Papi." Mamá shakes her head with a slow, determined rhythm. "And your abuelito."

"Of course." They both already know they can't refuse my request to leave again. The choice is neither mine nor theirs.

Mamá sets her lantern on the ground, then stretches out her arms. "I've been so worried."

We hold each other, her swollen belly against my maiden one. Neither her arms nor her lap have the magic to keep all things right, yet I reach into my past and want to believe in her power, in all the reassurances about life she gave me as a small child. Mamá sniffles. I beg my tears to stay inside my eyes.

My tears don't listen to my plea.

#

Papi, Abuelitos Ygnacio and Tomás, Jesús María, Santiago—they're all here, dressed and waiting to ride if need be. Likely ready for the past two days. How easy it was to put all of these family ties aside in the magical unreality of the cave, in the presence of Ángelo, with worrying about what Jedidiah would do or not. Now the mixed odors of men and sweat and tobacco in this room soak into me and overpower my very being, as if I am the small, square tapestry on the wall.

Abuelito Ygnacio and Papi sit at the table, one at each end. The rest of us sit on the long side benches, as we did the night the men invited me to join them for dinner and to discuss matters of importance. Much has changed, though, even with the same uncertain glances in my direction, the direct stares followed by lowered eyes. The fact that I'm here gives them relief and grave concern, I'm sure.

"When did you last eat, Catalina?" Abuelito Ygnacio asks.

"A couple days ago," I say. "There wasn't any food."

"Oh." Papi scratches the side of his nose.

"Are you hungry?" Tomás rests both his hands, clasped, on the wooden table.

"I don't think so. Ángelo—too many other matters—keep me from thinking about food." A strange situation. "My throat is dry, though. May I have a drink of water?"

Papi pours me water from the ceramic pitcher on the table. How warm, the liquid on my tongue. And hard to swallow. The corn flavor of a tortilla might taste good, just to savor in my mouth, if not to swallow.

"Wish there was a tortilla from last night's dinner," I say. The generous portions of leftovers always augment the servants' meals. No scraps ever remain.

"Josefa is preparing you some tea," Tomás says. "You're less likely to choke."

"Only two days have passed since I've eaten." I've gone longer than that with a fever or a Lenten fast.

"You keep the tea down," Papi says. "Then we'll talk about tortillas."

Abuelito just frowns and says nothing. They all act as if I'm seriously ill, with some sort of wretched pox or influenza. Well, I'll show them. I rest my first two fingers against my wrist pulse—or where I think it should be.

My fingertips don't feel anything but the smoothness of my skin. But I have to have a pulse. I'm here, alive...aren't I? Oh, dear Mother of God. I try my other wrist, detect a weak throbbing under the skin. Praise the Lord and the saints who watch over me. I haven't become Spirit Woman yet.

"I'm pretty sure I'm still alive." I shrug. "No need for great concern." Yet why does my pulse lack vigor?

"But there is need for great concern." The sadness in Papi's eyes bores into my own. "For the past year, I've watched you change from a child into a young woman. Now, Catalina, you move beyond womanhood. You are changing into someone—something—I no longer recognize."

Papi's words draw tears from my eyes. Does he no longer love me? Why does this all need to happen? I part my lips to reply. My tongue can't say the words boiling up inside my heart, and even the spirit of Señor Cervantes offers no advice.

"Such words, they are too harsh," Abuelito Ygnacio rasps in Papi's direction. "Catalina's destiny has traveled beside her for years. From her ability to rope a longhorn as a vaquero would, to her ability to charm the youngest son of Don Emilio Ortega. All the while she has tirelessly worked side-by-side with this ranchero's servants to keep our home in order and bellies full of good food."

Tomás pushes back his chair and stands. In another time, under another set of conditions, he might have been a tribal leader. Now I see a wise yet tired man fight to unravel one tragedy out of many that life has fired in his direction. Should I tell him I've seen his brother's ghost? Maybe that would upset him even more.

"My friend." Tomás turns toward Papi, his beardless chin tilted upward. "Catalina's destiny was shaped before her birth. Before the birth of Rain Falling. Perhaps when the priests and friars buried my family's surname. Nothing can restore what the Spanish white men took from this land's peoples. Lives. Dignity. Everything. Yet even worse awaits us, for the white men of the Bear Flag threaten to erase all of us, as if we never existed. They and their countrymen won't be satisfied until they leave the last of our men, women and children, slain, rotting and covered with flies."

Much of this I have heard or pondered about before. Faced when convenient, but not truly addressed. Hoped, somehow, to be spared. As these words and more pour from my Oljon abuelito's mouth, they confront me in a way I can no longer avoid.

Ángelo and I will never share a life where we raise a family and tend herds of cattle in the pastoral beauty of Alta California. The best I can hope for is that we share our life together, whatever that may bring. And even that remains uncertain. We will wed, in this world or the next. Didn't Ángelo promise me as much? Yet Friar Fernandoco at Misión de San José has said more than once that people aren't married or given in marriage in Heaven.

What is left for me to pray for? What should I believe?

Then, in my mind, the voice of the old vaquero calls my name from the inside of a longhorn skull.

"When the time comes," he says, "you will know what to do."

But how will I know when?

"*Suletu*," he answers, again using the word for flying or flies.

The buzzing of flies fills my ears for the first time in many days. When I was little, Josefa's Mamá told me flies arise from maggots. Papi claimed devils generate flies spontaneously from dead things and spoiled food. Both may be true, but I'm certain of a third way. Flies come to life when I pass by their spirits. I know not why.

"I'll take tea and a tortilla," I say to Papi. "So many strange thoughts fill my brain. I need to nourish them all."

I end up sipping several cups of medicinal tea—manzanita from a local *curandero*—praying Papi will let me eat the tortilla on my plate. I inhale the aroma of corn, count the brown spots, the uneven surfaces, the places where air pockets puffed up during cooking and later receded. So many physical characteristics give tortillas the feel against my tongue and the taste I love. At last, Papi nods in my direction. I take a bite. Last night, I wasn't sure I still lived. Now I'm certain I do.

I tell the men what happened the night of the thunderstorm—about the disappearance of Spirit Man, the strange knife of El Cid, the Bear Flagger struck by lightning, and Ángelo's rescue. I'm vague about some parts of my story, and say little about Jedidiah Jones, except that he helped me put Ángelo on my horse.

"I'm sure No Name will return tonight," I say. "I must ready a pack today with clean bandages, soothing herbs and a canteen. Plus a little food."

Tomás frowns. "And the musket ball, it is still inside Ángelo?"

"I saw no wound where the ball left, only where it entered." I avoid his eyes. "The cave, I think it has powers to heal. I dare not remove Ángelo before he awakens. And bringing someone else there—I don't think that would be a good idea. Spirit Man said I shouldn't."

"Did he instruct you to bring Ángelo there?" Abuelito Ygnacio raises his coffee cup to his lips.

Warmth spreads to my face. I feared he would ask such a question. Will my answer lead me to admit that Ángelo might never be allowed to leave Coyote's cave?

"He—he left without giving me instructions I needed." I stare down at my toes. "Ángelo wasn't breathing. I had to do something. Once inside of Spirit Waker Cave, he—" I tilt my chin upward. "He started breathing again."

I didn't expect such absolute silence. Not a creak of a floorboard or a swallowing of food. Not one of the men even shifts position on the long benches beside the table. And when Abuelito Ygnacio sets down his coffee cup, there's little sound of the two surfaces making contact with each other. A sick gnawing feeling in the pit of my stomach tells me I did something unforgivable.

"Catalina, start at the beginning." Jesús María's voice is soft, yet firm. "Tell us everything you remember about Spirit Man taking you away the other night, about him vanishing—about anyone you met at all in the process."

"Nothing is too small to neglect," Abuelito Tomás adds.

"Everything," Papi and Uncle Santiago say at the same time.

Abuelito Ygnacio mumbles a sentence or two I can't understand. "And dip no bitter truths into a jar of honey."

33. *Untidy Results*

IT IS ALL OUT. Every bit of the mess I've made of things. A Bear Flagger in the same cave as Coyote's gold. Ángelo helpless, and in an unholy state of being. The disapproving look from Salvador of the Eagles. How could I be so foolish? Selfish? How can I atone? No wonder No Name left me here instead of taking me back to the mountain early this morning. I finish lighting the candles in the family chapel, then kneel on the earthen floor.

...pray for us sinners...

Why, oh why, did Spirit Man lead me to Ángelo's body? Give me the freedom to decide where to bring the man I love? Did he test me again, as he'd done when he played the role of Spirit Man Two—the dark one? If so, I failed, leaving me with one big, fat, wretched problem. I don't know what to do now. Neither do Papi, Mamá, my abuelitos, nor my uncles.

...pray for us misguided sinners...

That's why I'm here, asking for guidance from God, the Virgin of Guadalupe, and any Oljon ancestor I have who might still be willing to speak to me. None of them answer.

...pray for us misguided and desperate sinners...

I stand, cold all over and shivering. When a cook's apprentice breaks an ordinary bowl in the kitchen, she apologizes to her mistress, sweeps up the fragments, then takes her flogging without a whimper. The breakage of a beloved bowl is a different matter. The apprentice should also reassemble all the pieces, glue them together, then sand and

185

retouch to yield a refurbished vessel for household display. I, like the apprentice, need to put back all the beloved pieces.

Piece number one: Return Ángelo to his family for burial and mourning. That includes returning the crucifix his family gave him. Piece number two: Convince Jedidiah Jones to leave Spirit Waker Cave and accept whatever fate awaits him. Assuming, however, he hasn't found the gold. In that case, he likely will have already left the cavern and died. Then I'll have to bury what's left of him and return the gold to the cave's inner reaches.

Number three: I can't expect No Name's cooperation. I'll have to find the hidden cave myself. This will mean gathering more bits of spilled tobacco off the floor and doing another vision quest. No, this time I'll ask the men to open their tobacco pouches.

Will Spirit Waker Cave reveal its location to me?

Some strange feeling, within the depths of my very soul, tells me it might, if I'm sincere instead of shallow, sensitive instead of selfish. If I will make my family proud of me instead of afraid or ashamed. Ángelo sleeps as if he remains alive, but he died the night of the storm. I must release his spirit to travel to his heavenly home.

...pray for us sinners who truly seek forgiveness...

A horse, I'll need one of those, and an Andalusian is not an option. I'll ask Mamá for Fandango. After all, much of this wild craziness started the day I repaired Fandango's corral latch. That morning, approaching riders changed my life forever. Meeting Spirit Man for the first time also started with Fandango and the runaway ride. My fingers reach for Ángelo's crucifix, as if not directed by me alone. Yes, this magnificent piece of sacred jewelry belongs with his parents. My plain silver crucifix on the string of rawhide belongs with me.

At first, the tears only moisten my eyes, then they overflow their borders and trickle down my cheeks. The flood that follows—accompanied by uncontrollable gasps and sobs—washes through me, waves of total misery. Yet the old vaquero predicted my future. My marriage to Ángelo on Earth must take this terrible path—ending before it even begins.

I don't want to lose him for the rest of my life, but I already have. Can my memories and faith comfort me in this time of sorrow?

...pray for us sinners who need strength...

#

Josefa and I sit side-by-side on my bed, the door to my room open to the oncoming night. My bedroom key continues to reside in my cloak's pocket, although Mamá has given up on locking us inside when I'm home. Josefa's own Mamá has doubled her prayers. In fact, Manuel's and Josefa's parents have agreed on a wedding date. The first day of August, despite the Mexican-Yankee war. Don Ortega has donated workers and money to build a small house for the couple on Abuelito's property, will even provide cattle for the feast. I think *Doña* Ortega insisted.

So much changes so fast.

Regardless, crickets continue to chirp. Crops grow. Longhorns fatten, Papi's stacks of cowhides for market now taller than I am. Kernels of maize soak in slaked lime—the promise of fresh tortillas. So much does not change, and for that I am grateful.

I stand and stretch. The candle lamp bathes Epifania's yellow dress and me in its glow. How does this garment stay so clean, still smelling as if newly laundered? How does it look as if a dozen servants have rubbed the fabric to remove wrinkles? I check the hem of my undergarment. The magical stone from Spirit Man remains secure within the hem. I do not know what may happen tonight, but I must prepare. I wrap myself in my cloak, the tobacco offering and matches stuffed into one pocket, the pouch containing the handkerchief and sand in another.

"Where will you burn the tobacco?" Josefa says. She doesn't look at me.

"Where the wind tells me to."

"Will I see you again?"

"I hope so," I say, "for your wedding, at least."

She raises her chin and stares into my eyes. "Remember to ride like a lady. Don't let your skirt bunch up and your underclothes show."

How brief, her smile is.

"I want to hug you," Josefa says, "but I don't think I should. You prepare to go somewhere sacred. Do something sacred. I don't know the rules."

"I don't think I know them, either." I smile and stretch out my arms.

We clasp hands as two maiden women. Our days of childhood truly have passed. Then I walk out the door and head for Fandango's small corral.

Fandango waits for me, already saddled and bridled, a packhorse beside her—a dun gelding laden with supplies. Mamá always calls him Tortilla. The men have been at work. I smile.

Papi approaches. "I packed extra bandannas for you."

"Thank you." My dearest Papi, how my heart aches.

He doesn't try to hold me close. We both understand why. Yet what is this woven into Fandango's mane?

A single feather. Based on size, pattern and coloration, I'd say it's from a hawk.

34. *To Find Spirit Waker Cave*

I HEAD EAST toward the Sierra Nevada, or where those mountains ought to be. Papi's favorite star helps, the big blue-white one he used to point out to me in summer, part of a triangle of three stars that keep watch over this section of Alta California.

The pace remains slow, more walk than trot or canter. No sense in Fandango stepping into a varmint's hole and breaking her leg. Besides, Ángelo is dead. The need to rush has passed. My primary mission is to find the secret cave.

The magical underground chambers have to be somewhere high up, although no guarantees exist regarding passable trails. Without No Name to fly me to this place and that, Coyote will have to take some responsibility if he wants this job done—that is, to return the cavern to an uninhabited state, and a place to hide evidence of Alta California's gold. At least for a few years.

"You'll have to trust me," I say, "trust I've learned my lesson."

Have I learned? Of course I have, although one part of my brain questions another, thinks I can't resist temptation when it raps on the door. I yawn. The one thing I still can't resist well enough is the urge to sleep when deprived of that pleasure. I do have better endurance than before. Spirit Waker Cave may have changed me. I doubt Spirit Man ever needed much sleep, maybe for the same reason. Come to think of it, did I sleep at all inside the cave?

The passage of time within that mysterious place might not equal the passage outside. Spirit Man and No Name's false daylight may change time, as well. I spent half the night traveling with those two and searching for gold nuggets. When I returned home, far less time had gone by.

Thoughts about rest bring another yawn. My eyes, adapted to the dark, detect a stand of trees. A good place to kindle a small fire and burn a little tobacco. If I manage to stay awake, I might have a vision. If I nap for a few hours, Coyote might bring me a dream.

#

I awaken in the dark. The sky holds no hint of dawn. No vision, no dream and not much sleep. My horses await, ready to travel. Didn't I remove their packs and saddles prior to lying down? Yes, I used Fandango's saddle for a pillow and covered myself with her saddle blanket. Beforehand, I built a small fire, then made a tobacco offering. Or did I? I feel for my tobacco pouch. It's full. A shiver shoots down my spine. False memories. Obviously, I simply dismounted, tied the horses to a tree and went to sleep on the ground.

"I'm sorry," I tell them. Papi and Abuelito always care for their horses before themselves.

Even worse, I still have no idea where to find the secret cave. I brush the dirt—not much—off my dress, then untie the animals. The time has come to climb into Fandango's saddle. The sky displays the guiding stars. There ought to be a southeast pass through the Sierra Nevada, however, I don't know if I want to use one. I need to travel upward, not through. For now, I'll ride until I reach a creek. From there, I'll travel beyond the larger ranchos.

As I set out, my mind drifts. Weeks ago, I never rode anywhere by myself. A chaperone—often Abuelito—always accompanied me. How I wanted to experience the freedom of riding alone anywhere I pleased. If only I could travel beside my grandfather just one more time now—even for an hour.

But that can't happen. This journey, this heavy burden in my heart, is mine alone.

The chirps of crickets swell, as does the rush of water over rocks. We come to one of the streams that still have water in summer. Fandango picks her way down a rocky bank. Incredible, the way she does so by starlight. Tortilla, on a lead rope, follows. They drink for a few minutes, then take jumpy steps and whinny.

I smell what they must: a strong musky odor, like the urine of a wolf or coyote. Obviously, not THE Coyote. Too bad. Directions to his mountain den would help. Wolves tend to run in packs. Coyotes don't, unless they're hunting down larger prey, such as a deer. Or a woman riding a horse?

No gun. No decent knife—I left Spirit Man's in No Name's saddlebag. Now what should I do?

I should have asked the stream permission to water my horses. Wherever Spirit Man is, I bet he laughs.

"Señora Corriente," I say, "I beg you to forgive me. My horses, they needed water, and I neglected to ask your permission."

The crickets stop chirping.

"I believe Coyote or Wolf is ahead of me in line. I will leave now, go burn an offering of tobacco as I should have done earlier."

Above the rush of water, comes panting, then a growl. The musky odor grows stronger. Someone or something I don't care to meet at the moment moves closer. A pair of yellow eyes stares at me out of the night. From the distance comes a howl, then another from a different direction.

Fandango rears. My legs cling to her sides. I drop Tortilla's lead rope. Both horses scramble up the stream's bank.

"Easy, Fandango. Easy!"

She calms as the odor of predators fade. I have no idea where Tortilla dashes to with all of my supplies—maybe back to Papi. I groan.

Ahead, false daylight brightens a stretch of trail. Tortilla stands in the middle of a grassy patch, facing the biggest coyote I've ever seen. Just stands there, calm. Munching grass. Fandango stomps, skitters and snorts. Calm, she is not. I climb off her back and tie her reins to a low tree branch. I make my way toward Tortilla and the coyote, my heart pounding hard.

The wild animal is sturdy enough to kill me. A good running leap—I would not have a chance. So why do I approach, defenseless? Still, Tortilla does not seem afraid. I face the beast, my arms by my sides, open palms forward.

"Thank you, Señor Coyote. Please forgive me for not burning a tobacco offering before I slept."

His tongue drips saliva, He turns and ambles back toward the stream as the false daylight fades. Who or what other than Spirit Man or his horse can make daylight shine from the darkness? He said his spirit was going to live inside of another person, didn't he? If that was true, how is he here tonight?

Or is that what Spirit Man said? Did he say "another person?" Or just "another?"

I need to put this aside, concentrate on what is most important: Finding Spirit Waker Cave. Only then can I bring Ángelo's body back to his family for burial and secure the secret of Alta California's gold. Really, as dear as Ángelo is to me, keeping anyone from discovering gold in California remains one of the most important duties I could ever accomplish. These thoughts bring pain to both my mind and heart as I burn my next tobacco offering to Coyote.

35. Witchcraft

JEDIDIAH JONES stands in the cave's witchlight. Well, that's what the pitch torch up there in the wall sconce has to be—a product of witchcraft. Been burning straight on for days. Simply ain't natural. He kneels—surely God'll know it's not from misplaced reverence—then unwraps the folded cloth he found tucked way back in a crevice. Might have been some vaquero's neck bandanna. He thought there'd been another cloth package too, but then it was gone. Odd. Then he sees the glitter from a patch of dried mud in the middle of the fabric. Gold? No gold in Alta California. The gold-crazy Spaniards would have found it years ago. Did that Catalina gal go panning for pyrite—fool's gold?

He clears away some of the dirt. The shine comes from little rocks, not pyrite flecks. He scratches one with his fingernail, leaving a mark. Jumping Jehoshaphat! Pyrite would be hard. These got to be nuggets, gold nuggets. How did they get here? Did some explorer carry them up from Mexico City? Hide them away for safety? He fingers the cloth. It's damp and filthy but not rotten. These nuggets weren't wrapped in it long.

The back of his neck itches. Always does when he's confused or needs a bath. Magical lightning and a flying horse—Catalina Delgado's a witch, for sure. Might she also be one of those alchemists he'd once read about? Have a special pact with the Devil to turn lead shot into gold? If so, Jedidiah better stay clear of the whole business.

Or should he?

Just a good spit away from him lies Ángelo Ortega, snoring like a hibernating grizzly. Ángelo had been dead for half a day and then some when Jedidiah and Catalina unloaded him off the back of the black Andalusian stallion. Something about this hole in the mountain brought him back to life. Well, not alive enough to piss into his britches, the way most knocked-out folk do after a couple days. Regardless, who knows what sort of evil being he'll become when he wakes up—maybe one of those Voodoo zombies? Saw one stumbling around down in New Orleans. Jedidiah rewraps the gold in the bandanna, then shoves it into his pants pocket. Might be a good idea if Ángelo's eyes stay shut for good.

Jedidiah stands and stretches. Catalina claimed leaving this cave might not be the best for his longevity or Ángelo's. Life's the better choice for him, given the opportunity, but maybe not in exchange for the eternal shoveling of coal in Hell. He's done a couple stints feeding a raging firebox with coal. Not to his liking. Of course, most of his jobs weren't to his liking. Dreams of running a rancho with Epifania—they're always much better.

And then there's Ángelo, in no condition to save his own soul. Epifania wouldn't want her brother damned—although he may deserve it. Would be nice to meet up with her in the future—on good terms—that future a long journey ahead. He climbs over rocks toward the falls and sits on one of them. Refreshing, all this chilly spray. He's always been partial to the power of cascading water.

The rowboat with the Mexicans on the beach. John C. Frémont and that Kit Carson fellow. The old ranchero and his twin nephews murdered. The sound of an unforgiving ocean. Bad, the way Carson shot those three men.

Yet so what if Jedidiah shot the Indian, the one about to send an arrow into Frémont's back? All Indians are heathens, aren't they? More like animals than people. At least that's what many say. Only problem is, he hasn't believed that crap for years, and the man he shot was one of Catalina's relatives.

Catalina's a person, sacred animal and sorceress—a powerful combination. And she is Epifania's dear friend, someday might put in a good word for him, once she realizes she's wrong about bewitching Ángelo. Jedidiah closes his eyes, even feels his smile forming.

Come sunrise, maybe he'll drag Ángelo through the waterfall, sit by his sleeping form out there—see what happens.

36. Strangers and Flies

AN ACHE SPREADS through me, from my broken heart to the tips of my fingers and toes. "The Tunnel of the Twin Falls." How many days have passed since Spirit Man spoke those words? "No map or chart marks its location and none ever will."

What a mistake, to leave Spirit Waker Cave and Ángelo, and then assume I could find my way back. I needed neither food for me nor medicine for him. I needed him next to me, and still do. Now another night wanes. The imposing Sierra Nevada and its foothills stand before me, defy me to ever find the man I love again. There will be no words of good-bye, no grasping of his cold hands, no final holding him close. The tears come. I can't hold them back.

Fandango picks her way along the uneven ground. If there's a trail through this area, we've not found it. My knees grip her sides as we head up another hill. Oh, to travel by way of No Name's magic. I sniffle.

Too bad I can't change my past actions, my misjudgments. Somehow, I made No Name angry with me. Because I questioned the actions of Jedidiah Jones—a Bear Flagger? Why did that bother him? Whose spirit occupies that stallion's body? Not Spirit Man's.

Bear Flaggers possess no honorable qualities, especially the man who shot Ángelo. Even Jedidiah Jones, who helped me with Ángelo, only did so because he was afraid of me or thought I was Epifania Ortega. And didn't he murder Salvador of the Eagles? How could a horse as humanly clever as No Name ignore that truth?

Fandango stops to nibble grass. What if Jedidiah has found Coyote's gold in my absence and tried to escape with it, or attempted to leave because he got hungry? What if a wolf or cougar discovers Ángelo, asleep and helpless? It's my duty to return Ángelo's intact body to his family for burial. Again, more tears. A plague of them.

Calm down, I need to calm down. That large coyote I met at the stream might help me navigate, maybe mark the trails I am to take. Jedidiah could realize he isn't hungry in the magical cave, will survive until my return. And he is a coward, won't go exploring where he shouldn't. Some being tests me, the way Spirit Man did. Surely, I'll find the location within a week or two. All will end as well as possible, considering the saints will claim Ángelo's soul.

Dearest Lord, how will I live without him? Fandango nickers as I sob.

#

The noise of many hoofbeats reaches my ears. All my muscles tense as I sit in the saddle. From which direction does the sound come?

Ahead, as the dawn arrives, shadows take form. Several riders approach, their horses similar to Fandango. The riders don't wear the clothes of rancheros, vaqueros or Bear Flaggers. In fact, they're mostly covered with animal skins and furs. Indio peoples are known to capture mustangs, the descendants of Spanish Barbs, the same as Californios have done. I squint. What tribes live in these foothills? Perhaps they've traveled down from the nearest mountain.

Some tribes are friendly toward Mexican rancheros— others aren't. That feather my uncles braided into Fandango's mane, I have no idea of its meaning. Is it meant to show friendship, or declare strength? I don't know the language of any tribal group, only a few words the vaqueros taught me.

197

Dear saints and angels, may the spirit of my mother, Rain Falling, guide me. If these people don't understand at least a little Spanish, may they interpret any hand gestures I can devise.

I ride at a walking pace in their direction, leading my packhorse. They—men—advance with apparent equal caution. What will they think of a lone *mestiza*, riding astride, wearing men's pantaloons and a frilly yellow dress? I rearrange my cloak to disguise the clothes underneath.

"*Suletu*," the voice of the old vaquero whispers inside of my head. At least he hasn't deserted me.

An all-too-familiar buzzing follows. A battalion of flies swarms out of nowhere and speeds in my direction. I've never seen so many all at once. The sound grows as loud as the world's tallest waterfall. I groan. Flies descend upon me, hundreds of them, maybe thousands. Fandango doesn't flinch, as if she neither sees nor hears them. They land on my arms, my legs, my chest—even the top of my head. A giant, droning, crawling blanket. I mustn't scream, mustn't shake. It takes all my inner strength to fight total panic. Then, I realize, the flies aren't on my face or Fandango. Not a single one. I stare in the men's direction, do the best I can to produce a welcoming smile, then say friendly words and express signs of greeting.

No wide eyes stare at me. No faces distort in terror or disgust. These men look at me as if nothing is wrong, or even unusual—like they expected my arrival and escort of *las moscas*. Their horses aren't the least bit jumpy. Why, I bet none of them sees my swarm of flies. After all, no one but me ever does.

"I am the child of Rain Falling," I say in Spanish.

I point to myself, rock my arms as if I'm holding a baby, then point toward the sky. I flutter my hands above my head, then move them downward. One of the men nods. At least he doesn't laugh at my attempt to communicate. So far, so good.

"I request your help." I add, "Have you heard of a cave that awakens spirits? On top of one of those mountains, possibly near a waterfall?" I point eastward.

I probably shouldn't reveal so many details, but there might be many caverns where tribes take their dead or where spirits dwell. I don't know their customs and beliefs. Will it help to mention Coyote? And what about flies? Do these men associate flies with death?

"Some flies," I say, "they told me to travel only to a special Spirit Waker Cave, and with great haste. They claim Coyote sent them."

The men don't come any closer. Still no fear in their facial expressions, but plenty of caution. None of them offers travel directions. Maybe they don't understand Spanish, or my mention of flies and Spirit Waker Cave is a bad omen. Maybe something else.

One of them points toward the south, not east.

"Thank you," I say, repeating the word in the various forms I know.

I continue eastward into the wilderness. Do these men wonder if I'm dead or dying? Searching for a loved one? A person with no fear of death wouldn't look back, so I don't. How horrid, the buzz and feel of my coat of flies. I don't shake them off, though. In their own way, I think they've gathered to protect me. They might even know the right direction I should head.

"If so, I'll never get angry with you again, never compare you to Bear Flaggers."

Fandango navigates her way up another rocky section of hillside. My guardian flies buzz. Abuelito Tomás and his sons are right about all things having spirits.

Abuelito Ygnacio, however, once told me a story about flies. How the Devil is their Lord. My flies are tricksters—want to be like Coyote. They annoy me, but I doubt they're evil. In my mind I see Berreyesa and his twin nephews, their bloodied bodies collapsed in the sand. The Devil is the Lord of Bear Flaggers, not of flies.

#

The rising sun warms my face. My coat of buzzing flies spirals away, as if I have just exhaled them.

"*Gracias*," I call to them. Thanks for a job well done, whatever that job was.

On Fandango's back, I head on yet another upward eastward climb, leading Tortilla. Still no trail, yet I don't expect one. Hooves clop against packed soil, then click against shelves of granite. Before me, snow-peaked mountains loom in the distance, both majestic and ominous. Deadly all year around, especially in winter. I'll find Ángelo before winter—won't I? I don't know how long the magic of Spirit Waker will stay with him. I couldn't bear to return and find him rotting.

Why did No Name desert me? To test my worthiness, or to display anger? All right, No Name's a spirit horse with a physical presence, knows things I don't. He didn't agree with my low opinion of Jedidiah Jones. If he let me in on the secret he apparently knew about Mr. Jones, I might change my mind. And, by the way, why did the fur men instruct me to head south instead of east?

I can't believe this conversation in my head. Guardian flies. A flying horse without wings who can think like a person does. Fur-clad men with impossible insight. All I ever wanted was to rope cattle, marry Ángelo, and have children. How has my life turned into this maze of strangeness and sorrow? I can almost hear the longhorn skulls in the wall of Fandango's corral laugh at my dismay. Does Spirit Man laugh at me too? Or groan?

A chill passes through me and reaches down into my bones. The wrong direction—I'm going in the wrong direction. That's what those fur-men tried to let me know. I need to aim for a river or stream, a place where water washes gold down from these mountains. I need to find more gold. Then No Name will have to show up, will have to take me back to Spirit Waker to hide Coyote's treasure.

This area of foothills must be where snowmelt forms the headwaters of many California rivers. But how did Fur Man and his people know about my quest?

I change directions, angle south.

V. Finding the Key

37. Plague of Yankees

I INTRODUCE MYSELF to the stream, then step ankle deep into it. Sunlight warms my back and the chill of snowmelt numbs my feet. Feels good. If I wade deeper and fall all the way in, though, the cold will suck my breath away—maybe forever. I'll never forget that night with Spirit Man, when the water attacked me. Can't let that sort of disaster happen again, not until I've freed Ángelo from his unnatural state of breathing while dead. I direct my feet along the stream's rocky bottom. The water reaches my calves. A trout swims by with a lazy swish of its tail. Clear water. No gold nuggets.

Should I search here at night instead of day? Is darkness the secret of discovering gold, or does the magic of false daylight begat more sorcery? Until now, I thought No Name only brought me places after dark to conceal the mysterious way he travels. Nobody is around this afternoon. I could ride for days and not encounter a single soul.

I sit down on a boulder, its flat top dry. My cloak and dress should be torn, filthy, ripe with sweat—yet they are not, even smell of the soap Mamá's servants make and scent with bay leaves. As with Ángelo, part of me no longer belongs in this ordinary world. Yet I am awake, a state Ángelo will never experience again. After I return him to his family, will I disappear the way Spirit Man did? No, I must continue to search California's rivers for gold, embrace my assigned quest full force. Better to collapse in bed exhausted each morning than to cry myself to sleep.

Water rushes around my boulder and the sun warms me through and through. I yawn. A dragonfly drones by. How tempting to take a nap. Because I'm so far from the cave? Fandango and Tortilla graze near the stream. I should have taken the pack off of Tortilla's back.

#

"Wake up," a voice screams at me. Josefa? Am I dreaming?

"Catalina!" The voice comes from inside my head. "Get up. Ride. Now."

I sit up straight. What's going on?

"Run for your life!"

I wade toward the shore as fast as I can, grab my shoes, then vault atop Fandango's saddle.

Which direction to flee? If I knew the problem, I could figure out the answer. My knees prompt Fandango's sides. She takes off in the same direction we were heading to before stopping, Tortilla following on his lead rope. There's no galloping—not even trotting—in this terrain.

If I'm to encounter something bad, I'd better find a hiding place, fast. The granite outcrop below might actually be a ledge—with a place underneath to conceal us from above. Unless the pending danger comes from the bottom of this hill and decides to pass by my hiding spot. Uphill or downhill, no time remains to guess. I'll head down before I'm shot down.

#

I squeeze between my two horses. There's barely room for the three of us under this ledge. If No Name were here instead of Fandango, he wouldn't fit. Too tall. I grasp Fandango's hackamore bridle and Tortilla's halter, whispering to both animals. Papi's vaqueros taught them not to raise their head and whinny in this stance, and I pray they remember the lessons.

I listen for any hints of danger. Other horses, men's voices, gunshots—nothing. Maybe I imagined those voices in my head. I must have drifted off to sleep on the rock, then awakened from a bad dream. Now I'm here, under a ledge, making no progress at all in finding Ángelo. I'm just wasting precious time. Yet Mamá used to say, "You don't waste time when figuring out the best way to do a job." Instinct and training tell me to wait a little bit longer.

Then comes the unmistakable crack of gunfire in the distance. My mouth turns dry as dust. My stomach aches. Perhaps horses from that place whinny, perhaps people scream. The gunfire continues, over and over.

"Stay quiet," I whisper to Fandango and Tortilla. "Please."

\#

We remain under the ledge, sometimes shifting position, never moving far. Papi's vaqueros trained Fandango and Tortilla well. Perhaps the spirit of that old vaquero keeps my horses calm. I say my Rosary within my mind. Mamá, she trained me.

I've heard no noises since the gunfire stopped, except for the wind and cries of birds. Who was shot, and how far away? Did the murderers leave? Are any wounded left alive that I can help? The sun lowers in the sky and the shadows lengthen. Dusk will arrive in an hour. I need to look for survivors soon. Oh, that I could evoke Spirit Man's false daylight anytime I need.

At last, I emerge from under the ledge, leading my horses. They're nervous, skittish. The wind carries the smell of death. Huge black birds circle in the sky—condors, back up the hill, not far from here. Maybe half a league? Fear brings a shiver that speeds from my fingertips to my toes. Without the warning I received, I would be dead too.

How slow, the ride up the hillside. The trek tilts me back and forth as we climb. We reach a level spot, and the place of death. Horses, people, so many of them. Not just death, massacre. I'm not ready, have to look away. The ground reveals the tracks of shod horses. Probably not owned by native peoples. I dismount and tie bridle reins and lead rope to a pine branch. Tortilla has smelled the blood of longhorn slaughter many times. Fandango hasn't. Best to tether them both at a distance, to keep each other company and calm.

I tie a bandanna around my mouth and nose, then walk by the body of a roan mustang, torn open and stained with blood. Musket balls must have hit him. Two other horses lie maybe a hundred paces ahead. Condors feed off them already. I reach the scattered piles of human remains. First, a woman, her infant in cradleboard strapped against her back—the elaborate beadwork discolored with blood. An old man hugs a child—no older than five. He must have tried to cover the little one with his own body.

My stomach churns harder, its unrest impossible to settle. I turn and vomit.

The grim picture repeats over and over as I search for anyone alive. So many slain. Then I see him, a man wearing what's left of a fur wrap. He's one of the men I met last night, I'm sure. I hurry to his side. His arm twitches, his guts spilled all over his clothing. There is nothing I can do to help him, only offer final comfort.

I grasp his bloodied hand. "Who did this? And what peoples are you from?"

He whispers several words I don't understand. I kneel in the dirt and bring my ear close to his mouth.

"Foreigners," he says in Spanish. Then his trembling hand points to himself. "Miwok."

"I can't heal your wounds. Only stay with you."

"Leave. Might—come—back."

"But the others."

"Gone. Checked—before—I—fell."

A condor, its wingspan twice my height, swoops down and settles on a woman's body several *varas* away. This vulture has no fear of me.

"That roan," the man says, "saddle—key—love—" His eyes close. "My knife. Take it." His body relaxes. Breathing stops. His spirit has joined the others. In my mind, Ángelo breathes, although he is as dead as this man in furs. Tears spill down my cheeks. I sob. For Ángelo, for these people, for my family—for myself.

I claim the knife and sheath Fur Man offered me, then return, sniffling, to the rest of the bodies. No sign of life. The roan. I only see one and stop there. A condor perches on the frame saddle and feeds off of the horse's bloodied rump. How do I chase away this vulture to check the saddle, hide blanket and saddle bags?

How did I ever prevent the river from drowning me?

"Señor Cóndor, my name is Catalina Delgado, daughter of Rain Falling. The Miwok man over there—his dying request was that I look at your meal's saddle and saddle bags."

Señor Cóndor turns his yellow-orange head in my direction. *Dearest saints, please don't let him decide to eat something that's not dead.*

"May I please interrupt you?" I stare at his neck instead of his eyes, the decorative collar of black feathers. "I won't take long. I promise."

Señor Cóndor's beak pulls another chunk of flesh from the roan's carcass. I wait, begging my stomach not to revolt. He swallows, then peers in my direction. Those red-brown eyes do not appear friendly.

Then he spreads his wings, the long, white patch of feathers on his underside like a giant skeleton's bones. He's going to attack. I cover my face with my crossed arms. Instead, he moves a few paces away from me and the roan. I exhale hard. The saddle, saddle bags and blanket wait for me. I have to hurry.

I've not got the strength to remove a saddle—even this simple frame saddle—and a hide blanket from a dead horse lying on its side. The saddlebag attached to the rear horn, however, rests on top of the animal—not underneath. With Fur Man's knife, I free the bag, then cut through the rawhide girth strap, reach under one side of the saddle and feel for anything odd. I work as fast as I can, cutting away a section of hide blanket, and getting out of Señor Cóndor's way.

"*Gracias*," I say to the huge bird. Longhorn skulls, swarms of flies, a buzzard—I'm acquiring an interesting group of allies.

What could be in the saddlebag? What revealing pattern will I find on the hide blanket? The last light of day glows from the horizon. I'm sure my horses are saddle and pack weary. Why not wend our way over the next hill, locate a sheltered spot, then remove their burdens from their backs? I could build a fire and examine what I've found. We could sleep.

Sleep. Eternal sleep. How disrespectful of me not to bury the Miwoks' bodies. There are so many, though. It would take me days to dig a grave large and deep enough, if I could at all. I have no shovel. The ground is hard. Too many right and honorable things demand I take action. Too many consequences await my potential mistakes.

"Run for your life." The memory of those words remains almost as vivid as the nearby scene of slaughter. We have to keep moving, at least for a couple of leagues. The stars and full moon will help me find a safer place to sleep.

I return to my horses, then tie the rolled hide and extra saddlebag to Tortilla's packs. Fandango's neck feels far too warm as I stroke her. I climb into her saddle. My hands, perhaps all of me, must be cold in comparison. So much has happened during the past few days. Have I eaten? I don't recall. I did drink water from a stream.

Those murdered children. The parents and grandparents who tried to protect the little ones with their own bodies. The expressions of distress frozen on their faces will haunt me forever, along with the words of the man wrapped in bloodied fur. On the softer sections of soil, the hoof prints of shod horses confirm the wretched truth. Yankees likely slaughtered those thirty Miwoks.

When the sun rises and I'm far away from here, I'll examine the contents of the roan's saddle bag and the section of hide blanket. Saddle, key and love—Fur Man told me those words with urgency. They must be important.

What if the saddlebag contains a dispatch, like the one I found when I stole that courier's horse? Written in a language I don't know? The day Ángelo left his home to join Comandante José Castro's military forces, he talked about planting false dispatches. Even if Fur Man's saddlebag contains a document and I can read its contents, doesn't mean the message is true. And how are a key and love involved? Do Miwok parents lock their daughters up at night to protect the girls' reputations?

#

I rise and stretch. So pleasant, the music of the flowing stream. Sad too, for I'll never share such a moment with Ángelo beside me. But I must save my tears for later. I need to inspect the saddlebag. My dearest love would agree. I shake the dirt from my cloak, splash water on my face, then drink from above the horses' watering spot. I take a deep breath.

I still can breathe air and drink water. My fingertips touch Ángelo's crucifix. Angels and spirits continue to help me move forward. I ready myself to face a puzzle beyond my ability to solve.

The saddlebag comes first, a long, flat, pouch made from an animal hide. Not the type my people use. A little beadwork here and there. Nothing elaborate though. I lift the flap of the pouch and peer inside, only to face two small, round eyes staring back. This fox pelt, unlike the ones Fur Man wore, includes the head. I remove the pelt. Empty—the rest of the bag is empty? How disappointing.

Wait. Something rests against the bottom corner of the bag. I reach my hand deep inside, feeling fur again. I pull the object out into the daylight. A rawhide strip holds a small bundle of folded pelt. Another deep breath of air fills my lungs and lingers. This is no letter. I exhale hard.

Part of me doesn't want to unwrap the little package. Those Miwok men, women and children could have been murdered because of what lies inside. No, then the murderers would have searched the bodies and their belongings. More likely, the murderers enjoy killing people who don't look like them.

I unwrap the package. A half dozen gold nuggets! I gasp.

Someone else has found gold. Not good. If Fur Man's people discovered this treasure, what about Bear Flaggers? My shoulders droop. My whole body sags. Several hundred years ago, Spanish conquistadors searching and mining for gold destroyed entire civilizations south of Alta California. Dearest saints—such a deadly invasion of Alta California by Yankees might already be underway.

Think, I need to think. *Please, Lord, spirits and saints above, help me make sense of my thoughts.*

I return to the stream and drink more water. I should eat something. Why am I never hungry? I go to my supplies and pull out a piece of jerked beef. Salty. Doesn't taste right. But I need to eat or I'll die. I chew, then swallow. The lump of food, as heavy as that dead roan, reaches my reluctant stomach.

I still need to examine the half of the saddle blanket I managed to salvage at the massacre scene. Three burps later, I unroll the hide—nap side up—on a boulder. Nothing unusual, just a well-worn section of bearskin. I flip it over.

Red stains mar the skin side, like spilled blood. But these stains have no blurry edges. A dye that doesn't easily wash out made them. What do the markings mean?

The symbols could represent a mountain, low hills, and a river or a stream. If I knew this Sierra foothill territory, I might have the skill to figure out a location. And where are the symbols of love and a key? Spirit Man and No Name, why did you both have to leave me? Ángelo, why didn't you wait to go to war?

Even as I ask these questions, answers wiggle their way into my mind. Spirits don't remain with the living. Spirits need to do what they must do. And the Bear Flaggers murdered Ángelo's dear friends. Ángelo had no honorable choice other than to avenge those he loved. Love and a key— the key to Ángelo's actions—and Fur Man's?—involved love.

Fur Man and his family were traveling from the eastern mountains, possibly from the northeast. Bear Flaggers may have followed them. Could I trace Fur Man's tracks back to the site where he discovered gold? More might remain trapped in silt. Will I meet murderous Yankees during my journey?

"All right, Señor Coyote—wherever you are—should we put this gold the Miwoks found in a safe place first? That is, in Spirit Waker? Don't worry, I'll also check on Ángelo and Jedidiah Jones."

I neither hear howls, nor detect the stink of coyote urine. No black Andalusian stallion appears either. My long sigh whistles. But, of course, such mystical creatures likely await the cover of darkness. My first encounter with No Name, when I rode runaway Fandango, wasn't his normal behavior.

A key and love. Love and a key. Fur Man's simple words form a complicated puzzle. For now, I must set aside my compulsion to reach Ángelo. That's a key. Duty calls me to retrace Fur Man's trail, travel to where the most personal danger waits. That's love. I don't appreciate my own reasoning. But men face puzzles and difficult decisions when they go to war. Ángelo left his family, me, everything, to prove he was a man, responsible enough to choose his own bride—me.

Well, I, Catalina Delgado, must prove I'm a woman, responsible enough to choose my own husband even in the afterlife. That Bible scripture, the one about no marriages in Heaven. Surely exceptions exist. If only I could recall the exact wording. Regardless, while I'm alive and able, I must accomplish the feats only a living person can. I must locate Fur Man's source of gold before Bear Flaggers decide to fill their canteens and find a special surprise.

I roll the bear-hide map, then arrange the packs on Tortilla's back. His tail swishes away a fly. *Suletu.* How welcome my dear plague of flies would be on this horrid journey of mine. A plague of Yankees, that's what I must prevent.

38. Sierra Stream

I RETRACE MY path north, then head east toward the Sierra Nevada. Sometimes unshod hoof prints guide me. Mostly, not. My bottom grows sore from time in the saddle. Vaqueros, they get used to it. I've spent too much of my recent life cooking instead of riding.

Cooking, Mamá, Papi, Abuelito, Josefa—how I miss our rancho. Does the baby inside Mamá grow all right? Is Josefa still afraid of our tureen? And Abuelito—who reads to him in my absence? These are activities I should be doing, weaving my family together like cloth. Bastard *mestizas* live on the ranchos of many Californios. Why am I the sacrificial lamb?

Rain Falling, I suppose that's why. Papi shamed Mamá, right before or right after their wedding, and I must pay the price. What I'm charged to accomplish bears no mark of shame, but one of duty and honor. Mamá gave me love and a strong sense of right and wrong. After all, did she not insist Papi and Abuelito better the lives of our servants and vaqueros? Pay them a wage in cowhides without charging them for food and shelter? Probably because she'd discovered the details about Papi's infidelity. As a result, my family is less wealthy than most rancheros we know. Our smaller land grant works against us too.

I'm the sacrifice because Rain Falling neither lived long enough nor had freedom of movement. I should accept the role. Yet not marrying, not bearing children, is a bitter herb I'm not anxious to digest.

The sun reaches its highest point in the sky, then starts to lower. So slow, this travel, all uphill. I yawn. Abuelito used to tell me mountain air brings sleepiness. Ahead, a stream runs through a little meadow in a flat section of terrain. I water the horses, tie them with rope to a tree, then relieve them of bridles, saddles and packs.

"Please dear saints," I pray aloud, "keep Bear Flaggers from finding me."

Again, I examine Epifania's yellow dress. No stains, no odor, no rips in the fabric. My cloak appears dusty, but three shakes in the air restore its luster. Clearly, this all has to do with Rain Falling, with the old vaquero, Spirit Man, and the black Andalusian stallion. Maybe Señor Cervantes—pleased I read his book—is involved too. No doubt about it anymore. I truly am part of two worlds—the world God—and Coyote?—created for the living and the one occupied by the dead.

Part of two worlds. I should put Fur Man's fox pelt around my neck, show the stream I'm picking up the search where he—a Miwok—left off.

Wearing the pelt, I return on foot to the stream, introduce myself, then follow its path. At a bend, the still shallows near shore wear green scum. Ten feet toward the center, murky water flows. No sandy bottom here. Who knows why? With Spirit Man, our best gold hunting had happened at night in muddied water. I'll wait until after dark to go wading.

How odd, the way one of the fur men directed me upon our first meeting. To choose the same route he and his people took instead of heading in the direction he'd come from. Did he realize Yankees followed him, think he'd chosen a safe path of escape? Or did he fear I'd find the source of those gold nuggets?

Yankees—a shiver crosses my shoulders. This very minute, Bear Flaggers might track me. Should I continue wearing Fur Man's fox? I stroke its softness. The stream needs to know who I am.

39. *Freedom*

JEDIDIAH JONES lifts Ángelo Ortega's body across his shoulders. He presses a limp thigh against one side of his chest and grips a wrist with his other hand. Dead weight, but the ranchero ain't particularly heavy. The height of the cave's front chamber gives Jedidiah room to stand.

He navigates up the rocky incline toward the cave's entrance. Tricky as blazes with a load on his back. Suppose he could have dragged Ángelo. When you're dead, what's a few more bruises? It's the eerie way that this Mexican keeps breathing—after he went without for more than half a day. That's why Jedidiah carries, instead of drags, him toward the waterfall and sunlight. Seems the respectful thing to do.

Another upward step, another step closer. That Catalina gal told him she's the only one who can leave this place without dying. Could be a lie. Women are good at deceit. Would Epifania ever try to deceive him? She's different. Probably not.

Regardless, living in a hole in a mountain with nothing to do but wait to be fed is like being in jail. Having a witch-woman for a guard is plain scary. Best to escape—if he can—while he still has possession of his own mind and soul.

Jedidiah doesn't cross through the falls yet. Standing beside the cool spray refreshes him. If death's going to come soon, might as well enjoy one last good feeling. Epifania's dark eyes and broad smile. The way her fingertips once touched the back of his hand when she and he thought nobody else noticed. Except Ángelo did. Life isn't fair, but Jedidiah's mama never claimed it would be.

He chuckles as he steps into the waterfall. The gold nuggets he found in the cave are stuffed into the pocket of his britches. At least he'll die a rich man. He walks into the sunlight and unloads Ángelo Ortega on the ground.

Nothing bad happens. Nothing at all. And Ángelo's still breathing.

"Well, I'll be a blue-tailed skunk." Jedidiah tosses back his head and laughs. "It's going to be one blazes of a long walk home."

Arms stretched out, he turns in a slow, full circle. The terrain don't look familiar at all. But he's alive! What does being lost matter? He knows how to catch fish and build a fire to cook them—and he can tell east from west, and north from south. There's more than one pass through the Sierra Nevada and this is only July, a long time between now and winter. Several Indian tribes make the area their home.

"Hallelujah!" he says, "Epifania, I'll get back to you yet. And maybe even bring you your brother."

Jedidiah leaps into the air, then lands on his feet. His entire body bursts into flames.

40. Always be Polite to Rivers and Streams

ANOTHER SUNSET ARRIVES, this one introducing a completely full moon. Not the false daylight I need, but at least there's no pitch-black sky. How many days have passed since the murder of Don Berreyesa and his nephews? Ten or eleven? Three days since No Name deserted me. I hold high the resin torch I made, and maneuver through underbrush and uneven ground toward the next bend of the stream I visited earlier today. Hope the water here runs deeper, as it travels to feed into a river.

I introduce myself to the stream, remove my shoes, then wade, the water less cold than expected. The stream's flow tugs at the bottom of my cloak and dress. Spirit Man always told me where to reach down into the water and find gold nuggets. How did he know? Why didn't he pick up the gold himself? Well, he did end up changing into someone else. He needed a student. He should have stayed around long enough to complete my lessons.

The storm that night, all the lightning. I couldn't have rescued Ángelo from the Bear Flaggers without Spirit Man's help. The memory brings fresh tears. Of course, I also had the help of Jedidiah Jones, a snake of a man—another problem I need to address when I return to Spirit Waker. And to get there, I better find gold in the next few hours, to be sure No Name shows up. I've got a feeling the Miwok's nuggets might not count. I wasn't the one to remove them from the water.

I pretend my feet have eyes, that they see each step I take. Abuelito Tomás claims all things, alive or dead, have spirits. Does gold have a spirit too? My toes and heels feel the irregularities in their underwater path, the rocks and little holes. My ears listen for whispers. Nothing, nothing, nothing. I give up.

No, I mustn't give up. Ángelo remains in danger. I can't find my way back to him, can't do anything. Discovering some gold nuggets is my only chance. I break into sobs, as loud as the rushing of this stream. My tears could drown a company of Bear Flaggers.

After a while, I splash my face with cool, silty water. What would Josefa do to find the gold? If she were here with me, we'd figure out a plan. But she's not here and we may never see each other again. Even more tears. Somewhere, do two companies of Bear Flaggers drown?

Oh, for a voice of wisdom. None arrives. I know what Josefa would say if she were present. I must not leave this stream without bringing handfuls of mud with me. I carry a red bandanna in my cloak's pocket. I reach in and pull it out.

I bend over and scoop several handfuls of muck into my bandanna. I fold the fabric around the ooze, stuff the bandanna into my cloak pocket, then head for shore. Soon my shoes are back on my feet. I climb up the bank of the stream.

What a soggy, muddy, mess my clothes are. Will they change by morning? Or will the reality of life conquer magic?

The torch flame has gone out. I return to camp and build a fire. Rub two sticks together—no one but Josefa's mom can do that better than I can. In the warmth of the firelight, I sit on the ground and examine the contents of my bandanna. Globs of mud—some small rocks—do I see a glitter? My heart thuds so hard I can hear it in my ears.

I've seen both real gold and fool's gold. I may be a fool at times, but not enough to misjudge what I see now. The nuggets in this mud are genuine. I'm sure.

All right, No Name, it's your turn now. I stand, then walk over to my pile of supplies, put the wrapped-up bandanna into Fur Man's saddle bag. I yawn. It's been a long day. Time

217

to get some sleep. No Name will make sure I don't miss his arrival. Better take a few swallows of clear water first. Earlier, I watered the horses above the collection of green scum. I'll fill my canteen there.

I stroll upstream, careful not to trip. I should have kept the resin torch, reused it. No matter. I've got enough moonlight for fetching a drink. The two-part drones of bullfrogs blend with crickets' chirps and burbles of flowing water. How lovely.

Then another sound, a click, grasps my attention. Dear God, I know that sound. No need to look behind me for a gunpowder flash.

I dive down the nearest bank, tumble through shadows and underbrush as a gun fires. Brambles scratch my face and arms. I've got to hide. A gun fires again. This time, the sound comes from a different direction. There must be two armed men. The next round fires even closer. I've got to get out of here before they reach the edge of the stream's bank. The water below moves fast. Is it deep enough to carry me to safety? There's only one way to find out. I scramble into the rushing water, push myself along from rock to rock as best I can. Now the water's deeper and carries me along.

More gunfire follows. A musket ball strikes a nearby rock. Too close! A horse whinnies. Tortilla? The image of the dead roan flashes into my brain. A different horse trumpets a challenge. That's Fandango's voice. A boulder slows my escape. The two gunmen stand on top of the embankment, aiming at me in the moonlight. They have entrapped me.

Fandango runs up behind them. She slams her chest against their backs, knocking them off the edge. They roll down the slope into the brush. Fandango—gripping something with her teeth—charges down toward me, using the men as steppingstones. Her wild eyes gleam yellow. Yellow? I manage to stand, then vault onto her bare back. My arms wrap around her neck. I cling for my life. I should have kept her saddled and bridled. She again tramples both men as she climbs up the incline, then leaps into the air. A wave of water—as tall as Abuelito's adobe home—rolls beneath us, swallowing the two gunmen. I see this all in magical false daylight.

Fandango is no black Andalusian stallion, but we're flying.

41. Return to Spirit Waker Cave

HAIL MARÍA, Mother of God. I know not what power keeps me on Fandango's back, but I give thanks. And thanks to Señor Rio, who created a wave to wash those awful men away. Were they Bear Flaggers? I suspect so. Perhaps they participated in the massacre of Fur Man and his tribe. Somehow they noticed me wearing the fox pelt and thought I had escaped their attack. Doesn't matter now, I'm safe, although Tortilla must have perished. Poor, faithful horse. Fandango still clutches something in her mouth. The saddlebag containing the gold I collected? Fandango must know where to find the storage cave, even if she didn't until now. Ángelo—surely I'll see him soon.

My dearest love! How will he look? How will he be? Still asleep? Or a moldy corpse? How can I remove him from Spirit Waker and end his life—no matter what I promised my family? And Jedidiah Jones, what to do with him? I left all the supplies beside the stream. With the giant wave, they likely washed away. If Jedidiah's waiting for a meal, he'll have to wait longer.

Jedidiah and Ángelo passed through the waterfall and into the cavern several days ago. Spirit Man had said, "Those who enter the Tunnel of the Twin Falls alive, do not leave that way." Are Ángelo and Jedidiah now spirit people who require little or no food and water? Certainly I'm part of two worlds, have been since Spirit Man first whisked me onto No Name's back. But I also carry the protective pebble he gave me.

The cave has other glowing stones. How foolish of me, not to have slipped one into Ángelo's pocket. No, my little rock probably protects me because Spirit Man selected it. Or because I'm Rain Falling's daughter.

Well, Jedidiah entered Spirit Waker alive, but Ángelo didn't. At least I think Ángelo didn't. I'm no *curandera*. I can't tell for sure if a person is alive or dead, if part of them resides in the spirit world but might return. Spirit Man never told me I shouldn't bring Ángelo to the cave. He wouldn't have neglected such advice without good reason. Unless he wanted to give me more time to grieve and say good-bye. If only I could figure out the truth.

My tears arrive, enough to water Mamá's corn plants. The night wind lifts those drops of water into the heavens.

#

At the brink of dawn, I ride up a section of mountain. Which one, I've no idea. A waterfall—the waterfall—lies ahead. "Oh, Ángelo," I whisper, "just a little longer. I'm almost there."

I dismount, go through the motions of straightening my cloak and yellow dress, brushing off the dirt of travel. But, of course, I need not do so. My clothes remain in perfect condition. Either I'm dead or enchanted, there's no other explanation. I recall the night Spirit Man insisted I wear the dress Epifania gave me. I'll probably have to wear it for eternity. At least it's beautiful, a frock I love.

Fandango, now ahead of me, halts. She lowers her head as if to graze, but she doesn't. Her tail swishes. She looks back at me and nickers. Is something wrong? My heartbeats come faster, a sign of life—unless they arise from my imagination. I reach my horse's side.

Nuggets, gold nuggets sit on the ground. How did they get here? Why were they left? Dear saints! A powdery gray substance—ashes?—surrounds them. Spread out, as if the wind's been carrying the flecks away. The ground, the surrounding plants, are blackened, singed. Only a dozen or so horse-lengths away, grasses and bushes appear healthy. A small and special fire struck here. These nuggets came from inside of the mountain and somebody removed them. Then that person paid the mystical price.

Either Jedidiah Jones or—Ángelo. Or both. I've got to find out if Ángelo sleeps safely inside where I left him.

I race through the waterfall, scramble down the rocky incline into the familiar chamber. The magical torch in the wall sconce burns and flickers, the light as sparse as before. I reach the flat section of the cave's floor, where I left Ángelo sleeping.

Nothing but the blanket I used to cover him with remains. Fresh tears fill my eyes.

"Ángelo! My love, where are you?"

No answer. I call again.

The ashes outside, are they from both Jedidiah and Ángelo? Mountain wind has scattered part of the pile, no knowing how much. A spirit or magical spell must have set one or both of them on fire. A living person would have stolen the gold.

"Ángelo," I cry out.

Should I be outside, scooping up every fleck of ash I can, preserving what little may be left of the man I love? Or is he inside this cave, in a section I've been too scared to explore? All right, Catalina, think with your brain instead of your emotions.

If Ángelo dwells inside, I'll find him now or later. If he's outside, I might not unless I act with haste. I leave Sprit Waker, then grab Fur Man's saddlebag. I scoop up the gold nuggets and, with the help of a flat stone, as many ashes as I can, depositing them in the leather pouch.

"Ángelo! If you're out here, come back to the waterfall."

No one answers or returns. All right, time to search the various chambers. If I find nothing, at least I probably have some—maybe even most—of my love's remains. More tears flow. Please, not yet. My eyes need to see the whole truth without grief clouding them.

Fandango follows me into the cave. She's a mystical mare, now, can't possibly be subject to the cave's death-upon-leaving curse. I smile. Fandango is more friend than horse, as if she blends with Josefa. How ridiculous. Spirits may be able to take this form or that, but ordinary people don't. When did I stop being an ordinary person? As daughter of Rain Falling, maybe I never was one.

I set down Fur Man's saddlebag of gold and ashes. I left my canteen and all other supplies at the river with the trampled Bear Flaggers. At least this cave has a waterfall if I ever decide I'm thirsty. Another sigh. Concerns about my future thirst are like concerns about washing Epifania's yellow dress. Unnecessary.

Time to hide the gold, the ashes, and then explore. I mustn't take the torch in the wall sconce. If Ángelo is alive and somewhere outside, he'll need light when he returns. Not good reasoning. By now, he's either a spirit or a spirit person. In either case, he'll eventually find me in here. Although I'm part spirit, existing between life and death, I need light for the job ahead.

"Fandango," I say. "If you know the secret of false day—the way No Name does—I could use some additional light exploring the inside of this mountain."

Fandango snorts, as if my request breaks mystical rules. I pat her on the neck, then remove the torch from the wall. First, I enter the side chamber. She can't fit through the opening. I hide my treasures in the same crevice as Papi's bandanna, then rejoin my horse.

Next, we pass through several chambers leading deeper into the mountain, each new ceiling lower than the one before. By the fourth chamber, the torch sputters as much as it flickers—threatening to leave me in darkness. Fandango balks. Even a mystical mare may need more fresh air than this part of the cave holds.

I'm able to breathe and must continue alone.

Abuelito worked in a silver mine as a boy and once lost his way. I feared getting lost inside of a mountain when I was an ordinary living person. Still a fear, but not for the same reason. What if Ángelo returns to the entry chamber and needs me? What if I can't find my way back to him? That's my main fear now.

Do I worry too much as the darkness around me deepens?

Darkness—only a few weeks ago, that word symbolized the Devil's very being. Then, the unforgivable actions of the Bear Flaggers. Next, my lack of self-knowledge shrouded me from light—that and the strangeness surrounding Spirit Man. What will the word, darkness, mean to me tomorrow?

I navigate several more chambers. They angle downward. A glittering beckons me, maybe fifty paces ahead. What's in the next room of this maze? Another magical torch? I climb inside the opening and blink from the brightness. Like polished blue-and-white jewels in sunlight. What place of mystic miracles is this? Raising my torch, I approach and touch a cavern wall: rock of some sort. The sparkle doesn't rub off. My eyes adjust. The ceiling of this room must be many times my height. Elongated rocks extend from both the cave's ceiling and the floor. The old vaquero told me of such rock structures once. So did Papi and Mamá. What I see are crystals. So magnificent, they are. Something else catches my eye. In the distance, light streams, and not from rocks or a resin torch. Sunlight accompanied by the sound of falling water.

#

I edge my way upward, over piles of small rocks, toward daylight and a thin curtain of water. At least I think it's daylight. Such a lovely, warm yellow glow beckons me.

Fandango plods behind me. She somehow squeezed through the smaller passages while finding enough air. Another miracle. Yet, now, I'm the one who must lead, make the decisions that could bring wonder or horror. How exhilarating to stand on this mysterious threshold and behold the land ahead. Green grasses cover hillsides. Animals graze: longhorns, goats, buffalo, horses. A wide river runs through a valley. Snow-capped mountains stand in the distance. All so clear, as if I am down there. Yet no vaqueros tend the animals. No sign of people at all. The paradise waits for travelers to move in.

"Catalina!"

Ángelo's voice behind me? I turn. No one.

"Don't step out there," he pleads. "I almost made that mistake. Please do what I say."

"Where are you, my love?" My heart beats so hard, it might leap out of my chest. "What happened?"

"Walk back into the chamber of crystals. Sit down. Then I'll tell you."

I do as he says. If only I could see him. At least his voice is here. I sit down beside pale blue crystalline rock formations shaped like giant clubs or spears.

"All the time I was in the cave asleep, I could hear and see you. When you left to return home, my mind could follow you there as well. You couldn't hear me though. When you heard Josefa's voice, telling you to run from the river, the warning came from me. Then that Yankee, the one who tried to court my sister, dragged me outside. He burst into flames. I did too."

"Oh, dear God—"

"Hush, my love," Ángelo says. "Let me finish."

"Can you touch me? Touch my hand?"

"Not now. Not yet. If we're lucky, maybe later."

That's something. Far better than nothing. Tears roll down my cheeks. I ought to have run out of them by now. My Oljon mamá should have named me Tears Falling.

"When our bodies turned into fire, our spirits didn't know what to do. Where to go. But there was a compulsion to return to the cave and find where it leads. We both had it."

Ángelo then tells me how he floated through the chambers until sunlight gleamed ahead, but all the way there, rage filled both Jedidiah and him. Jedidiah wanted to shoot Sutter and Frémont. Ángelo wanted to do in Kit Carson as well—all of the Bear Flaggers, as a matter of fact. Then arose the vision of peacefulness and the other end of the series of chambers, a small waterfall and a rainbow—everything Heaven should be.

"But we couldn't set aside our anger," Ángelo says. "We couldn't forgive. Jedidiah walked down the path to potential paradise, screamed and—and disappeared." A raven calls from beyond the cave. "I've waited inside here ever since. I couldn't leave. I had to warn you."

I nod and lower my eyelids. The falls! Of course, the second of the twin falls. Spirit Man warned me about this place. I lean my back against the tapered crystal pillar.

Stalagmite, that's the name of this formation, or so Papi claimed. I never thought I'd see a stalagmite, couldn't imagine why I needed to know such a strange word. Mamá, Papi, Abuelito, they all know so many things I don't. Who will teach me now?

Something else gnaws at my mind: the death of Salvador of the Eagles. "That Yankee, the one who pulled you out of the cave," I say. "He murdered the brother of my grandfather Tomás."

"I know. But he took me with him when he left here. He thought witchcraft was at work, that stepping through the little waterfall would save both our souls."

"How could he—anyone—think that?"

"What did you think, the first time you rode on a flying horse?"

Ángelo is right, but wrong too. Trying to save the soul of one person doesn't make the murder of another right. Saints in Heaven, what am I thinking? I'm here and I'm alone with the man I love—or at least with his spirit. After tonight, who knows if I'll ever be with him again? And I'm arguing about the worthiness of a Yankee?

"Riding through the sky, I—I worried about my reputation, as well as the true meaning of what was happening." Now that I need reassurance the most, I can't even hold Ángelo's hand, let alone kiss him on his forehead or lips. "Do you know the way back through the chambers?"

"Quite well by now. Is there something you need to learn?"

"I wish I knew if I'm tired, or ever will be again. I sleep far less inside of this cave." My face warms at the thoughts going through my head. "But I want so much to sleep where I can hear the lullaby of cascading water. Do you think—"

"Do I think what, Catalina?"

"That you could—" How can I say this? What will he think of me?

"Could what, Catalina?"

"Do you think you could stay close to me, tonight? Under my cloak. But maybe not any closer."

"I think I can manage that." A little laugh follows. "Although you probably won't be able to tell I'm there."

We return to the other end of Spirit Waker Cave, a thousand Monarch butterflies fluttering inside of my stomach. I walk over the uneven ground. Does my head float somewhere in the sky?

I shake out the blanket I used to cover Ángelo days ago. I curl up on my side on top its coarse weave. The ground is hard. Fandango's saddle and blanket are back at the river. Too bad. My spine and neck ache.

Then something pushes at me, slips under me where my clothed body touches the ground. Ripples my cloak but not my dress—settles between the two garments. So comfortable. It is as if I sleep upon Epifania's fancy, soft mattress. Magic of the most beautiful kind.

"I love you," Ángelo's spirit says from underneath me. "Sleep well."

"I love you too." Death hasn't parted us, at least not yet.

Hail María, full of grace—and kindness.

42. A Skunk's Rear End

JEDIDIAH JONES needs to puke. Well, that ain't going to happen, a least not anytime soon. Whatever form he's taken, a creature with a stomach isn't one of them. Dang. Mama always said Hell is a place full of fire. Hellfire killed him—burned him down to a pile of ashes. The place he's in now has no fire. It just plain stinks.

One minute he was in a cavern full of crystals, rock icicles growing from the floor and the ceiling. Would have taken his breath away if he still had any. Next, he faced the gates of heaven. Well, no gates. No Saint Peter, or any of that. Just the most peaceful scene a person could imagine. Open land extending forever. No sign of people, just animals grazing or sleeping in sunlight. Talk about the lion lying down with the lamb. He couldn't blame himself—just his stupidity—for stepping into that welcoming world. All was fine until a skunk swallowed him.

Now, far as he can tell, he's sitting in that skunk's gut. Right up the damn thing's ass, judging by the gross smell. And he doesn't get to escape when the animal drops its dung. Nope, he's like a piece of the skunk's innards. What did he do to deserve this?

Oh yeah, he shot one of Catalina's relatives. But the Indian was about to send an arrow through the man Jedidiah was hired to protect.

Americans all over the place murder Indians. And forget the fact slavery is illegal in Mexico. Most rancheros in Alta California treat Indians like disposable personal property.

Hell, John August Sutter not only forces hundreds of Indians to live in squalor on his land, he's likely killed hundreds more. As for good old John Charles Frémont, he's massacred entire villages. Even the Spanish missionaries—for all their supposed godliness, weren't free from guilt. Jedidiah only eliminated one Injun: Catalina Delgado's great uncle.

Guess he killed the wrong one.

The stench of rotten eggs returns full force. How long is an eternity? Is there room for negotiation? Sutter and Frémont, they should be the ones stuck up here. Jedidiah should have sent them both to their graves when the opportunity arose.

Or maybe the fate of both Sutter and Frémont will first include hell on Earth. What would they hate the most? No wealth and no position of power. Yeah, let them live a long time under those circumstances, then top it all off with eternal imprisonment inside this blasted skunk.

43. Always be Polite
to the Spirits

I WAKE UP, the ground underneath my blanket rock hard.
No surprise, it's rock. My neck aches. The eternal torch casts
its glow in my direction. I shift, turn toward the sound of
cascading water. No daylight filters into the cavern. Either
this is still the night I slept upon Ángelo's spirit, or I've been
slumbering ever since. But I couldn't have slumbered for long.
Being in the cave makes me less likely to sleep, not more.

Of course, my recent experiences in blackened skies
and lightning storms could all be parts of dreams—Flying
Fandango no more real than No Name. Ha! That, I don't
believe. I'm the daughter of Rain Falling, aren't I? I'm Mamá
and Papi's daughter too. I sit up, stretch, then manage to
stand. My back and leg muscles disagree with the decision. I
must be more alive than dead—or less enchanted than more.
Ghosts can't possibly get this sore from curling up on their
sides.

I pass through the waterfall and greet the moon and stars
peeking through a partially overcast sky. Not ideal flying
weather. Weather never bothered No Name or Spirit Man. In
that respect, Fandango and I are beginners.

It's too dark to see what's left of the ash pile. I already
stuffed what I could into that saddlebag. The rest will scatter.
If I'm called to fly tonight, Ángelo may want to travel with me.
What if wind scatters him? Best for my dearest to ride in my
cloak's inner pocket.

Under my cloak. My face warms from the memory. My skin tingles where he would have touched me if he'd wisped underneath my dress. Is it wrong for me to think of this? We're not married. Still, one doesn't feel the touch of a ghost. We can hear each other's words of love but can only touch each other through our imaginations. Ángelo and I, being together as we were last night—or even closer—isn't wrong.

That Bible lesson from Friar Fernandoco. In Heaven, no one shall marry or be married. That's not exactly what he said. The quote refuses to surface.

"Hope." The voice of Señor Cervantes, the man who wrote *Don Quixote*, has returned. "Hope shares its birthday—its very moment of birth—with true love."

#

Inside of Spirit Waker, I comb my fingers through my hair, then weave the usual two braids. No tangles to remove. My braids from yesterday looked almost as neat as today's. All a matter of habit, the daily arranging of my hair—like brushing off my dress and cloak.

I enter the side chamber with the torch and stare up at the crevice where I've hidden Fur Man's saddlebag and the various cloth-wrapped gold nuggets. The crevice wasn't difficult for Jedidiah to find. Should I select a new location?

Perhaps the gold belongs in the huge cavern, the one loaded with crystalline rock formations. There, the call of the vision of Paradise ought to distract thieves. They won't bother hunting in nooks and crannies.

However, going in there could prove dangerous even for Ángelo and me. The temptation to step into that beautiful world would grow greater over time. Spirit Man warned me not to explore for good reason. I climb a pile of small rocks and push the saddlebag deeper into the hole.

Then the fact hits me. I've been awake for at least an hour. No trace of Ángelo. Has he gone exploring where he shouldn't? But he knows better—doesn't he?

I close my eyes and count to ten, then keep going to twenty-five. The man I love is dead, reduced to a spirit. A person can't get deader than dead. It does no good to imagine the worst each time we're not side-by-side. Neither Ángelo nor I are children. Important matters require his attention, just as finding Coyote's gold demands mine.

Speaking of gold, I ought to go be polite to a river. Each night that I reach my hands into wet sand or silt and find nuggets, I delay the arrival of a plague of Yankees. I whistle for Fandango. The cave echoes my call. I whistle again. No whinny, hoof beats, or horse. Maybe she's gone looking for her saddle.

I pass through the waterfall a second time. Under a blanket of stars and scattered clouds, all my clothes drip. Then I see a gleam—a lantern—in the direction of the burned plants. I press my lips together so hard, they hurt.

"Catalina?" a voice calls.

Josefa! This time for real? "How on Earth or in Heaven—"

Fandango's nicker and the smell of horse tell the story. So that's where Fandango has been. I stumble toward horse and light. Josefa sets her lantern onto a flat rock.

"Ángelo's dead, isn't he." Josefa does not ask the question. She states it. The mountain wind whips at her dress and cloak.

"Yes, but he's still with me, I think."

We wrap our arms around each other and weep.

#

Josefa already knows she mustn't venture into Spirit Waker. She's here to take Ángelo's remains home to his family. She removes a large cook spoon and a cloth sack from Fandango's saddlebag. Even in the dark, I know this saddle: Mamá's favorite. Another gift to me—one worth all this world's gold, as far as I'm concerned.

"The Ashes are not just Ángelo's," I say. "That Yankee who liked Epifania—Jedidiah Jones—they died together. Jedidiah thought he was helping Ángelo. It didn't end up that way."

We locate what little is left of the ash pile. The wind has done its work.

"I rescued what I could," I say. "I'll be back. It could take me a while."

"I'll collect what's left here."

Back through the waterfall I walk, then amble down the rockslide, my arms extended sidewise for balance. I'm getting better at this. My eyes adapt to the meager light with ease. I head for the side chamber and return carrying Fur Man's saddlebag. If Ángelo's spirit doesn't show up by morning, I'll visit the regular sparkling stalagmites and the upside-down ones hanging from the ceiling—whatever they're called. I've got some questions to ask them.

"We have to take care," I tell Josefa after I step through the waterfall and back into the night, "There's a secret in the bottom of this saddlebag and it must stay there."

She hands me the spoon, then holds her sack wide open and shuts her eyes. I remove a spoonful of ashes from Fur Man's bag, probe them with my forefinger, then add them to Josefa's sack. When I finish the transfer, few ashes—and hopefully all of the gold—are left inside of the beaded saddlebag. Josefa knots the top of her own bag, then binds the closure with a length of rawhide cording. Do the ashes under my fingernails belong to Ángelo, Jedidiah, or both?

"You must never open this sack," I say, "nor should anyone else." I'm sure my face conveys the importance of my words. "The cave's magic killed Ángelo. The Ortega family must bury this deep—very deep—or else something terrible could result."

Josefa bites down on her lip and nods. Then comes a shy smile.

"I'm the same person who refuses to use that haunted tureen, remember?" Now Josefa grins. "Your message, it will travel to the necessary ears."

How brave, this young woman has become. But, wasn't she always, in her own way? We maneuver her sack into her leather pack, a third as tall as she is. I harness the pack against her back, then help her climb onto Fandango. We clasp hands.

"Ride safely, my dearest friend."

"And you, as well."

Fandango leaps upward.

I touch Ángelo's crucifix, the chain around my neck. I meant to return the jewelry to Don Ortega. The night sky swallows both horse and rider. Too late. Once more, the Ortega family will need to forgive me.

#

I sit in the cavernous chamber, my knees drawn to my chest and my back against a crystalline stalagmite. An uncomfortable stalagmite, I must admit. I tried three others and settled for this one. Some spirit woman I am. Beyond this chamber, morning beckons from the place of pastoral beauty—the place where Ángelo heard Jedidiah's anguished screams. The entrance to both Heaven and Hell? Does Coyote's world even contain a place of eternal punishment? Voices call my name, the voices of my Abuelita, the old vaquero, maybe even my natural mother, Rain Falling.

"El Campeador," other voices say. "El Cid." They use both the Spanish and Moorish names for that warrior from medieval times. "Love and the key. And never forget the power of hope."

Hope... The war with the Bear Flaggers does not go well. All Californios risk losing their lives and lands. The Oljon, Miwok and other native peoples lost their lands to the Spanish—Papi's ancestors—many years ago. Yankee Bear Flaggers are even more brutal. I'll never forget the horror of that massacre scene—Fur Man and his family, the infant's bloody corpse.

By gathering gold I postpone the inevitable—people from Los Estados Unidos overrunning Alta California. But my people—including my Oljon mother's people—need some victories they can remember, stories to pass down to their children and grandchildren. Stories to give them hope for a better future.

I stand and study the crystalline garden around me. How many years did it take to form? The friars would insist, "Not that many." They claim to know the exact date God created this entire world. Coyote might have other opinions to contribute. Love. Hope. The Key. I walk toward the light, to the edge of the vision of paradise.

"Good evening," I say. "Or good morning, I'm not sure which. My name is Catalina Delgado, daughter of Vicente Delgado and Rain Falling, raised on the little rancho of the Delgado family in Alta California. I do not deserve your attention but beg you to listen to my story and my plea."

44. A Suit of Armor

I RETURN TO the chamber closest to the entry waterfall. I have prayed what I must pray. Strange, the relief washing through me. I cannot change the world, only postpone a string of many horrors. Not a happy thought, yet the full responsibility of my peoples' futures no longer rests upon my small shoulders. I will do what I can—complete the mission I've inherited. Yet I've requested the aid of all those who've lived before me to help stop the massacres of the innocents, the children. If such is not possible, at least give Californios, other Mexicans and the tribes hope for a better future.

Fandango whinnies for me from beyond the waterfall. Dark out there. She must be ready for another night's ride. When was the last time I saw daylight at this end of the cave? I touch my fingertip, the one I used to explore Ángelo's beloved ashes. Another whinny. More gold nuggets await to dwell in Fur Man's saddlebag.

"I'm almost there, Fandango." I step through the water barrier, my hand in my cloak's pocket. How refreshing, the cascading water feels, more than ever before—yet I mustn't wash away that last bit of ash under my fingernails. "Let's go."

But what is this? A light far stronger than from the moon and stars hits my eyes. I blink over and over. No Name trumpets a battle cry. He stands saddled and bridled next to Fandango. The light glows around him. My eyes keep blinking. Someone—in a suit of armor?—straddles No Name's back. He holds a bulky sword in his hand. Not comical, as Don Quixote would be. Heroic, like El Cid. The knight lifts the visor on his helmet, revealing those deep, dark eyes and bushy eyebrows I know so well. And I could never fail to identify the downward curve of his trimmed mustache. I gasp.

"Ángelo!" What joy to look upon his face. "But you had no form the other night, when—when we—"

"Well, I do now, Señorita Delgado." Ángelo laughs. "And the legend claims a dead man in a suit of armor rides an Andalusian into battle. Although his faithful steed was white or gray, was he not? Do you know spirits gossip that El Cid might have actually died years later in the comfort of his own bed?"

"Oh, my love, my dearest—" What is he doing, talking about the color of a horse or what spirits have told him?

Wait, that suit of armor he wears looks familiar, as does the shield patterned with a huge golden cross. Ángelo and Epifania's Uncle Julio. I've seen these items in Don Julio's home, southeast of Monterey. Now I laugh and fold my arms across my chest.

"Bear Flaggers. They know nothing about El Cid." The night breeze blows loose strands of my hair. "But, by now, I bet plenty of them have heard the news of your death."

"That's what I'm praying for. And if I still have my bodily form tomorrow night." His laugh grows more playful. "We'll find a friar—alive or dead—to marry us."

Marry. That word is so wonderful to hear. Ángelo stares at me with loving eyes. He lowers his visor, his face again shielded—but not from my memory or imagination.

45. A Second Chance

SOMETHING TUGS at Jedidiah Jones. Havoc's happening inside this damn skunk's gut. Worse than ever. But now he's part of what's moving—the waste material—the dung. A river of rotten eggs. He rides the fecal rapids to open air, lands on the top of a puddle of liquid crap, then rolls himself in a different direction. The Blessed Lord must have heard his prayers for a second chance. But now what is he supposed to do, without a body and stinking of shit and skunk?

One thing at a time. First, he's got to free himself from this hell—once in the disguise of paradise—float through Catalina's cave, then wash off in the waterfall. By then, maybe some being will make it known what's next. Then a breeze picks him up, whisks him away—in a different direction. Jedidiah groans, or the best he can under current circumstances. Either he's headed someplace better or worse. He's got no choice in the decision-making process.

He does have one choice, though, that might improve his uncertain prospects. Whatever task he's assigned by the powers in charge of eternity, he'd better sweep his personal grudges under the rug, step up to the mark and do one heck of a first-rate job.

46. Believe the Unbelievable

FANDANGO'S MANE fans out in the waning night's wind. I travel on her back, far beneath the overcast yet high enough above the treetops and ground fog to stay concealed. An encampment lies below us, whose I do not know. The likely battlefield stretches between the two hillsides where opposing armies gather. How long will it take for one calvary to charge to the other end? Ten minutes? Or will they decide to meet in the middle?

No Name's wild mane—two or three times the length of Fandango's—must make it difficult for Ángelo to survey the scene at all. But then, maybe not. Ángelo has experienced both death and the magic of Spirit Waker. I'm alive, though spirithood—without death, so far—grows closer with each passing day. A month ago, I could not have believed any of this possible. As a rider of a flying horse without wings, I'm learning to believe the unbelievable.

"On the right," Ángelo says to me from No Name's back, "those are Yankees."

He wears his Uncle Julio's decorative suit of armor, including the helmet with the visor lowered. It ought to be difficult to hear Ángelo speak to me, but it's not. His helmet has such narrow eye slits. I bet he sees right through the steel.

"They've more muskets than I can count," Ángelo says.

"It seems like a lot because our men have so few." I remember what our officers told me earlier this month. Surely Comandante José Castro informed his young recruits, including Ángelo, of the sad situation when they enlisted.

"Your father's muskets may not have reached these soldiers. I've even heard most of our cannons anywhere don't work right."

"Speaking of cannons, the Bear Flaggers have a portable one."

A cannon? The Yankees will hold their position and wait for our soldiers to try and reach them. Oh, dear God.

"If we can disperse the enemy here, my love, we can at least claim one cannon that does work."

I squint, trying to assess more about our troops' preparedness—or lack of it—while Ángelo concentrates on the Bear Flaggers. Most of our gathered soldiers are lancers—our fearsome horsemen who ride into battle, ready to drive their long, heavy lances into their opponent's chests. Perhaps less fearsome though, to well-armed Yankees who hope to shoot those lancers off their horses—or the horses from underneath their lancers—during the advance.

"We have to set up a distraction," I say.

"We think alike."

Whatever we plan, lead shot won't hurt Ángelo, although it ought to do significant damage to Uncle Julio's suit of armor. No Name's probably safe from harm too. He's been a spirit horse for a long time. Now Fandango and me, that's a different pot of beef stew. We both drift between form and spirit. We're vulnerable, despite the magic of Spirit Waker Cave.

"What possible military strategy does our side have?" I say. "The power. It's all too one-sided."

"No particular strategy, except to demonstrate bravery and honor. Try to survive, then return to our ranchos and families."

"And on their side?"

"To kill as many on our side as possible. By any means, without mercy. You should know that by now."

When my brothers used to play soldiers, they often pretended to form a line of musketeers in battle. They would take turns firing their imaginary cannon. They even begged me to play the part of the lady in distress. Such innocent times. One lesson I did learn from the game. The range of a musket is limited, and those guns and cannons both take time to reload.

"I've got an idea," Ángelo says.

"I might too."

The pink line creeping along the horizon and the lightening sky announce the coming of dawn. We have to land on the ground now. Behind our own lines? On top of the enemy? Or somewhere in-between?

No Name lands in full gallop on flat ground, in front of our forces who make their way down the hillside. How handsome Ángelo is in medieval armor, broadsword raised and shield on his other arm. No Name bears the heavy load as if a charger in an old Spanish tale. On Fandango, I follow my dearest love. For sure, our own soldiers can see these impossible feats. I pray none of them has a weak heart. Enough ground fog remains in front of us to hide us from the Yankees for a few minutes more.

"El Cid," I shout from deep within my chest, toward the thinning fog ahead and then back over my shoulder. "Make way for El Cid." May God forgive me for this untruth.

My cries trigger the combined roar of many men. "El Campeador," our comrades shout from behind me. "El Cid."

Then I see the animal with big pointed ears mere *varas* ahead of us, galloping straight for the Yankee forces. A burro has appeared out of nowhere. Did this creature also drop out of the sky? I've never seen any burro with such a flea-bitten coat and swayed back—poor thing. The burro brays an ear-splitting call to action. How can such a small and sickly beast possess this powerful voice and race faster into battle than No Name and Fandango?

Believe the unbelievable.

Then the ground throbs with the sound of hoofbeats. Our lancers following Ángelo and me have reached level ground and charge. I don't need to see them to know. Ahead, the sun erases the fog. Enemy musketeers have formed their deadly lines, far less than a quarter-league ahead. I bow my head. Please let our lancers go home alive to those they love.

"El Campeador!"

"El Cid!"

If I die, I die. Death is not my choice, yet unknown beings marked me at birth to lose my life long before old age—to be returned to my deceased mother, Rain Falling, once I'd hidden Coyote's gold. This morning I must accept my fate. All I ask is for my spirit and Ángelo's to find each other afterwards. *Hail María, full of grace.* There, I've said what prayers I can.

I straighten in the saddle, as if I too, wear a suit of armor. Fandango and No Name race with all their strength, however, the little burro remains in the lead. What sort of spirit drives the determined creature forward? For its sake, may it feel no pain. Musket shot will hit Ángelo second, then me. Only God—and maybe Coyote—knows what will happen after that. If I get through, I'm going to rope a cannoneer and put his team out of action.

Muskets fire, one round, then another and another. Smoke fills the air. Nothing hurts. I don't even cough, just keep riding onward. A huge boom follows: the cannon. The ball flies through the front of the burro's head, slams into No Name's chest and keeps going. Neither animal falls. My turn is next. I brace my entire body. Now I'll discover how much of a Spirit Woman I really am.

The massive ball of iron crashes through Fandango and rips into my stomach. I feel the pressure of the hit but no pain. No blood spurts from me. I think I'm all right. So are Ángelo, No Name, Fandango, and the burro. The impact didn't slow any of us down. The next round of musket balls doesn't either.

"Ghosts," a Yankee shouts in English. "They're all frigging ghosts."

I grasp my riata, now, ride toward the group of artillerymen and their cannon. The huge gun is on some sort of wooden frame with wheels. I've got to interrupt the firing of that thing to protect our lancers. Which soldier is the most essential to its operation? The one with the ramrod? The one who lights the fuse? I've only got seconds to decide. I twirl the riata over my head and cast it.

The loop sails through the air and lands around the barrel of the cannon. Praise God! I pull the noose tight and keep going. Fandango's mystical strength and momentum pull the cannon over on its side. No Yankee dares to challenge me. Mexican lancers will soon ride within musket range. Yankee musketeers hurry to reload their weapons. Ángelo has gone on to cut the ropes tethering their horses.

"El Campeador!"

"El Cid!"

The lancers are almost within musket range.

Then from the east, the direction of the bright sunrise, part of the sky blackens. A distant buzzing drone reaches my ears, even above the noise of two opposing armies beginning battle. The buzzing increases with each passing second. What I see and hear can be only one thing. Battalions of big, fat, horseflies ride the wind in my direction. None of the Yankee soldiers point toward the darkening sky. They are too busy fussing with powder and shot. I smile. My plague of flies are hungry for their blood meal.

This time, I won't be the only one who can see and feel them.

Now the buzzing grows louder in my ears than all the hooves pounding the ground, the battle cries of lancers, and the whinnies of horses set loose and scattered by a ghost in a suit of armor. I raise my own ghostly sword, pointing it in the direction of the enemy. Sword? I do not know where this weapon came from or who placed it into my hand.

"*Suletu*," I shout. "Attack the Yankees!" The turn of flies to eat spiders has come.

My living ammunition bombards the Bear Flaggers, coating the men's skin, their eyes, even their tongues when they open their mouths to scream. Enemy soldiers scatter on foot, on horseback, any way they can. Muskets, boxes of ammunition, the cannon and many horses—the foreigners leave all of them behind. Mexican lancers arrive and give chase. Flies and lancers disperse the plague of Yankees, at least, for this day.

"I claim all horses and weapons for the glory of México," I holler. I have achieved true spirithood.

But now what? My final hope for a simple life on a small rancho with Ángelo vanishes with the last strands of morning fog. The dead do not bear children.

#

The cavalry of Californios returns. Little blood soils the soldiers' lances. These are good men of peace. They may enjoy bullfights and bear hunts at annual cattle roundups, but they have no love for killing men. They have won this battle with bravery and honor. Given the enemy something to think—and talk—about. In that respect, they are braver and wiser than I. My hatred of the Bear Flaggers would have driven me to seek additional revenge. Cornered, the Yankees would have fought. Many men on both sides would have died, leaving friends and families to mourn. Perpetuating the drive to get even.

Yet, I cannot erase the image of the earlier massacre from my mind. The blood-drenched bodies of Miwok men, women and children, the baby on the cradleboard. What chance did Fur Man and his people have? Oh, that I could use true magic, make the Yankees respect all Mexicans, including the native tribes. Even teach many of my fellow Californios—as Mamá taught us—it's wrong to treat workers like slaves. Wrong to think "different" means "inferior." Perhaps in the future, that day will arrive.

May God, the Holy Virgin, and Coyote help me to make it happen.

I look up to face our soldiers and their leader, whom I recognize. My family and I handed him the dispatch about Don Ortega that night, the letter I stole. Ángelo joins me and removes his helmet. More than one soldier gasps. No wonder. Mid-morning sunlight shines through Ángelo's head and horse.

We have stayed here too long. We can't return to Spirit Waker Cave until tonight. A young lancer dismounts and walks in our direction.

"You are welcome at the rancho of your uncle, Don Julio Pacheco," he says. He bows his head and kneels before No Name and Ángelo. "You and your lady."

"I'm humbled to accept your gracious hospitality," Ángelo replies. He lowers his voice. I can't hear the rest of what he says, but I can guess. I smile.

The flea-bitten donkey ambles into our group, to a rousing cheer. Something about its facial expression seems familiar. Heaven only knows why. He's a hero, although he could use some grooming. I catch a whiff of excrement and skunk. Correction—he could use a lot of grooming. Well, I've no intention of leaving the poor little fellow behind, even if his spirit form reeks for eternity.

Too bad he's not alive. Epifania would consider him cute. And I do owe her something special for the yellow dress I'll wear forever. I wonder....

47. Marriage Below Heaven

FRIAR FERNANDOCO agrees to marry us inside of Uncle Julio's hacienda. The officer in charge of the lancers gives his blessing. No time to send for family, friends and Comandante Castro, not when this bride and her groom could spontaneously vanish. Even now, the wife of one of the soldiers has to hold my bouquet of flowers for me. I have problems when I try to clutch real objects. And who knows how long it will take the Bear Flaggers to regroup and threaten my peoples? Time is critical for more than one reason.

Ángelo and I do our best to take communion during the wedding ceremony. I hide my mouth, throat, and chest behind my bouquet of flowers as I swallow. I'll die of embarrassment if the holy sacrament tumbles out of my ghostly gullet and lands on the tile floor. A young lancer helps Ángelo out by shielding him with a sombrero. Spirit people can wax and wane—a cycle I've yet to understand. Being one isn't easy.

The Bible verse I've been unable to recall, drops into my memory. *For in the resurrection they neither marry nor are given in marriage, but are like angels in heaven.* What has happened to Ángelo and me can't be the usual type of resurrection. A cannon ball passed through me, but I've never officially died. Friar Fernandoco must surely agree with my reasoning—or our presence simply terrifies him.

"Yes."

"I will."

"I do."

Ángelo and I say all the expected words. Friar Fernandoco makes his final pronouncement. Ángelo and I reach out our hands to each other. Our first kiss ever happens behind the sombrero. Our noses press through each other's faces. His whiskers tickle the inside of my cheek. My lips end up kissing the back of his tongue. We're going to have to practice this or figure out the secret to taking normal human form, the way Spirit Man did.

Whatever happened to him? Who did he become? I suspect I'll find out soon. We've got gold to gather and he may be the only one of us able to stuff muddy nuggets into a sack, unless we enlist another volunteer.

Servants place platters of fresh tortillas and honey on a long wooden table. The mixed fragrances of corn and honeycomb smell so good. Too bad I can't eat. Other servants roll out a cask of aged brandy. I motion to one and explain what I need. She takes several plates of our festive food—and a pile of raw beef—outdoors to the patio and sets them in beds of flowers.

"Bless you," I tell her, and she leaves.

My special comrades gather, my army of flies. Many of them may prefer blood rather than honey, but they all deserve this invitation to celebrate my happiness. Hard to believe, the way they used to annoy me, even frighten me as a child.

"Thank you, God, for love, for family and for all your creatures. And I thank Coyote too." But I should have bowed my head to pray.

I do so and lower my eyelids. Countless dots of golden light sparkle inside of them, as bright as Spirit Waker Cave's blue-and-white crystalline chamber. The tiny glittering points flow, not like flecks of fool's gold in a stream though. They coat me inside and out. This gold, so very real, I call love. My spirit fingers touch the key to my room in my cloak's pocket, the one Manuel forged for Josefa. Unselfish love is the secret to opening many doors.

For this night, anger and hate drain from my heart. Does Ángelo feel the same way? If so, the day may come when we can linger without fear beside the second of the twin falls, let the vision of pastoral paradise become our spirit rancho.

I've no doubt the old vaquero hears my thoughts, then grins. Rain Falling, Salvador of the Eagles, and the spirit of Señor Cervantes probably smile in my direction too. Mystical threads connect us. I ought to weave such connections between myself and the living people I love: Mamá, Papi, my brothers, abuelitos and uncles. Josefa and Epifania as well.

I laugh. Another daunting challenge won't discourage me. Armed with love and hope, I'm ready. I've found the key.

CPSIA information can be obtained
at www.ICGtesting.com
Printed in the USA
BVHW080815310821
615687BV00007B/99